The sound of a car behind her had her scooting off the road.

Annie broke her stride to check over her shoulder. Gray government car.

Nate Dufrene.

He slowed beside her. "Wanna ride?"

"I'm almost there. And I'm pretty sweaty. Wouldn't want to mess up your seats."

"I don't mind."

Her mind screamed *get your butt back to the house and leave sexy Nate Dufrene the hell alone.* Her libido, however, told her to take the candy the man offered and climb into his car like a naughty little girl.

"If you don't mind," she said, pulling open the passenger door.

"You look like you could run circles around me."

"Don't know about that. You look fit enough," she said.

"Oh, yeah? Maybe we can go for a run together."

Her body tightened unwillingly as thoughts of other things they could do together flitted through her mind. Lord, what was wrong with her? Goal: prove to Sterling she could do a phenomenal job as an investigator so she could make more money and get better assignments. Barrier: hunky detective.

She made a noncommittal sound.

"Tell me, Annie. Is that a *yes* or a *maybe?*"

Dear Reader,

The people of Louisiana have a joie de vivre that spills over and encourages visitors to get up and pass a good time. Whether it's slurping gumbo, listening to the sounds of zydeco or watching the pageantry of Mardi Gras, this place is unique.

I love my state, from the winding piney hills of the north to the flat delta of the south and all the places in between. We live, we love and we eat...a lot!

I hope you enjoy my venture into Acadiana with the odd and sometimes kooky matriarch Picou Dufrene and her three disarming boys. If the food isn't a good enough reason to visit Bayou Bridge, the sexy Cajun men will seal the deal. Life is good here on the bayou. Tru dat.

Look for the other two books in this The Boys of Bayou Bridge miniseries. *Under the Autumn Sky* will be out in July 2012 and *The Road to Bayou Bridge* will hit the shelves in September 2012.

I love to hear from my readers, so drop by and leave me a note at www.liztalleybooks.com or drop a letter in the mail to: P.O. Box 5418, Bossier City, LA 71171.

Happy reading,

Liz Talley

Waters Run Deep
Liz Talley

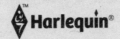

TORONTO NEW YORK LONDON
AMSTERDAM PARIS SYDNEY HAMBURG
STOCKHOLM ATHENS TOKYO MILAN MADRID
PRAGUE WARSAW BUDAPEST AUCKLAND

Recycling programs
for this product may
not exist in your area.

ISBN-13: 978-0-373-71776-7

WATERS RUN DEEP

www.Harlequin.com

Printed in U.S.A.

ABOUT THE AUTHOR

From devouring the Harlequin Superromance novels on the shelf of her aunt's used bookstore to swiping her grandmother's medical romances, Liz Talley has always loved a good romance. So it was no surprise to anyone when she started writing a book one day while her infant napped. She soon found writing more exciting than scrubbing hardened cereal off the love seat. Underneath her baby-food-stained clothes, a dream stirred. Liz followed that dream, and after a foray into historical romance and a Golden Heart final, she started her first contemporary romance on the same day she met her editor. Coincidence? She prefers to call it fate.

Currently Liz lives in North Louisiana with her high-school sweetheart, two beautiful children and a passel of animals. Liz loves watching her boys play baseball, shopping for bargains and going out for lunch. When not writing contemporary romances for the Harlequin Superromance line, she can be found doing laundry, feeding kids or playing on Facebook.

Books by Liz Talley

HARLEQUIN SUPERROMANCE

1639—VEGAS TWO-STEP
1675—THE WAY TO TEXAS
1680—A LITTLE TEXAS
1705—A TASTE OF TEXAS
1738—A TOUCH OF SCARLET

For the people of Louisiana who may face hurricanes, crooked politics and record droughts, but who never fail to invite a neighbor to the table to share their delicious dishes and their lives. I'm honored to live among you.

Special thanks goes to Caddo Parish Sheriff Detective Mick McDaniel and to the Medeiros family who showed me true Cajun hospitality.

CHAPTER ONE

The marshlands off Bayou Lafourche, Louisiana, 1986

SAL COMEAUX GLANCED in the rearview mirror for the fifth time that night and muttered a curse. The child still stared at him with those freaky blue eyes. No longer crying, just gazing into his soul with stabbing accusation.

He clutched the steering wheel tighter, trying to ignore the weight pressing down on him. Guilt. God. Whatever. It threatened to suffocate him. Cold sweat rolled down his back as he searched the inky night for the dirt road. Ten years ago if he'd a blinked, he'd a missed the turn. Much had changed in his life, but one thing was constant—the turn to the Cheramie homestead.

"Almost there," he said to the void surrounding him, not bothering to look back at the girl.

He felt so alone.

Why had he let Billy Priest talk him into doing something so dadgum stupid? His friend had ulterior motives that had nothing to do with mere money. Billy hated Martin Dufrene. Thought the man responsible for all his problems, for losing his family. Dufrene was a bastard, but he'd not caused Billy's wife to leave taking their son with her. Her leaving had been a result of Billy's alcoholism and quick fists—the reason the man had lost his job at the Dufrene mill. "An eye for an eye, and money for us both," Billy had said, knowing Sal was soft—and that he owed half the bookies in Baton Rouge, guys meaner than a water moccasin and just as dangerous. Self-preservation had won out over loyalty, and Sal had convinced himself no harm would come to the child. He was weak, true, but he was no monster.

He'd not have the child's blood on his hands.

He risked another look even though the girl's eyes felt like God's sitting upon him, like in that damn Gatsby book he'd had to read in eleventh grade. The child's gaze was steadfast, her small mouth slack, her tear-streaked cheeks pale.

She gave him the creeps.

An old white fence post materialized in the tangled brush beside the dirt road like a specter. Relief flooded him. The old landmark tilted crookedly in the headlights. He hooked a turn left and bumped down the pitted road toward the old house where his *grandmere* lived.

The place wasn't welcoming. Old, wooden and leaning like half the stumps in the land surrounding it. Though he couldn't see it, he knew a tributary of the Bayou Lafourche sprawled behind the old house, a dark ribbon unraveling across lank swamp grass. He loved Mere's house almost as much as he hated it.

He braked on the crushed shell drive and shut off the headlights of the stolen truck as the screen door cracked an inch or two. Then he saw Pap's shotgun muzzle appear.

He rolled down the window. "It's me."

Moonlight flashed on the metal of the gun. She didn't lower it. "Who's 'me'?"

"Sal."

The gun disappeared and the door opened. "Why you here? I ain't seen you since your mama ran off with that Morgan City boy."

"Sorry, Mere. I—"

"Didn't need you around here no how, so why you here tonight?" Her voice sounded tired, disinterested. She'd never liked him much, but he was her only known grandson.

He eased out of the truck, mindful *Grandmere* might decide he wasn't worth a damn and hoist the shotgun again, but he knew the old woman was his only chance to hide the child until he could figure something out. What, he wasn't sure, but he wasn't killing no child and feeding her to the gators. Billy and his threats be damned.

"I got a little girl here."

His *grandmere* shut the door and stood in her bare feet and flannel housecoat. Her face sagged in the light of the moon. She'd aged. Life was hard on the bayou and Enola Cheramie wore that life like a badge. "A girl?"

"Yeah, uh, my kid." He hesitated. Hadn't thought much more beyond getting the child here. Mere wouldn't keep no child that wasn't blood. "Um, my old lady's strung out, beats the ever-loving shit out of the kid. She tried to kill the girl tonight. Grabbed a—"

"You got a child? Off who?"

"Some gal from Houma. You don't know her. She's batshit crazy, and I should have never taken up with her. Just need the girl to stay with you for a spell."

Grandmere shook her head. "I can't keep no child. I'm still fishing. Got no one to watch her."

He jerked the girl from the backseat of the cab. She didn't make a peep. Just allowed herself to be dragged toward the porch. Her hair was tangled and her dress stained with the black dirt of the bayou. He'd tried to do what Billy had wanted. Tried to kill the child. He'd stood holding a trembling gun on her. He wasn't weak. He'd killed dogs when they'd needed putting down, but this child was different. And she wouldn't close her eyes. Just looked at him. Like Christ on the crucifix had looked down on him at Our Lady of Prompt Succor. Vacant. Hopeless. And he couldn't pull the trigger.

So he'd lowered the gun, knowing God spoke to him through the eyes of the child. Knowing he had to find a way to save her and placate Billy. Knowing his own sin would lead to pain.

Enola Cheramie was his only chance for redemption.

The little girl was pretty and barely three years old. No woman, not even a tough, old crane like Enola, could resist a child like this one.

"She'll go with you. She's a good girl." He pushed the child toward his *grandmere*. The little girl clutched her pink blanket and turned those strange eyes on Mere.

"She don't look like you" was all his *grandmere* said before beckoning the child forward.

The girl didn't move. Just stood unblinking at the foot of the rickety stairs. His *grandmere* wasn't much to look at. Wizened like fruit sitting out too long in the sun, with a square face and broad chest. He'd likely not go near her either. He pushed the girl again between her shoulder blades. "Go on. Mere will take care of you."

"I didn't say I would," his *grandmere* said, but Sal could see it in her eyes. She'd watch over the girl until he could figure out a way to fix what he'd done. What Billy had done.

"I gotta go, Mere. I'll be back to get her. Don't let no one know too much about her. They might send her back to her mama and then she'd be as good as dead."

Enola crept down the steps and reached out for the child. The little girl didn't move, merely turned her head and watched as the old woman's hand clamped down on her shoulder. Then the little girl did something surprising. She held her arms out.

Mere lifted the child into her arms. "She ain't bigger than a minnow. What's her name?"

Sal pretended he didn't hear the old woman. The less she knew the better. News would sweep across Louisiana, and though Mere lived on desolate Houma land far off Bayou Lafourche, she went to town upon occasion. Four times a year or so. He climbed back into the cab and cranked the engine. He glanced at where his *grandmere* stood, cradling the child, muttering words of comfort. As he shifted into Reverse, he saw the child rest her head upon the old woman's shoulder.

From the open window he heard Mere say, "Don't worry yourself, minnow. Ain't no one gonna hurt you or my name ain't Enola Cheramie."

Something crept round Sal's heart and he knew somehow he'd done the right thing. He crossed himself at that moment even though he hadn't attended Mass since he'd left Holy Rosary and headed to Lafayette over fifteen years ago. Yes, God approved. This he knew.

He backed up and left the old woman and child, heading back toward the dirt road that would connect to the highway, which would connect to the interstate that would take him back to Bayou Bridge where he was currently in an ass load of trouble.

The night draped around him, oppressive and warm for February. A mosquito buzzed near his ear. He fanned the pest away, rolled up the window of the old truck and turned the AC up two notches, but obviously the owner hadn't bothered with the expense of Freon. Warm air blew from the vents, failing to cool his body, now drenched in sweat. Was it from the damn Louisiana humidity or the sheer terror rising in him?

Both.

He clicked the brights, haloing the grasses growing on

either side of the dirt road. No one was out this early in the morning, not even the shrimpers. The road was uneven, jarring him, but there was no other way out except by boat. He reached the turnoff and headed north on the highway hugging the Bayou Lafourche. Businesses and houses lined the highway on either side of the water. He crossed a lock bridge to reach the other side and rode thirty miles in silence toward Houma. Each mile brought him closer to a no-win situation.

He'd go to jail. Maybe even Angola.

He swallowed and tried to focus on the smattering of businesses outside Houma. The interstate would be quicker, but Sal didn't want to go fast. He knew what lay ahead. Billy wasn't smart enough to pull the scheme off. Sal should have known better than to mix himself up with a piece of bayou trash like Billy. He turned past the entrance ramp for I-49 and took Highway 182 instead, finding peace in the old highway that would eventually cross the Bayou Tete, the very bayou he'd spent so much time on, fishing and contemplating what a failure he'd become.

The road twisted like a serpent, winding around the Louisiana wetlands before brushing against the tangled trees, sad against the February darkness. It made Sal feel melancholic. He yearned for better times. Bait on his hook, Pabst Blue Ribbon in hand, herons gliding to perches on the bayous off the Atchafalaya. How had he come to this?

His headlights caught a shape in the road. He jerked the steering wheel hard, standing on the brakes at the same time. Too late. The image of a gator in the road flashed through his mind at the same time the truck crashed through the guardrail and went airborne. Cypress limbs blocked his vision just before a sickening thud jarred the vehicle. Sal threw his hands in front of his face as the trunk of a tree hurtled toward him. His head snapped backward at collision and he vaguely registered falling, flipping, hitting the water with a loud crack.

Sal gasped for air as water the color of weak coffee poured into the mangled cab. "Hep!"

His mouth felt stuffed with cotton and he couldn't make his legs move. His lungs starved for oxygen. He gulped at the air, hoping to drink it, telling his body to move. No use. "Hep!"

His mind raced though his body could not move. Broken rail. Someone would see. Water deep. Truck sinking. He could taste the fecund water of the swamp. It filled his mouth, stinging his nostrils as he inhaled the essence of Louisiana, his birthplace, his home.

His hands flopped useless beside him, like large oars adrift in a current. He couldn't move. Couldn't save himself. He'd cheated death one victim that night when he'd taken the girl to Enola, but it would wait no longer to claim a replacement.

Sal said a prayer as the water reached his eyes, but there was nothing to comfort him. Nothing except the sound of justice and regret roaring in his ears.

And the last thought to register before he slipped into a place of darkness was no one would know what had happened to Della Dufrene.

CHAPTER TWO

South Louisiana, 2010

Anna Mendes, aka Annie Perez, stared down at her charge and cursed her bad luck for being the only woman at the agency fit for the job. Masquerading as a nanny? Not exactly easy. More like impossible. "Please tell me you're joking, Spencer."

The five-year-old stood next to a potato-chip display making a horrible face. "I'm sorry, Annie, but I think I'm gonna fro up."

Annie looked down at her shoes—her new running shoes she'd bought with her first paycheck—then back at Spencer, who had squeezed his eyes closed. He did look green around the gills. Perhaps the chocolate milk had been too much. She glanced desperately around the gas station/deli as if there might be someone lurking around the overcrowded shelves to help her. Her gaze landed on a bottle of pink bismuth. Perfect. "How about some medicine? Something to settle your—"

Too late.

Spencer jackknifed forward and reacquainted Annie with the pint of chocolate milk he'd guzzled after they'd left the outskirts of Baton Rouge.

"Oh, God." Annie jumped back about a yard and stared at the child, waiting for his head to spin around. Then it registered. She was in charge. Of the child. Of the situation. She needed napkins and cold water. "Okay, Spencer, okay. It's fine. We'll get this cleaned up."

The boy looked up, tears welling in his big brown eyes. "I'm sorry, Annie. I didn't mean to."

Her heart melted even as she felt queasy herself. Poor kid. The whole thing was her fault. A child probably wasn't supposed to drink that much on a road trip. She should have known, but no discussion of chocolate milk had been in any of the parenting books she'd pored over in preparation for this assignment. It hadn't been in *Know Your Child: A Study on Child Behavior* or in *So You Think You Can Parent?* She knew. She'd read both from cover to cover, and still had no clue what in the hell she was doing.

She grabbed a stack of napkins from next to the slushie machine and mopped Spencer's face. "Don't worry, Spence. Are you feeling better?"

He nodded his head, "Uh-huh."

"Good. Let's go wash up. I'll find the store manager and report our little accident."

"What in the name of—" a voice shrieked behind her.

Annie spun around. Obviously, the gas-station manager had found them. "We had a little accident."

Spencer whimpered so Annie placed a reassuring hand on his shoulder.

"A little accident?" the woman said, screwing up her nose. She had bleached-blond hair and wore a Breaux Mart T-shirt three sizes too big for her small frame. Deep pocketed eyes, tanning-bed faux tan and smoker's lips made Annie think of the prostitutes sitting on stools of the clubs surrounding the military base where she'd worked security years before.

"Yes, an accident," Annie said, hardening her gaze. Spencer settled his head against her thigh so Annie moved her hand up to rub his head. The books had been very emphatic about young kids needing constant affection and praise. She rubbed harder.

The older woman spread her hands. "I can't believe I gotta clean this up. I just got through cleanin' all the johns this morning. Jesus."

"Good to know the bathroom is clean. Come on, Spencer. Let's let this nice lady do her job."

The manager stared hard at Annie, making her glad she had combat training. If looks could kill—well, Annie would be on the floor forcing another cleanup on the paper-product-and-automotive aisle.

Spencer allowed himself to be tugged toward the neon bathroom sign in the back of the store, only putting the brakes on when he saw the candy aisle. "Hey, Annie, can I have—"

"Don't even think about it, bud," she interrupted, toeing the bathroom door open with her foot. She'd made a mistake at the airport giving in to the milk. She wasn't stupid. Spencer wouldn't see candy until he was returned to his mother.

"But I want candy!"

"Too bad." Annie shoved him into the dark bathroom and flipped on the light. Yep, the bathroom was clean. Sorta.

"You have to give it to me. I've been good. You said if I was good on the airplane I could have a prize. I want a candy bar."

No more relying on advice from a book. She went on instinct. "No. You puked all over the floor, and now that lady has to clean it up. The last thing you need is candy."

He stuck out his bottom lip.

"Wash your hands," Annie said, in the voice she'd used on suspects she apprehended.

Spencer didn't move.

"My way or the highway, bud." She flicked the faucet handle so water gushed into the sink and glanced in the mirror as Spencer finally got the message and shoved his hands under the flow.

Lord, she looked terrible.

Her normally tamed hair had slipped from its clip and frizzed around her face. Usually her olive skin glowed, but today it looked mottled. Her gray eyes looked tired. Confused. Resigned to a crappy life she had never intended.

Oh, she knew how she'd gotten back to square one. She'd dared to hope for a normal life back in her home state of California, throwing away a perfectly good career for a man, his daughter and a shot at being happy homemaker— all because she watched *It's a Wonderful Life* and decided she needed a do over.

She'd been beyond naive. Okay, bordering on stupid.

So now she worked on a trial basis for Sterling Security and Investigations, LLC, as an undercover nanny. God, it sounded like a movie starring Sandra Bullock. No, she'd been a beauty queen or something. Still, having her first assignment encompass planning playdates and scrubbing mushy graham crackers off her T-shirt wasn't what she had in mind when she told former FBI agent Ace Sterling she'd take the job. Typing reports for the firm would be better than being stuck in BF, Louisiana, with a conniving, adorable five-year-old and his celebrity parents.

"I'm done," Spencer said, holding out his dripping hands.

Annie grabbed a paper towel. "Good job. Always wash your hands. Germs can make you sick."

"And chocolate milk," Spencer observed gravely.

"Yes, and chocolate milk."

They exited the bathroom, passing the unhappy manager, and walked out into the oppressive heat. First day of fall, her ass. Felt more like a mid-August heat wave. No wonder her hair looked like it belonged in a Twisted Sister video. But, really, why did she care? She had never worried about her hair, her makeup or wearing kicky little kitten heels. Annie was a professional. Hair got in the way. Makeup wasn't necessary. And she'd be damned if she ever wore anything on her feet like Tawny Keene did. Spencer's mother was asking for a broken ankle.

She pressed the button on the key fob, unlocking the doors of the rental car sitting by the pump. Spencer wriggled into the booster seat in the back and grabbed his iPod touch. Annie made sure the seat belt was snug and then swiped the credit card issued by the Keene family and filled the car.

Even though they were only thirty minutes from their destination, Annie knew a full tank of gas was always a good idea. Be prepared. First as a security officer in the Air Force and later as a field agent in the FBI, Annie had taken pride in expecting the unexpected. She had never been without extra ammunition, money, false IDs or any other necessities an agent might need.

She glanced around, taking stock of her surroundings. No one had followed them from Baton Rouge. Whoever had been sending threatening messages to the Keene family was likely back in California, but she couldn't be too careful. Her job was to protect Spencer while helping to investigate the threats. That's what she was getting the not-so-big bucks for.

Annie set the gas handle in its cradle and screwed the lid on the tank. She had to stop beating herself up. She'd gotten herself into this situation and she'd have to make lemonade from the lemons. She could always toss in some vodka to make it less painful.

But not on the job. Never on the job.

She slid behind the wheel and started the engine, determined to have a better outlook—after all, she'd avoided vomit on her new shoes, hadn't she?

Just as she pulled forward a government car swung in front of her. She held one hand over the horn, but pulled it back as the car slid into a parking spot in front of the gas station/deli. The door opened and one long leg emerged followed by its owner.

The man wasn't in uniform, but Annie knew automatically he was a cop. Or a detective, more likely. Something about him had that aura. Smart. Disciplined. Sexy.

She shook her head at the last thought and inched forward, wondering if the heat had gotten to her.

The man turned toward her, giving her a nice view of a strong jaw, dark hair and crooked nose. The nose, whether acquired in a bar fight or merely a hazard of the job, made him more interesting. He worked out, that was certain. His chest was broad, but he looked quick enough. He must have felt her perusal because he zeroed in on her as the car swooped by him.

She saw the antenna raise and bleep in his mind. Awareness of something different. *Rental car. Note license plate. File away in recesses of mind for later use if necessary.* It was exactly what she'd have done.

Spencer started humming as she pulled onto the highway, glancing at the GPS affixed to the windshield. Twenty-two more miles until the turnoff for Beau Soleil, the plantation home where Carter and Tawny Keene waited for them. The mansion served as a backdrop for the movie Carter was directing, some mystery or horror movie starring Spencer's mother as the dumb blonde who ironically doesn't get axed in the opening. Or something like that. Annie hadn't paid too much attention—horror films didn't interest her. She liked period pieces, so maybe the old house would be interesting. She would be staying there with the Keene family while the rest of the cast and crew stayed at a local motel.

The drive to Bayou Bridge, the town nearest the plantation home, was uneventful. Tangled woods with palmetto lurking beneath branches lined the highway with the occasional pasture interrupting. Then there was the long bridge over the mysterious swamp basin with thin trees and brackish waters giving rise to the flight of the odd egret. It had a unique beauty that drew Annie's eyes from the monotonous asphalt more times than it should.

The cell phone sitting in the cup holder chirped. She looked down. Tawny again. The woman was a high-maintenance nightmare, but she worshipped her Spencer. Annie ignored the jittering phone since they would be there in ten minutes and she didn't want to pull over and waste time.

"Is that my mom?" Spencer asked.

"Um—" She didn't want to lie. The books had said be truthful with children. "Hey, we're almost there. Then we can see about getting some of those crawfish for dinner, huh?"

"Really? Cool."

Mission accomplished.

She exited the interstate and drove through the charming Bayou Bridge before taking the turn on the highway that hugged the Bayou Tete. Annie wanted to stop the car and indulge in the sight of colossal live oaks fanning their branches over the snaking river, but didn't. Beau Soleil sat on the bank of the bayou so there would be plenty of time to contemplate the land of Evangeline later. She could only imagine the breathtaking sunsets and her footfalls on the hidden paths beside the water. Maybe she could sneak a run in that very evening.

"Am I gonna get to see a real alligator, too?" Spencer interrupted her yearning for tranquility and a good sweat. She never knew kids asked so many questions, but they did. Lots.

"I don't know."

"But this is Wouisiana. I gotta see an alligator." Spencer allowed a little whine into his voice. She'd given him a picture book about the bayou state when she found out they'd have to go. He'd studied the thing on the plane, pointing out Mardi Gras floats, crawfish and his absolute favorite subject—alligators. Then she'd found a book called *Mr. Breaux Bader and his Ghost Town Gator* at the airport and read it three times while they waited on their luggage.

"It's *Lou*isiana, and I'm sure we can find someone who will take us to see an alligator."

"Cool. I can't wait."

The trees hung over the road, blocking out the afternoon sun, and as Annie took a big curve, she saw the iron gates opening to Beau Soleil. First impression was stately, old and very Southern. Annie felt a shiver as she drove through. She wasn't sure if it was a sense of homecoming, which would have been weird, or a sense of foreboding, which would be alarming. But something snaked along her spine.

"We're here."

She heard the iPod touch thump against the seat.

"What's that?" Spencer asked.

"What's what?"

"That."

Annie swiveled her head to see a small patch of ground ringed with an old iron fence laced with rose bushes. Concrete tombs surrounded a huge mausoleum sitting in the center. "Um, a cemetery."

"What's that?"

The questions the kid asked. Jeez. They hadn't addressed

death in those books she'd studied. Wasn't that a parent's job? Be truthful. "It's where they bury people when they die."

"They put you in a box like that? I thought you got put in dirt or something. That's where they put my gram. They covered her up with dirt."

"Well, usually they do, but this area is below sea level so they can't do that here in South Louisiana."

"What's sea wevel?"

Lord, help me. She glanced in the mirror. He looked perplexed. "Ask you mother."

Explaining death, burial and the fact bodies would float if they were buried below sea level wasn't in her job description. She had to draw the line somewhere.

The car crunched down the gravel road framed by thick woods on either side. Finally, the view opened to reveal a huge yellow plantation home.

"Wow," Spencer breathed from the backseat.

His response was an understatement. The home sitting at the end of the drive was beautiful in the way a grand old dame was. Clinging to the vestiges of beauty, showing the good bones beneath but helpless against the ravages of time. It was the perfect house for a Southern Gothic horror flick.

Spencer bounced around in the backseat.

"Hey, are you out of the booster?"

"Yeah. We're in the driveway." He said it with a teen-ager's "duh" tone.

"Doesn't matter. If I applied the brakes, you could get hurt." She tapped the brakes a bit to show him. Spencer flew forward and smacked his head on the console.

"Owwww!" he cried.

Crap. She smothered another stronger curse under her tongue and stopped in the middle of the drive. She turned to the boy who had started wailing. "Oh, Spencer, I'm sorry. Let me see."

"No!" He cupped a small hand over his forehead. "You're mean."

Great. Just what she needed. Tawny and her accusing blue eyes. Frankly, after four nannies in a year, the family was lucky to find even someone as childcare-challenged as Annie to take on the job. Tawny had a reputation, especially when it came to her son, but she had no clue Annie was undercover security for her child. Only her husband, Carter, knew the truth. Ace wanted everyone in the household to react naturally to better her chance of identifying the person threatening the child. The police thought the threats were perpetrated by a crazy fan and recommended standard precautions. But Annie's boss had agreed with Carter Keene—they would take no chances.

"Come on, Spencer, I didn't mean to hurt you."

She reached back and tugged at his arm.

"Don't," he snuffled, finally removing his hand. There wasn't even a mark on his forehead.

She cupped his chin, angling his head left and right. "It looks fine. I'm sorry. Okay?"

He nodded.

She let out a sigh. "Now get your fanny back in the seat and buckle up. We don't want you to get hurt again. Never know when a driver might need to brake for a squirrel or dog."

The little boy wiggled his hind end into the booster seat and swiped at the tears. The child had beautiful chocolate eyes with envy-inspiring lashes. "So can I have the Skittles in your purse since you hurted me?"

Damn. Swindled by a five-year-old. She glanced at the purse she'd bought when she'd taken on the nanny assignment. It was big and floppy. She hated it, but it allowed her to carry things Spencer needed, like wipes, hand sanitizer, extra socks, bandages and the ever-present iPod touch with charger. She'd hidden her Skittles in the zipper pocket. "It's 'hurt,' not 'hurted,' and you can have them."

She glanced in the rearview mirror. He smiled. "Cool."

Annie pulled into the large circular drive in front of the mansion. As she put the car in Park, the double doors flew open and Tawny emerged and clacked down the porch steps heading for her child.

"Mom!" Spencer struggled against his seat belt, kicking his legs and squirming.

"Birdie!" Tawny shouted, flinging open the back door and climbing in. "Oh, I've missed my boy so much."

Tawny smacked noisy kisses on Spencer's cheeks and neck as the little boy laughed and threw chubby arms around her neck. Annie couldn't contain the smile twitching at her lips. Those two were totally gaga for one another. If it hadn't been so damn sweet, it would have been nauseating.

"Hello, Tawny," Annie said, pulling her purse along as she climbed out of the cool car and into the moist heat of the Deep South. Her breath caught and immediately she felt sweat pop out on her upper lip. Why did sane people live in such oppression?

Tawny looked up. "Hi, Amy, and I thought I asked you to call me Mrs. Keene."

Spencer slid from the car. "Her name's not Amy. It's Annie."

Tawny blinked. "You're such a smart boy. Of course, it's Annie. I forgot."

Spencer ran up the grand stone steps of the large home. "Where's the alligators? I wanna see them. Annie said maybe we'd eat some crawfish."

Tawny followed, her platinum-streaked hair swishing

with the rhythm of her steps. She wore towering stilettos paired with itty-bitty blue-jeaned shorts and a halter top and looked as if she'd tumbled from a Hooters ad.

Annie tucked a piece of brown frizz behind her ear and climbed onto the wide veranda of the house that Tawny and Spencer had disappeared into. She hesitated a moment, stretching her toes in her running shoes, dropping the bag at her feet and rolling her head side to side in order to work out the kinks the torturous hours of travel had given her.

"I can work that out for you if you want."

The voice came from Annie's left. She flinched, appalled to have been caught unaware, and turned toward the person standing stock-still in the shadows.

The older woman was about as odd a sight as Annie had ever seen. Dressed in a pair of faded black yoga pants and a skintight tank top, she stood poised like a crane. Her long thin legs bent at odd angles while her sticklike arms curved in midair. Thick silver hair lay in a fat braid over one shoulder as if it grew from the bright green bandana wrapped round the woman's head. Serene violet eyes stared unflinchingly at Annie.

"Oh, I didn't see you there," Annie said, trying to tamp down the alarm in not sensing someone within her immediate perimeter. Were her skills that rusty?

"That's the point," the woman said, unfurling and moving into another unnatural position. "That is the essence of Tai Chi—to ebb, flow and become centered. At one with the universe. A calm fixture within chaos."

"Right," Annie said, rehoisting her bag onto one shoulder and moving toward the open doorway.

"I'm serious about the massage. I've studied tension points in the body," the older woman called. "Your aura is deep red. You need untangling."

Annie turned around. "Untangling?"

The older woman smiled. "Or maybe a mint julep?"

"Who are you? And do you really serve mint juleps on the veranda down here? I thought that was a touristy trick."

"Ah, maybe. I prefer good bourbon straight up, myself. Oh, and we call it *the porch*."

"Me, too. On the bourbon." Annie stuck her hand out. "I'm Annie Perez, Spencer's nanny."

The older woman smiled, but didn't move toward Annie. She flowed into another position. "You don't seem like a nanny."

Unease pricked at Annie's nape. "Yet I am."

The older lady unwound, placing both bare feet on the planks of the porch. She took Annie in from head to toe. "I'm Picou Dufrene and this is my home. Welcome to Beau Soleil, Annie Perez."

The woman seemed to possess the uncanny ability to see beyond the outer wrapping. Most people saw a young Hispanic woman and put her in a category. For the past few weeks, no one questioned her being the worst nanny to ever hold the position. Annie walked to the rail of the porch and rubbed a finger along the spidering paint as she surveyed the wide span of lawn with its moss-draped twisted oaks and allowed the romance of the place to seep into her bones. Maybe Louisiana wouldn't be so bad for the next month. It wasn't palm trees and balmy ocean breezes, but its earthy beauty tugged at the soul. Plus, the quirky Picou Dufrene interested her. "Thank you, Mrs. Dufrene."

"It's Picou."

"Annie! You gotta see this!" Spencer exploded onto the porch, nearly tripping over himself. Annie put a steadying hand on his shoulder.

"Slow down," she said, pulling his little hand into hers.

"I saw a bear!" His brown eyes danced with excitement.

Picou's laugh was smoky. "That's Chewie. My son Nate named him after the wookiee in *Star Wars*."

Annie allowed Spencer to tug her toward the house. "I'm hoping this one is stuffed?"

Picou gave her a secret smile. "One can never be too sure at Beau Soleil. What seems benign can sometimes bite."

Picou's words followed Annie into the house, dancing around her mind, making her wonder if the kooky owner had some otherworldly sense about life and the people who trudged through it. Annie didn't believe in magic hoo-ha crap, but she knew from her late grandmother some people were more perceptive than others. Or maybe merely more observant.

Better to heed Picou's words and trust no one. Spencer's life might depend on it.

CHAPTER THREE

NATE DUFRENE WATCHED Sandi Whitehall hurry out of the liquor store with two bottles of grain alcohol and a carton of Marlboros. Not good. Paul was drinking again and that meant the next day Sandi would likely be wearing heavy makeup and moving slowly. Not that the woman would ever admit to her husband beating the crap out of her every time he fell off the wagon. The whole damn town knew about the Whitehalls, but he couldn't do anything if Sandi wouldn't press charges. Which she wouldn't.

He shook his head and watched the traffic creep by, nearly everyone braking when they caught sight of him sitting in the borrowed sheriff's cruiser under the truck-stop sign advertising cigarettes, video poker and boudin. It was almost comical.

His mind flipped back to the brunette in the rental who'd pulled out of Breaux Mart a few hours before. She'd known he was law enforcement even if he'd been in his unmarked. He'd seen it in her expression as she'd pulled by him.

At first he'd thought her a regular soccer mom, replete with a rug rat in the backseat, properly restrained, until he'd caught sight of the rental tag. Of course, nothing wrong with renting a car for a trip. But still, she'd given off a strange vibe, and it had raised a flag in his awareness. Likely she was halfway to Alexandria or Lake Charles by now, heading to Grandma's house or something equally harmless.

He settled into the seat and closed his eyes. He hated sitting out here, but Buddy Rosen's wife had unexpectedly delivered a baby boy early that morning. Nate had "gifted" them with covering Buddy's shift for the afternoon even though he'd sworn he'd never sit in a patrol car again. It hadn't seemed like such a sacrifice until he'd had to change a flat tire on the drive from West Feliciana parish and then discovered Buddy had been assigned to watch a four-way. So much for his day off.

His cell phone rang.

Picou.

He sighed. "Dufrene."

"I know very well who you are. I called, didn't I?"

He sighed again.

"Get over here right now."

His mother sounded winded. Panicky. He hadn't caught it in her initial greeting but now his Spidey senses kicked in. "Why?"

"The boy has gone missing."

"The boy? What boy?"

His mother sucked in a breath. "The director's son. His nanny took a shower while Tawny was playing with him, but then Tawny got a call and went to another room. When she came back, he was gone. Just hurry."

The phone clicked. She'd hung up.

Nate started the cruiser, but didn't put the lights on. His mother had good reason to overreact to a missing child, a fact well-known to the Bayou Bridge Police Department and the Sheriff's office. She'd called in his younger brother Darby as missing many times over the course of his childhood. This boy had probably done what most little boys do—traipsed off into the woods to explore or play a game of hide-and-seek in the many rooms of Beau Soleil. But, still, some children didn't come home.

Just like Della.

Regret hit him hard, as it always did. Her disappearance had been partially his fault. But he didn't want to think about that February day no matter how much it stayed with him, like Peter Pan's shadow sewed onto his conscience.

Della. Gone. His fault.

He glanced down at the manila folder sitting in the passenger's seat as he pulled onto the highway and headed toward his childhood home. Another detective had handed it to him when he'd left the station that morning, but he'd yet to open the file. Instead he'd allowed it to sit like a ticking bomb, afraid it would explode and crack the thin layer over the wound festering for the past twenty-four years. He refused to watch his mother crash and burn all over again. Because even though he was a big, tough St. Martin Parish detective, his mother's tears brought him to his knees.

Never again.

His murdered sister was gone and there was little sense in digging it up again. Every other lead over the past had played out, and this new wrinkle would, too. But following up was his job—for both his family and this girl asking questions.

He shrugged off the burn between his shoulder blades and increased his speed, hugging the twisting road. He'd not been to Beau Soleil in over a week. Not since the gypsy had visited Picou. Or was it a mambo? Either way the woman had given him the creeps. For one thing she was blind, and for another, she looked like one of the witches from Macbeth.

Huckster. That's what she was. Had his mother believing all sorts of nonsense about setting suns, righting wrongs, and prophesies about birds or some such crap. Picou's quest for answers was ridiculous. He could tolerate the occasional trip to Baton Rouge to consult a palm reader because that incorporated a visit to her cardiologist, but bringing those sorts of people out to the house crossed the line.

The gates greeted him before he bumped down the long, winding drive faster than normal. He needed to seem as if he were in a hurry. Otherwise, he'd hear about it for the next few weeks. The Arch Angels Feast Day was coming up and he'd been hoodwinked by the parish priest into serving on the church's committee, so there'd be no escaping Picou, who was the chairwoman of the celebration.

He rounded the corner and saw her. Not his mother. Or the actress. But the woman from the rental car he'd seen outside the Whiskey Bay gas station.

She stood calmly in the center of chaos, hair damp, brow furrowed. All around her people scurried, left, right and in circles, calling out and craning their heads in that universal motion signaling something lost.

In this case—a child.

He rolled to a halt and climbed from the car.

"Oh, Nate, thank heavens!" Picou called, drawing the attention of the people milling about. The woman who he now assumed was the freshly showered nanny caught his gaze. Her eyes widened slightly, but she didn't move.

A well-endowed blonde tumbled toward him, and he recognized her from the pictures in the local newspaper.

"Oh, God, please help us. My baby. He's gone!"

He placed a hand on the woman's shoulder as much to keep her from crashing into him as to hold her up. "Okay, Mrs. Keene, take a deep breath and tell me what happened."

The blonde burst into tears, shaking her head and swiping at the streaking mascara on her cheeks. Her thin shoulders shook and she covered her face with both hands and sobbed. The presumed nanny stepped forward and took the actress's elbow. "Go sit down, Tawny. I'll talk to the deputy."

Her voice was nice. Kind of low and gravelly. It had quiet authority, probably from all the nannying she did.

Tawny nodded and allowed a pale Picou to lead her away. Nate looked hard at his own mother. She looked shaken and he felt every tremble of her hand as it stroked the actress's back. His mother's clouded eyes met his and he tried to convey *reassurance* in his nod, but as usual, he failed to comfort her.

He turned his gaze back to the nanny.

"I'm Annie Perez," she said, stepping forward without extending a hand, as if recognizing the situation didn't call for niceties but rather expediency. "I work for the Keenes as Spencer's caretaker."

People still scrambled around them. Many looked to be part of the production crew, if their sweaty T-shirts and baggy parachute shorts were any indication. He would expect the nanny to be searching desperately, but she wasn't. Her calm struck him as peculiar.

"Lieutenant Nate Dufrene."

"Dufrene?"

"Picou's my mother."

"Oh."

"Time is of essence…"

She stiffened. "Right. Tawny took Spencer to her room to spend some time with him. She said he fell asleep while she read to him, so she stepped out to make a phone call. When she hung up, he was gone. I've searched the rooms on the second floor, top to bottom."

"Closets? Bed—"

"Thoroughly," Annie interrupted, pushing a piece of hair behind her ear. Sweat beaded her upper lip, reminding him to wipe the sweat from his own forehead. Too hot for mid-September.

"The first floor?"

"Your mother and Mr. Keene searched the bottom floor—"

"Third floor?" he interrupted.

"The housekeeper—I've forgotten her name—and the production assistant are searching now. Mr. Keene brought some of the crew to search the grounds and outer buildings."

"Lucille."

She frowned. "What?"

"The housekeeper's name is Lucille." He realized that had nothing to do with the task at hand. "What about personal security? Does Keene have it?"

"His name is Brick, but he was with Carter on set. He's out there searching now," she said, with the slight lift of her shoulder. Any other time and he would have thought it sexy, but not in the middle of a crisis. Or that's what he told himself.

"Where do you think the child is?"

"If I knew, you wouldn't be here."

Okay, it had been a dumb question. "Best guess?"

"I don't know. We had a long flight from L.A., and he could have gotten up to look for me or Tawny and fallen back asleep somewhere. He's done that before, but if he dozed off elsewhere, it's somewhere very strange." She averted her eyes and he knew there was something she wasn't saying. Something darker and more worrisome.

She started walking toward the door of the house. She didn't invite him to follow. He followed anyway. She turned around. "You may want to talk to Mr. Keene. He's in the kitchen on the phone with the FBI."

"FBI?" Nate stepped inside the house. "The child has been missing for all of thirty minutes, why would Keene call the feds?"

"That's not my place to say."

"Humor me. There's a child missing."

He saw reason overcome duty. "Fine. The family has been receiving threats for the last several months, directed at Spencer."

He studied her in the gloom of the entryway. Alert, no-nonsense and levelheaded, this woman seemed once again something more than what her job title hinted. "You sure you're just the nanny?"

A flicker of something appeared in those quicksilver eyes. "What do you expect? A bodyguard? The Keenes have one of those."

Her words didn't drip with sarcasm, but it was there. She seemed offended he didn't trust her. "Sorry. You don't talk like a nanny and with the threats, other precautions might have been taken."

Another lift of her shoulder. Again, kind of sexy. "Look, I'm just a former real-estate agent. The housing market sucks, and I needed a job. Besides, the only threats have been letters and, maybe, a rock through the production office's window. Nothing to necessitate locking down the kid. The FBI is looking into it as a courtesy to Mr. Keene since he consults with them on his films. My job is to keep the kid with me when he's not with his parents…something even a former real-estate agent can manage."

He couldn't stop his lips from twitching. He liked her prickly and smart-assed. Suited her. And made those mysterious gray eyes crackle. "Okay, I get the picture. So why aren't you as concerned as everyone else?"

"Who says I'm not?" she challenged, lifting her chin. Her skin was smooth and golden, her cheeks broad and high. Her hair frizzed around her face, making her hard edges a bit softer. She was altogether an intriguing woman. "Do I have to run about like a chicken missing its head in order to be worried?"

"No." Yes. Every woman he knew reacted in that way. Were real-estate agents any different?

"So I don't panic. Won't help find Spencer. Oh, and by the way, I don't know what was in the notes they received. Only what I heard from the staff. You'll have to ask Mr. Keene."

She'd anticipated his next question. Odd.

He stood a moment watching her as she pushed through the swinging kitchen door. Then he followed and found Carter Keene, careworn and sweat-soaked, holding the corded phone Nate's mother insisted on keeping. He spoke intently to whoever was on the other end of the line. When he saw Nate, he cupped a hand over the mouthpiece. The cavernous kitchen felt oppressive with the man's apprehension. Nate preferred Annie's calm assurance or Tawny's wailing melodrama over the desperation in Carter Keene's eyes.

"Nate? Thanks for coming. You know about the threats against Spencer in California?"

Nate nodded. "Ms. Perez told me a little."

The former star of *Miami Metro,* now turned director, looked at Annie. "Tell him what he needs to know. I'll join you out back when I finish talking to Agent Burrell."

Annie gave Carter a look, as if communicating something. Were they involved somehow? With Carter's former reputation, it wouldn't surprise him. Nannies had to be easy plucking, but this one didn't seem the type to dally with the boss.

Yet after ten years in law enforcement, nothing truly surprised him.

The nanny motioned Nate through the back door and onto the bricked patio as if she were the hostess of Beau Soleil. As if she were the one in charge. He bristled. This was his damned house. Okay, not his, per se, but his family's. Something about this woman both soothed and rankled.

"Look, I need to call for backup. Do you know if Keene has talked to Blaine Gentry about the situation?"

She shook her head and averted her gaze. "I don't know who Blaine Gentry is."

"The sheriff."

"Oh," she said, her eyes searching the property behind the house. "What's out there?"

She pointed to the horizon toward where the land sloped off toward the Bayou Tete. She also ignored his question.

"The bayou." He combed his hand through his hair, wicking the sweat from his forehead. "So is the sheriff aware of this threat situation? He's hasn't mentioned it to our department. And is there anything you can tell me about Spencer that might help me? A special toy? Activity? Perhaps he did something naughty and doesn't want to be discovered?"

Annie's eyes glazed into thoughtfulness, and he could almost see the cogwheels in her mind turning. A furrow crinkled her forehead. She blinked once. Then twice. "You know, I think I know where he might have gone."

"Where?"

"To see the alligators."

"Alligators? We don't..." His voice trailed off as she turned, breaking into a jog as her feet hit the thick grass of the lawn. He snapped his mouth closed. "Hey, where are you going?"

"He wanted to see a real alligator. I told him we'd find one later, but he's not good at waiting," she called back.

Nate jogged after her. "Surely he wouldn't wander off with no one seeing him? To the bayou? By himself?"

"You don't know children well, do you?"

He didn't answer. No, he didn't know children at all.

Why would he? But he didn't think a child could make it down the stairs, through the kitchen and across the wide lawn without making noise or at least one person seeing him. It didn't seem plausible.

The distance to the bayou was a good piece. Thanks to numerous hurricanes, fallen oaks lay uprooted, their grotesque limbs stretching toward a cloudless sky, blocking their progress to the river. Finally they reached the edge of the property. "To your left."

She veered, spying the worn path leading down the embankment toward the river. Her footing was steady, though the path was steep. All the while her eyes methodically searched the silted bank below.

"Spencer!" she shouted, quickening her steps.

Nate pounded behind her, slipping often on the eroded bank, before catching his footing. He skidded to the bottom and saw the boy, standing near the water, kicking at an old tire that had lodged in some reeds. Nate held up at the bottom of the path, but Annie made a beeline for the boy.

Spencer turned his head and grinned. "Look what I found, Annie. A tire. We can make a swing like Tony made in the book."

Annie scooped him up and gave him a tight squeeze.

"Ow! Stop it, Annie." Spencer squirmed, kicking his legs.

"I ought to paddle your behind, Spencer Keene," Annie said, setting the boy on the bank away from the river. "You've nearly given your mother a heart attack."

He wrinkled his nose. "What's a heart attack? And I don't want to get a paddle. Why would I get a paddle?"

The nanny sighed and sent her pretty eyes heavenward, mouthing something. Was she counting? Then she dropped to her knees and cupped Spencer's chin.

"Hey, who's he?" the boy asked, trying to rip his face from Annie's hand. He pointed a chubby finger toward Nate.

"That's not important now. I want your eyes to meet mine. Now." Her voice was firm. Very firm.

Spencer stopped struggling, his gaze moving to Annie's, the first inkling of *uh-oh* in his eyes.

"Don't you ever, ever, go somewhere by yourself without asking first. Ever." Annie's voice shook and at that moment, Nate knew that however the woman had first appeared to him, she'd been frightened for her charge. Or maybe she was overcome with anger.

What he could see of Spencer's chin started to wobble. "I wanted to see the alligators. You said I could."

"That's no excuse. You did not have permission to come here by yourself. Do you know how dangerous this is? We've talked about this. About how you aren't allowed to go anywhere alone."

A fat tear plopped onto Annie's wrist. "Don't be mad at me, Annie. I just wanted to see the alligators—"

Annie shook her head. "No. I am mad at you because you could have been hurt. Badly. Don't ever do that again."

Nate started to intervene. They needed to alert everyone at the house, Spencer had been located and was safe, but as he watched Annie tug Spencer into her arms, saw the small boy cry on her shoulder, something stayed him. Annie wrapped her arms about the boy and rocked him slightly, before lifting and carrying the child toward him.

"Here," she said, shoving the boy into his arms. "Carry him up the hill. He's too heavy for me."

Nate flinched as the child wriggled. So much for tenderness. Spencer cocked his head back and stared at him with big brown tear-filled eyes. "Who are you?"

Annie started scrabbling up the hill, not bothering to

look back at where Nate stood holding the child. "Obviously, I'm her minion."

"Oh," the child said, pursing his lips into an O. "What's a minion?"

Nate sighed and walked toward the little-used path that would take him back to Beau Soleil. "Someone who has to follow the directives of a master."

"What's diwectives?"

Nate smiled. "What she tells me to do."

"Oh. Then I'm a minion, too," Spencer declared. "I want down. I can climb good."

Nate set the child down because his calves screamed and his back didn't feel much better.

Spencer dropped to his hands and knees and made like a monkey scrambling up an incline. The child's bottom wagged in the air, and he started making monkey sounds. Nate almost smiled because he'd forgotten the silliness of children, but he remembered the seriousness of the situation and recalled Annie's face as she passed him, handing off the boy. She'd been too emotional to deal with the child.

A twinge of something unknown plinked in his chest. Odd, and not comforting, was the knowledge he'd become fascinated by the plucky nanny in such a short time, almost from the moment he'd first spotted her behind the wheel of the rented Chevrolet. Some primal urge inside him wanted to crack her veneer and dig beneath her mask of supreme capability to the sweet vulnerability he'd just glimpsed.

Hell. Not what he needed. A prickling awareness for someone obviously not interested in him. For someone staying a few weeks at the most. For someone hiding something. His instincts told him so, and if there was one thing Nate could claim about himself, it was having good instincts. Something was off about the nanny.

By the time he emerged from the path, Annie had Spencer by the hand and people were bearing down on them, including the director and his wife.

Catastrophe averted.

But something told Nate things were just starting to heat up. Or maybe that was his blood. He never thought of himself as a Mary Poppins man, but that nanny was doing weird things to him. And he didn't like it.

SEVERAL HOURS LATER, after a supper of Creole fried chicken and a summer salad, Annie sat in the wood-paneled den of Beau Soleil, watching as Tawny balanced a teacup on her knee and stroked Spencer's head. He sat on the floor putting puzzles together while his mother read a fashion magazine and occasionally chatted with Picou about psychics, mediums and the truthfulness in séances. For once, Spencer seemed content with the task, biting his lip as he tried to force pieces where they couldn't possibly fit.

Annie knew how that felt. She'd been living a giant jigsaw puzzle for the past year. Not fitting no matter how much she tried to shove the pieces in.

Like this job.

First, she was less than good in her nanny undercover role. She'd probably screw the kid up before she finished the assignment. And second, she had no leads on the perpetrator. Zip. Zero. Nada.

This afternoon had scared her. Putting her in as the nanny hadn't been fair to Spencer. Prime example— alligators. Why hadn't she explained to him how dangerous alligators were? Or the truth about animals with sharp teeth? Why hadn't she gone over rules with him about where he could go at the old mansion, and who he could go with? She should have briefed him on what to expect at Beau Soleil.

But she hadn't. She'd been too tired. Wanted a shower.

And had been more than happy to hand the child over to his mother.

She'd have never done something so sloppy when she'd been with the Bureau. Of course, she'd never been in charge of a kid. Never had to go undercover. But it had proven to her yet again she wasn't cut out for raising children. She didn't have the knack. Her failed almost-marriage to a man with a daughter had proven as much. She and Mallory had been oil and water.

Spencer looked up at her and smiled. Her heart unwillingly swelled in her chest.

Damn.

Okay, so she could see the attraction of kids. They were a pain in the butt, but when they smiled like that, or lay their little heads so trustingly on your shoulder, well, all bets were off on the old ticker. Spencer's smile did funny things to her.

She smiled back.

He went back to work on the puzzle, and his mother turned toward her. "I hope you're planning on doing a better job of keeping up with my son, Amy. We fired the last nanny, you know."

Annie shoved her magazine onto the table crowded with knickknacks as irritation gnawed at her. She needed to grab hold of some coolness. The last nanny had been fired for sexting with her boyfriend while hiding out in the pool cabana during Spencer's fifth-birthday party over a month ago. It had been an awkward discovery especially since her boyfriend sat right next to her, naked and at attention. Annie really didn't see sexting in her future.

Spencer looked up. "Mom, her name is Annie."

Tawny wrinkled her nose. "Funny birdie, you remember everything."

"Taw—Mrs. Keene, my aim is to take care of Spencer

every moment he's in my care." She wanted to point out he'd not been in her care when he disappeared. He'd been in his mother's. Instead she silently counted to ten.

"He was with you when he went missing, Tawny," Picou interrupted, licking her thumb and turning the page of her *Southern Living* magazine.

Tawny frowned. "Well, she was on duty. Her day ends when Spencer's does."

"But you told her to leave him with you," Picou persisted, her eyes on the magazine, but her intent clear. "That sends mixed messages. Either he's with you or he's with her."

Tawny didn't say anything more. Her silence was almost petulant. She picked up the magazine and her lips started moving as she read silently.

"Are you ready for bed, Spencer?" Annie asked, hoping to shift the tension in the room. It was tough being on the Keenes' payroll even though technically she wasn't. She didn't know how much longer she could hold her tongue over Tawny's unreasonable expectations.

"No," Spencer said, shaking his head emphatically.

Tawny dropped her hand onto his head and rubbed his silky brown hair. Her message was unmistakable. Spencer wasn't going to bed until the actress was ready. For some reason Tawny was hostile to Annie. She'd yet to figure out why the normally bouncy actress went all snake eyes on her.

Annie shifted in the comfortable armchair and glanced about the room. A floral rug anchored the space beneath a bank of windows that allowed a study of the bricked patio with its still-blooming containers of verbena and begonias. Comfortable, slipcovered furniture scattered the room, with built-in bookcases taking up a whole wall. The room was feminine without being nauseating, and Annie liked it better than any other room she'd seen in the colossal house.

A huge portrait of the Dufrene boys dominated the space over the fireplace, tripping her thoughts back to the man who'd rattled her today. Nate Dufrene had suspected she was not really a nanny. Almost blew her cover. Thank goodness Ace had the IT guy build her a real-estate site in Nevada. Hopefully, if someone went looking, they'd see Annie Perez as a failed chica real-estate agent desperate to make rent. Outside of the fake career, that's pretty much what she was anyway. Well, half chica.

But then again, most "someones" weren't detectives with prying chocolate eyes and a nose for truth. If Nate poked around too much, he'd discover she'd never sold a house in her life.

She studied the portrait. Nate's dark hair had been clipped short and his expression was a mixture of boredom and tolerance. He'd not been happy about sitting still in button-up clothes next to his younger brothers. It was fairly obvious.

"Those are my sons," Picou said, catching Annie staring at the portrait. "Nate is the tall one. The others are Abram and Darby."

Annie smiled politely. "All nice-looking boys."

"Aren't they? Yet I can't seem to collect any daughters-in-law, which is a shame. I'd love to have a grandson like Spencer someday."

"Like me?" Spencer asked, scrambling to his feet, abandoning the puzzle pieces. He preened and gave the older woman the same dimpled smile his father had been delivering since his *Tiger Beat* magazine days. Killer.

Picou's eyes widened. Yep. Got her.

The older woman wore a patterned blue caftan, replete with a girlish bow pinned on the side of her platinum hair.

It looked utterly ridiculous, but yet, somehow fitting for the matriarch of the Dufrene clan. "Just like you...or a girl might be nice."

"A girl? Girls are dumb. They like purses and stuff." Spencer delivered a disgusted look.

Annie glanced back at the young Nate and recalled how the older Nate made her feel. Not just apprehensive, but interested. He'd grown into a long, tall, sexy drink of water, his youthful cheeks melting into a lean jaw and whiskered chin. Bright eyes fading to weary. Hair curling just behind his ears. Broad shoulders tapering to square, masculine hands. Yes, the man was on her radar, damn it.

Why couldn't her rational mind control her irrational desires?

It was not like her to feel so attracted to a cop. Or, rather, someone so similar to her. She'd always liked the shy guys, the ones who seemed bumblingly inept, with sweet smiles and simple outlooks on life. Seth had fit the bill.

Nate Dufrene did not. He felt dangerous. Not biddable. Not sweet and complacent—more like intense, deep water with a strong current.

Annie had a job to do and the farther she stayed away from Nate Dufrene, the better. She didn't need him hanging around, chipping away her façade, tempting her with his haunted eyes. Something about him compelled her to draw near when she needed to pull back—especially since she still had to split an astronomical mortgage on a condo with the last mistake she'd made. And that note was due at the end of the month.

She caught Picou regarding her with a thoughtful expression. Annie pulled her gaze away from both the portrait and Picou. The glint in the woman's eye made her squirm. *Not going to happen, lady.* Annie wasn't barking up that particular tree.

"Time for bed, Spencer." This from Tawny.

Finally.

Annie rose from the chair and held out her hand. Spencer took it, rubbing his eyes with the other hand while yawning. Once again something warm stole across her heart. He reached up for her to pick him up, so she did, enjoying his arms curling around her neck. He looked back at his mom and Picou. "Mom, Annie's not in trouble, is she? She told me I could see the gators, but I didn't wanna wait."

Annie froze, her back to Tawny and Picou.

"Of course not, birdie. And I'll take you to see the gators, okay?"

"'Kay," Spencer murmured, stifling a yawn.

"Good night, birdie. Love you," Tawny called as Annie walked to the door. "And goodnight to you, too, Amy."

Annie bit off a retort.

Tawny had gotten that one in on purpose.

CHAPTER FOUR

NATE LEANED BACK AGAINST the supple leather of his desk chair, his heavy sigh interrupting the silence of his office. He'd been through the files for the third time that week, looking for anything that might grab him, might stand out enough to follow, but there was nothing. Dead end in every direction.

He grabbed the files and bagged evidence and carefully placed them back into the cardboard box, setting it on the short filing cabinet. His office needed organizing. In fact, his whole house could use a good cleaning. His house-keeper, Gloria, cleaned the toilets and changed the sheets once a week, but she couldn't make heads or tails of the cold-case boxes lining the wood floor of the living room.

Damn it. Radrica Moore's killer would go unpunished.

He shoved the lid onto the box. Then he hesitated. He didn't want to give up. Wouldn't be fair to Radrica. To her mother, who still mourned the death of the thirteen-year-old honor student. He pulled off the lid and propped it against the box, staring into the contents.

There was very little physical evidence in the case. The body of the African American girl had been found in stag-nant water of the flooded timberland just off the Mississippi River, badly decomposed. The cause of death had been inconclusive, though the coroner found evidence of pos-sible defensive wounds. The Rapides sheriff's department classified it as a homicide, but had nothing else to go on.

Nate padded into his kitchen, opened the fridge and surveyed the contents: six pack of Abita, leftover barbecue from the Wing Shack and a package of luncheon meat he didn't remember buying. He grabbed an Abita and shut the door.

As he cracked open the beer, he shifted his thoughts from the cold case lying dead in his office to the incident at Beau Soleil that afternoon. Even though the boy had been found safe and sound, something bothered him about the whole deal.

Annie Perez.

Maybe that's who had him at attention.

And not in a way he welcomed.

When he'd reached the reunion between the "missing" Spencer and his over-the-top mother, he noticed how easily Annie faded into the background—purposely, it seemed.

She'd skirted the gathering, melding herself into a quiet statue on the perimeter, but her eyes had been searching the group of people gathered as if weighing some unseen force.

But maybe that's who she was. Cautious, still and serious. Nothing wrong with being quiet, even if intensity flowed out of every pore of the woman.

Desire snaked into his belly.

Exactly what he didn't need. He lifted the bottle and took a swig, swiping a hand across his mouth. It had been a while since he'd dated. Maybe too long. He'd been busy this past summer with more requests for help on cold cases than he could handle. The state budget had police and sheriff departments cut to the bone, and word had gotten out about his talent with homicide cases that had no pulse. His consulting jobs were freebies, and sometimes when things were slow, Blaine gave him leeway. Not that it really mattered. He didn't work them for the money anyway. He worked them for the satisfaction of getting what he'd never have—completion.

He walked back to his office and stared at the database open on the computer screen. The Annie Perez he'd met earlier today hadn't been a real-estate agent in California. Didn't mean she hadn't been one someplace else, which was why he reserved judgment on the woman and stopped poking around looking for info on her. He had no real reason to check her out—she'd done nothing wrong. Still, something told him it wouldn't be a bad idea to get to know her a little better.

The only thing he couldn't figure out was whether his interest was strictly professional. He really didn't want to think about it being anything more. He was good at hunches; bad at lying to himself.

WHEN ANNIE WOKE UP the following morning, she felt as if she'd been run over and left for dead. Spencer had ended up in her bed at some point. She'd forgotten when. Some vague notion of 2:24 a.m., muttering "climb in" and then spending the rest of the night being kicked by a mule.

She rolled over and looked at the mule sleeping peacefully on his back, mouth slack, brown hair sticking up like Billy Idol and jammies riding up over a plump little tummy.

Little devil should be on a soccer team.

She yawned in the bleary light escaping into the room through the heavy brocade drapes over the long windows. Had to be around 6:00 a.m. Her internal alarm clock woke her whether she needed to sleep longer or not. Leftover habit from high school when getting up had rested squarely on her shoulders.

She slipped out of bed, brushed her teeth, pulled on shorts and running shoes. Spencer would likely sleep until seven-thirty or so. Plenty of time for a quick exploratory run. She'd head out to the highway and get a lay of the land and be back before Spencer demanded his Fruity O's. But first she needed to let someone know she was leaving. After yesterday afternoon, she wanted the boy to be covered.

She nearly ran into Carter Keene in the kitchen.

"Up early," he said, dumping creamer into his coffee. He glanced at her briefly before picking up a spoon. "Have you checked on Spencer?"

"He's in my bed still asleep. Are you the only one up?"

"Yep. I need to get this movie in the can as soon as possible. The studio has another one lined up. Filming in Maine starts in December, so time is of the essence. We're already behind."

He looked around as if on a covert operation. She looked around, too, wondering why he overdramatized everything. Then she remembered. He was a director. Hazard of the job.

"So have you made any progress?" he whispered.

Carter hadn't talked to Ace in over a week, so the report was left to her. "We've done background checks on several of the investors of the *Goliath* movie, but haven't found anyone indicating a desire to harm you. Mad at you? Yeah. Enough to do something to Spencer or Tawny? No."

He nodded, his gorgeous blond hair catching the weak sunlight, causing a sort of halo to frame his pretty-boy face. And Annie knew from the rumors surrounding Keene that he was far from angelic. "What about Rudy Griffin?"

"Ace has one of his best guys working on his current whereabouts. From what we've learned, Rudy was on location in Oregon when the first note appeared. Right now, we're not sure where he is." Rudy was a stuntman who'd been injured on the set of *Goliath,* a big-budget movie that not only had a lion's share of production problems, but also tanked at the box office. Carter Keene had earned plenty of disgruntled non-fans on that one, but none more so than the stuntman who accused Keene's production company of unsafe and substandard practices. His burned arm had inflamed his need to bad-mouth and threaten Carter.

Carter shook his head. "It has to be him. When I found that note, I knew he'd gone off his rocker."

Annie nodded. "Rudy Griffin made threats, but lots of people make threats. Doesn't mean they'll carry through with them. This could be a random crackpot, and we may never find out who sent the notes."

"But they feel so ominous…and personal."

"They do. But we may be grasping at straws. Ace will be in touch if there is nothing more we can do. And by the way, I appreciate you not blowing my cover yesterday, Mr. Keene. It's best I stay hidden for now."

"Call me Carter, Annie."

"I'd rather not." Hadn't Tawny reminded her of her place yesterday?

Annie could see he liked to call the shots, but he shrugged. "Whatever's best."

She nodded, headed toward the back door of the kitchen and peeked out the glass door of the mudroom. Sunlight streamed through the coal-black trunks of the live oaks, throwing golden confetti on the grass beneath. Perfect morning for a run.

Spencer.

Damn. She'd forgotten to ask Carter to send Brick to babysit the door to her bedroom. She turned back around to reenter the kitchen and heard a scream come from the other side of the door.

"Spencer's not in his bed! He's gone!" It was Tawny's voice.

Annie intended to push through the kitchen door and tell Tawny the child was safe in her bed, but Carter beat her to it.

"Hell, Tawny, he's asleep in the nanny's bed. Don't you bother thinking before you start carrying on? You need to try processing something in that brain up there before opening your mouth."

Tawny closed her mouth and her eyes narrowed. "You've always enjoyed my brains, if I recall. Open mouth, too."

Neither of them saw Annie at the door and for a moment, she felt like an interloper, but didn't move. Maybe understanding the couple's relationship would help her with the case. She'd not spent much time with Carter or Tawny.

"Oh, and you're good at it, aren't you, sweetheart? That's what Mick's been saying." Carter's voice held sneer, disdain and hurt.

Whoa. Carter thought Tawny was messing around with the lead on the production, the wickedly debauched Mick Manners, who was playing the deranged killer in *Magic Man*.

"Oh, you're listening to someone other than yourself? You're telling me the great and mighty director actually realizes there are other people in the world besides himself?"

"What's that supposed to mean?"

Tawny shrugged. "You figure it out 'cause I got better things to do. By the way, after we wrap, I'm taking Spencer up to Mama's for a visit."

Carter snorted. "Why? So he can learn how to shuck corn and make crystal meth?"

"Yeah, that's what I'm going to teach him." Her voice sounded venomous and offended. She took a steadying breath. "I promised Mama I'd bring him. She's been stressed about Teri leaving Braden with her and going off with some guy from Georgia, so I thought I'd go up and make her feel better. She's having to take care of Braden all by herself."

"You haven't sent any more money to Teri, have you? That won't help her."

Tawny put her hands on her hips. "You know very well I cut her off after the Fourth of July incident. I'm just paying for some stuff for Braden. That's it."

Annie felt a pang of sadness for Tawny—nothing like family putting their hooks in and looking for a free ride. She took a step back, holding the door with the flat of her hand, letting it close slowly so she remained unseen. But her not-so-stealthy action caught Tawny's eye. The actress raced across the room and pulled the door back before Annie could escape. "What the hell are you doing? Hiding?"

Her words were accusing. Jealous. Oh, no.

"I'm going for a run, but I forgot to ask Mr. Keene if Brick could keep an eye on Spencer."

Tawny's hair was knotted and there were circles under her eyes. She gave Annie a disdainful lip curl then looked back at Carter. Her gaze held a question. "Maybe you better do your job and take care of my son before you pursue other activities."

Ouch. The woman thought she'd caught them in flagrante.

"Get your mind out of the gutter," Carter said from where he'd sunk on the old-fashioned banquette in the breakfast nook, but Annie didn't miss the gleam of satisfaction in his eyes. He liked her jealousy. "Annie passed through to let me know Spencer was safe in bed so no one would worry. That's all."

Annie stood stock-still, knowing she made for an easy target. She looked at Tawny, refusing to duck her chin or make any excuse. "Mrs. Keene, I'll check on Spencer again before I go, but I'd like to go for a quick run before starting his day."

Carter nodded. "Of course, that's fine. I'll tell Brick to keep an eye on him."

Tawny echoed with "Fine."

Carter refocused on his wife. "Be on location at eight o'clock sharp. Oh, and call Linda so she can work some makeup magic. The camera picks up every line and wrinkle, and we've got night scenes, long day coming up."

Annie pushed through the kitchen door but not before she caught the pain in the actress's eyes. Tawny was a prima donna extraordinaire, but Annie didn't like seeing the hurtful words the couple threw at one another, not when she'd seen the photographs scattered around the Hollywood Hills mansion of two people truly in love. Happy, laughing, loving couples were hard to find amid celebrity. Tawny and Carter Keene seemed to have had it.

At one time.

Annie decided to peek in on Spencer again. He still slept, and Brick already skulked in the hall, so she slipped out the side door and set off down the drive, the gravel crunching beneath her running shoes, the air already heavy with moisture. Sweat sluiced down her body before she hit the highway. By the time she'd gone a mile, her breathing was ragged and her legs heavy. Louisiana in September might kill her.

She rounded a curve, intending to do another mile even if she ended up with a toe tag, and nearly crashed into Tawny's former roommate and current best friend, Jane McEvoy.

"Annie," Jane breathed, leaning over and grasping her knees while gulping in deep breaths.

Annie stopped and mopped sweat out of her eyes, surprised the woman had remembered her name. They'd only met once. "Morning, Ms. McEvoy."

"Jane, please. And it's killer out here, isn't it? I've been here for almost a month and I still can't get accustomed to the humidity."

Annie glanced down the highway in the direction from which Jane had come. "What are you doing all the way out here?"

"Marathon," the woman panted, pulling the breathable tank from her torso. "I've been training for months around the shooting schedule. Beau Soleil's ten miles from the motel where the rest of us are staying, so it's a perfect training run here and back."

Annie nodded. Jane was okay. Much better than Tawny, but then again, Jane was a serious character actress appearing as an extra on police procedurals and the occasional big-screen film. With a wholesome look and a trust-inspiring demeanor, Jane was also frequently cast in commercials. As a close friend to the Keenes she'd snagged a part as the killer's girlfriend. Something about being whacked in the first scene only to reemerge at the end of the film as the mastermind who faked her own death.

Annie checked her watch. No time for another mile. "I can't handle that much running. Gotta get back to Spencer. Good luck with getting your miles in."

"Glad he was found yesterday. Scary, huh? He's such a rascal. I'm not surprised he slipped off. Tell him I'll bring him a lollipop when I get a break. I promised him one when he beat me at Candy Land last month." Jane straightened and glanced in the direction of Beau Soleil.

Annie nodded. "I'll do that."

"We should catch up. Maybe drinks in town? Tawny might come if Carter or that crazy lady will watch Spencer."

"Sure," Annie said, knowing Tawny would rather hang out with a leper than with the nanny.

"I'm so bored out here," Jane said with a shrug, as if that

explained why she was so hard up for company. "All the other girls on the film are twentysomethings who spend their time banging the crew. Although there is this one gaffer who's to die for, but he's such a baby. Okay, TMI. I'm heading back. I'll call the house later."

Jane set off back toward the motel, which sat right outside the city limits of Bayou Bridge. Annie had studied the map of the area, noting the bayous, tributaries and low marshland surrounding the small town. She needed to do some snooping around the production site, and Jane had given her a perfect reason for dropping by the motel if she could get some time off. Several members of the film crew worked directly for Carter's production company and she'd told Ace she'd try to get a feel for how they regarded the Keene family. This tentative friendship with Jane would be her ticket into that world. So drinks would work.

She headed back to Beau Soleil, sucking wind and praying she wouldn't crumple on the highway. The occasional car passed her, along with plenty of huge pickup trucks with dual exhausts and mud-splattered flaps. One passerby gave her a wolf whistle. She refrained from flipping him off.

By the time she made the gate to the mansion, she was done. She gulped air as she crunched down the long, winding drive at a slow walk. The cemetery appeared as she rounded the corner and she shivered despite herself. Her grandmother had claimed to have second sight and the ability to commune with the dead. The sudden prickly feeling had to be a leftover freakazoid gene rearing its ugly head.

The sound of a car behind her had her scooting off the road and checking over her shoulder. Gray government car.

Nate Dufrene.

Her heart took a gallop that had nothing to do with the run she'd just completed.

He slowed beside her.

She stopped.

"Wanna ride?"

"I'm almost there. And I'm pretty sweaty. Wouldn't want to get your seats wet."

His gaze traveled down her body and up again before meeting her eyes. The look was leisurely, not perfunctory, and his checking-out of her sweaty body made her throat tighten and awareness ignite in her blood. "I don't mind."

Her mind screamed *get your butt back to the house and leave sexy Nate Dufrene the hell alone.* Her libido, however, told her to take the candy the man offered and climb into his car like a naughty little girl. Damn, it was hard to ignore candy like Nate.

"If you don't mind," she said, walking around the car and pulling open the passenger door. She sank inside and angled one of the vents onto her face. Nate turned the AC on high and shifted into gear, rolling slowly toward the historic home where he'd been raised.

The car smelled like plastic, mingled with the slight scent of citrus cologne that suited the man sitting next to her. She inhaled, sucking in cool air and Nate Dufrene. Both were good.

"You run often?" he asked, casting an inquisitive look her way.

"Three or four times a week," she said.

"You look like you could run circles around me." He drove really slowly. On purpose? Or did he hide pawpaw tendencies behind his gorgeous brown eyes and lumberjack body? Maybe he wanted more time with her?

"You look fit enough," she said, glancing out the window. No sense in trying to sound flirty. That had never been her game. Besides, she shouldn't have climbed in the car with him, shouldn't have gotten close enough to drink in his clean smell and seductive voice.

"Oh, yeah? Maybe we can go for a run together," he said, as the house came into view.

Her body tightened unwillingly as thoughts of other things they could do together flitted through her mind. She glanced at him, unable to help herself and shrugged as though his presence wasn't affecting her at all. Which it so was. Lord, what was wrong with her? Goal: prove to Ace she could do a phenomenal job as an investigator so she could make more money and get better assignments. Barrier: hunky detective.

"Is that a 'yes' or a 'maybe'?" Nate asked, swinging into the gravel parking area out front. "Because I'll be around. I think keeping an eye on the Keene family might be something our department needs to consider in light of the threats they've received."

"Really? Figured we left danger back in L.A., so I doubt it's something the local authorities need to worry about. I'm sure you have much more exciting things to pursue." She reached for the door handle, but his big hand on her arm stopped her. His touch was warm, even on her heated flesh.

"Just a second," he said.

She glanced at him, not able to read his expression or his eyes. "Yeah?"

"What did you say you did before becoming a nanny?"

Alarm uncurled in her belly, choking out the weird sexual energy that had been humming for the past few minutes. "A real-estate agent."

"With what company?"

"Why? You looking for a house in the Valley?" she asked, jerking her arm away. "I worked as a real-estate agent for several years in Nevada. What's it to you?"

"You lived in Nevada?"

No. "Yeah. Are you checking up on me or something?"

"Why so touchy?"

She gave him a dead stare. "I don't like people implying I'm a liar." Even if she was one. This undercover gig was hard to keep up around a guy like Nate. He seemed to smell bullshit from a mile away. She'd have to be extra careful to not let her guard down around him. Or anything else.

"I didn't imply you were a liar."

She arched an eyebrow and climbed from the car. "I'm not an idiot. You implied all over the place."

She didn't wait for him to say anything more. She needed to get away from him. Get a shower before she had to pour Spencer's cereal and play happy nanny for the day. Hopefully, Ace or his best hound, Jimmy, would break the case by finding the weirdo who threatened five-year-olds back in California so she could go home and pick up another assignment, preferably something that didn't involve watching *SpongeBob* twelve times a day. But until then, she'd do what needed to be done, even if it meant lying her ass off.

Nate stared at her as she gave herself a mental pep talk. He didn't turn off the engine and he didn't follow her, which was probably a good thing. She felt way too vulnerable around that man. What was he doing here anyway? Didn't he have a job to do? Something more important than skulking around Beau Soleil implying she was something other than she was?

Her thoughts tripped over each other as she walked around the flowered path toward the kitchen door. She'd grab a yogurt smoothie before she went up to her bedroom.

Nate's mother met her on the path.

"Did I see Nate pull up?" The woman looked worried.

"Yeah, he actually gave me a ride."

"Good. He needs to see this."

For the third time that morning, apprehension flooded her. "What?"

"Someone left a present on the back doormat."

CHAPTER FIVE

NATE STARED AT THE dead bird lying on the sisal mat. A folded piece of paper lay beneath the fanned wings framing the missive with grotesque flourish.

"Who would do such a thing?" Picou asked, staring down at the poor creature. The mockingbird's soft gray head was flung back with beak open, giving a tragic appearance.

"Did you touch it?" Nate asked his mother, glancing to where she stood with lips pressed together, arms crossed as if warding off a chill, which was ironic since the day felt smothering already.

"Of course not." Picou sniffed. "I watch *Law and Order*."

He nearly smiled. "Good, Mom, good. I'm going to go back to the car to grab my kit and call this in. Stay here and don't touch anything. Where did the nanny go?"

Picou shrugged. "Inside? Maybe to check on the boy?"

Made sense. Yesterday had proven the boy's mother wasn't exactly the most responsible person on the face of the earth, so Annie's instinct to find and secure the child was good.

His mother looked a little spooked, but that was to be expected. Dead birds and presumably threatening notes brought back bad memories—memories that were about to be waded through regardless of the movie people and their harassment problem. He'd read the file on Sally Cheramie early that morning when sleep escaped him—the results had left a wake of acid churning in his stomach. Part of him wanted to toss the file aside, smother the query into his sister's disappearance, but facts didn't lie. The woman might be more than a desperate charlatan looking to get rich quick. This inquiry might bite.

He went around to his car, grabbed a kit from the trunk and pulled out his phone to call in the threat. This time it would be official.

He hung up with dispatch and shifted his mind back to the task at hand just as Annie appeared at his elbow. He stopped. "Spencer?"

"Safe with his mother. Both are unaware anything is amiss. In fact, Spencer is modeling his mother's shoe collection while she's getting a facial. The makeup artist arrived twenty minutes ago. Might want to question her and see if she saw anything."

He looked at her. "Oh, so you watch *Law and Order,* too?"

"You don't have to watch police shows on TV to use common sense. If someone put the bird on the mat, then Linda, or whatever her name is, might have seen him."

"Or her."

Annie glanced sharply at him. "Or her. That reminds me. I did see someone on the highway—Jane McEvoy."

He gave her a questioning look.

"She's Tawny's former roommate and BFF. She might not be involved in this threat thing, but you never know. Could be anyone with a grudge. Or a loose screw."

He didn't comment. She was right. If the threats were connected, it could be anyone who'd made the trek from California. He'd start with the production crew and work his way to those closest to the boy, including Annie.

He started walking again, noticing Annie's steps matched his stride for stride as they approached his mother, who wore a bright caftan along with flip-flops with sparkly doodads on them. She looked a little like a circus fortune-teller, but her purple-blue eyes were grave.

"You can go inside now, Mom. Just use the side or front door so we don't contaminate evidence out here." Nate studied the "crime" scene before placing his case on an out-of-the-way table. He opened the kit, aware he carried more than the average detective. His time in med school studying pathology had taught him some tricks that gave him an edge. Or at least he thought they did. He knew his success rate came from good old-fashioned research with a side helping of gut instinct.

"That's a lot of stuff in there. Do all detectives carry—" she picked up a spray bottle of luminal "—stuff like this?"

He took the luminal out of her hand and placed it back in the kit. "I was an Eagle Scout. I'm always prepared."

"What's this for?" she asked, picking up a vial containing fingerprinting powder and holding it up to the sunlight streaking through the overhanging trees.

"Something I may need. Put it back, please." He pulled out the high-resolution camera and caught a gleam in her eyes. He couldn't get a handle on this woman at all. She didn't look disturbed by the dead bird like most women would. He turned and caught his mother crouching beside the note and bird. "Don't touch."

"I'm not. Just making sure it's dead."

Annie walked over. "Oh, it's dead, Mrs. Dufrene. Birds don't lie that still if they're living."

Picou rose and took a step back toward Annie as Nate snapped photographs of the bird at several angles. After photographing the entire patio, he pulled on gloves and placed the dead bird in an evidence bag.

"You're not going to throw it away?" Annie asked.

"You'd be surprised what a lab can do with 'evidence'

like this. We can learn if the person who did this killed the bird or found one that had died of natural causes. And sometimes we can lift prints or find fibers that might give us a clue to help solve the crime."

"Oh," she said. He didn't miss the fact Annie acted out of character. Since he'd met her, everything had been deliberate, careful and no-nonsense. Now she asked him questions she must know the answer to. Hell, half of America watched *CSI*. He sealed the bag.

She shifted, pushing back her hair. "So what about security cameras? Don't you have them?"

"Why would we?" he asked.

"Well, with the disappearance of—I mean, Tawny said—" She stopped herself, looking for the words. "Some families who have suffered tragedies are more protective and plan against other—"

"We're not paranoid," Picou interrupted, her tone marginally defensive. "Our daughter was taken and it didn't matter whether we had dogs, fences or guards on every corner of the property. Bad things happen despite our best efforts."

His mother's response didn't surprise him. Even now, she tried to tell him she was sorry—that Della's disappearance had nothing to do with him. But it couldn't erase his mother's accusations the day Della disappeared. Couldn't wipe away the way she'd shrieked at him, accusing him of not watching out for his sister, labeling the kidnapping his fault. To a ten-year-old boy, it had been devastating. Picou had spent years trying to apologize.

At times, he felt the emptiness in her words. Felt the unreasonable blame. His mother didn't want to feel the way she felt. She couldn't help herself.

"I didn't mean to offend, Mrs. Dufrene. Just trying to help."

Nate looked at Annie. "Since you're in the mood to help, give me your opinion. You think this is related to the threats in California or just a simple prank?" He watched her gaze hit the bag dangling in his hand.

"I'm not sure. Most of the staff and crew know Tawny calls Spencer 'birdie.' The whole thing could be a sick joke. No one has tried to hurt him, so it could be someone wanting to get the Keenes' goat. Someone who wants to use fear against them."

"Nice thinking, Watson," he quipped.

"What? You asked," she snapped, her happy-camper vibe gone. He liked her better serious with her feathers ruffled. Felt right.

"I thought it sounded good." Picou nodded, her eyes earnest.

Actually it was valid. Someone was using terror as a weapon against the couple. He knew how powerful the love between a parent and child was. Not firsthand. But he'd watched his parents' marriage unravel with Della's disappearance and murder. They'd never healed. His thoughts flickered back to the folder. He needed to talk to his mother before word leaked out at the office. Someone, namely Kelli—the bigmouth in the unit—was bound to squeal about the woman asking questions down in Lafourche.

Nate set the bagged bird on the wrought-iron table and turned to Annie. "Did you use this door this morning?"

She shook her head. "Almost, but I went back to talk to Tawny. After that, I checked on Spencer and slipped out the side door. I didn't see anyone around Beau Soleil, but I wasn't looking either. The only person up this morning was Mr. Keene and he was in the kitchen fixing coffee. Maybe he heard someone."

Briefly the idea of Keene staging the threat for press or to suit his own needs crossed Nate's mind, but he quickly discarded it. Only someone with no soul would falsely threaten his own child for attention. Keene wasn't a nominee for Humanitarian of the Year, but he didn't seem to be lacking in love for his son, not to mention he'd tried to keep the threats quiet. No, someone else was playing a sick game with the Keene family.

As far as Nate was concerned, the dead bird on the doormat meant game on. The need to best the perpetrator welled up inside him. "Let's find out. Is Keene around?"

"His Jeep is." Annie pointed toward the gravel parking area at the side of the house.

"Grab him for me."

Annie narrowed her eyes. "Just because I'm the Hispanic nanny doesn't mean you can order me around. I don't work for you."

"Just like his father," Picou said, putting her hands on her hips.

Nate stiffened. "I'm not like my father."

Picou shrugged. "You could have fooled me. Annie may work for the Keenes, but she's a guest in this home. Go get Carter yourself. We'll watch the crime scene until someone from the department gets here."

Nate hated being compared to his domineering father, though he knew there was much of the man in him. For one, he looked like Martin and for the other, he had abnormally high expectations of those around him. Hard to fight the need to command and have people jump to fulfill his orders. He'd been called asshole more than once. Just like his old man.

"Sorry. I didn't intend it as it came out, and it certainly had nothing to do with your ethnic background or gender."

Annie nodded. "Apology accepted. I'm heading inside to shower and assume my duties, so I'll tell Mr. Keene you need him."

"Thanks." Nate looked at his mother as Annie headed toward the side door. Picou studied him, a hint of a smile on her lips. He knew then and there she approved of Annie Perez, which both pleased and distressed him. He knew his mother. She'd been throwing women in his path for the past five years, groaning about dying without having grandchildren. She'd be pushing the capable, sexy nanny his way every chance she got. The question was would he be waiting? "Don't you have something better to do, Mom?"

"No," she said, folding her thin frame into a patio chair and stretching her arms overhead. "You know I'm fascinated by police work, so I'll enjoy watching you in action. I won't have to watch *Cold Case* reruns this afternoon."

"Not much to watch, Mom."

"You trying to get rid of me?"

He drew a deep breath and held it for three seconds before releasing it. His mother was many things, topping out at fascinating, but she also had a childish, bratty nature. He looked at her, and she smiled winningly.

"Actually I'm here because of you."

"I know. I birthed you."

He gave her a deadpan stare.

"Okay, not funny, but I am glad you came by to check on me. Gets lonely out here all by myself."

"With all these people around, I can see you're starved for attention." He buried his guilt under sarcasm. He should check on Picou more. It was his duty.

The crunch of several cars sounded in the gravel.

"The cavalry has arrived, so I'll leave you to it. Come in later and tell me why you're really here. In the meantime, I'll hope it has something to do with that adorable little nanny. She's got spit and fire."

He heard car doors slam and the voice of Blaine Gentry, the St. Martin Parish Sheriff. "I'd hate to smother your matchmaking plans, but this has to do with Della."

Picou stopped in the middle of the path. "Della?"

Nate swallowed, wishing he could snatch back his flippant words. Wrong move. Should have waited. "Probably nothing, but a deputy down in Lafourche called me about a woman asking a couple of flag-raising questions. They sent a file on her, but we'll talk later."

Sheriff Blaine Gentry tromped onto the patio. "Morning. What we got here?"

Picou muttered "morning" before heading inside. Her shoulders were taut and he didn't miss the way the sunshine had been sucked out of her. Yeah, talking about Della did that every time.

"A dead bird."

Blaine's eyebrows chased his hairline. "You called us out here for a dead bird? Kelli said you found a body."

Nate stifled aggravation. Along with a big mouth, Kelli was known for exaggeration, one of the main reasons he'd hot-footed it out to Beau Soleil to tell his mother about the query in Lafourche. "And a note."

Nate's sometimes-partner Wynn Mouton ambled toward the bird sitting in the plastic bag. He lifted the bag and eyed the contents.

"Wow, you bagged this all by yourself and wrote the date on it, too. Your talent amazes me." Wynn grinned like the smart-ass he was.

Nate ignored him, walked to the mat and lifted the folded paper, opening it. "Yeah, I can write my name, too, asshole. But you can write my name when you write up the report."

"The hell I will," Wynn said, dropping the bag back onto the table. "It's a dead bird. Why we running lab on it?"

"You owe him, Mouton," Blaine said, his dark eyes taking in the perimeter. "And this ain't no regular dead bird. Feels like an iceberg case with lots underneath we can't see."

"Ah, hell," Wynn muttered, absentmindedly rubbing the shoulder he'd had surgery on after falling during a foot chase.

"Take a look," Nate said, holding the letter toward Blaine but not allowing him to touch it since he wore no gloves. It was regular copy paper with typed words centered on the page. Times New Roman font. Size 12.

"Twisted bastard," Wynn said, looking over the sheriff's shoulder.

Birdie, Birdie in the sky
You will pay an eye for an eye
Tell your whore mother to draw a line
Or her precious baby will soon be mine

"A rhymer," Nate commented, sliding the letter in the bag he held in his other hand. He sealed it. "Anger's directed toward the mother, so the kid's a tool."

Blaine nodded. "Sounds right, but let's try all angles. LAPD should have files and we'll make a request, but let's come at this fresh with our own guys. Dufrene, you take lead. Mouton, you assist. Start with who has a grudge against Tawny. Maybe someone she beat out for a part? Or one of Keene's ex-girlfriends?"

"I'll start with family and staff then move on to the production company looking at anyone who's been nursing a grudge for even the slight offense. Never know when taking the last donut might break someone." Nate slid the sisal mat into a large plastic bag and swept the patio with his eyes. He often did the work for crime-scene investigation. Dez Shaver, head of CSI, hated fieldwork and trusted

Nate to preserve the scene. Nate would put in a call for a few more deputies to do a complete sweep, including that of the perimeter.

He looked up and surveyed the familiar line of trees extending outward on the huge estate. The entire property was slightly over a hundred acres with many places to hide. Chances were, the perp had snuck through the woods and left the "gift." They needed to broaden the crime scene and look for footprints. It would be the first step on the path to finding out who might have it in for Tawny. "We'll need more help. Widen the search perimeter. Digging into Keene's past will take a huge team. I hear the man fancies himself Casanova."

"Not anymore." Carter Keene stepped out the back door, directly onto the spot where the mat had lain. Nate suppressed a wince.

"Mr. Keene." The sheriff replaced his cowboy hat and held out a hand. Keene took it, but didn't look impressed.

"You might want to watch what you say when you're insulting a man on his own movie set," Keene said, addressing Nate.

"Which happens to be owned by my family," Nate finished. "And it's not an insult. It's a compliment. Wynn once dreamed of catching a tenth of the action you got."

Wynn played along. "Hey, I did all right. Married, ain't I?" He wiggled his left hand.

Carter smiled, his ego apparently stroked as he sank into the chair Nate's mother had vacated minutes before and crossed his long legs at the ankle. Very nonchalant. "All in the past, gentlemen, all in the past. Now Annie said you wanted to see me? What's with the gloves and glowering police faces? Someone on set get out of line?"

"Sheriff's department," Wynn muttered.

Blaine regarded Keene with piercing blue eyes. The

sheriff's hat sat low, nearly glancing the bushy gray eyebrows beneath. On the surface Blaine looked very much a good ol' boy, but he'd been elected after serving an integral role on the task force that caught the Baton Rouge serial killer. Blaine had been the first to develop a geographical profile and pinpoint the area in which victims disappeared, earning himself a spot as the poster boy. "There's been a definite threat this go around."

Carter bent forward. "A definite threat? Against me? Or Spencer?"

Blaine picked up the protected note and handed it to Carter. Carter blanched, handing the note back to the sheriff. "How? I thought we'd left this nonsense back in L.A. Thought yesterday's scare was a fluke."

"It was," Nate interrupted, "but this isn't. This is someone getting serious with your family." He nodded his head toward the dead bird.

Carter's gaze slid to the gruesome talisman lying on the table. "Christ."

Blaine motioned toward the house. "We'll need to ask some questions. Why don't you go inside with Wynn?"

Carter shook his head. "I've got to get to the set. We're behind and—"

"Your son is more important, don't you think?" Blaine said, nodding toward Wynn. "Get a statement from him and the mother. Nate, talk to your mother, Lucille and the nanny. Let's make this official. I'll put a call out to Hollywood division and see if we can get what they have. Then you can take it from—"

"Call Burrell," Carter interrupted. "He's at Quantico and has all the files."

Blaine looked at Nate, communicating what they both knew. This FBI agent had humored Keene. High priority would not be given to a threat such as the ones received by the Hollywood couple...unless it went public. And it really didn't need to be made public at this point. Later Nate would call the agent Carter had an "in" with. Relatively speaking, the FBI was rather useless on something like this, but he'd be courteous. Never know when he might need a favor of his own someday.

Carter rose without another word and followed Wynn inside the kitchen. A few more deputies arrived, and Blaine gave them instructions for canvassing the area. That left Nate to find Annie.

The mysterious Annie Perez. Could she be in on the threats? He didn't want to think so, but she was hiding something and she'd had opportunity that morning. But setting up a kidnapping? His blood ran cold at the thought.

His gut told him Annie wasn't the perpetrator. She'd seemed genuinely concerned about the boy yesterday, and she'd have to be a consummate actress to fake the emotion he'd glimpsed.

But he'd been fooled before.

Hadn't his dad trusted the gardener?

Hadn't a young Nate, along with his siblings, laughed as the man wheeled them at dizzying speeds in the wheelbarrow? Hadn't Della always followed Sal as he plucked roses and trimmed the thorns so she could twine them in her curls? The man had smiled at them with manufactured loyalty as he plotted to poison them with his greed.

Nate shouldn't trust Annie any more than he trusted the town drunk. And the town drunk was the president of Homestead Bank and Trust.

ANNIE SLIPPED INTO THE house, ducked into the empty library and pulled out her cell phone. Ace answered on the second ring.

"Sterling."

"We got a big problem," Annie said, checking to make sure no one was around. She shut the door with a soft snick. "Whoever's been making threats is here in Louisiana."

"Damn," Ace breathed. She could almost see him in his trademark Bermuda shorts and surfer T-shirt, tugging on his shaggy hair in frustration. "Jimmy got a lead on a bit actor for Keene on *Miami Metro*. The dude got into a fist-fight with Keene on the set during the last episode. Had something to do with Tawny. No alibi for the night of the vandalism either. I thought we might be close to shutting this one down."

"I don't think so," Annie said, moving toward the floor-to-ceiling windows flanking the large antique desk. She moved on the balls of her feet, her footfalls making no sound on the Oriental carpet. The stuffed bear stared at her from the corner. "Someone left a note this morning, along with a dead bird."

"A dead bird?"

"Birdie."

He paused. "This is escalating."

"Maybe. Nothing for weeks and then as soon as we get here, we get a bump. Whoever's responsible is here. Part of the crew. Or the talent."

"Bump is right. No clue what's beneath the surface, but it has big teeth and likes to play. Damn." For a few seconds, he said nothing. "Okay, guess I'll send Jimmy down to help."

"Might be crowded. Locals are on the case."

He sighed. Annie knew he'd dealt with the cold shoulder from local law enforcement before. Most cops disdained private investigators, but Sterling Investigations had recently contributed on several high-profile cases, even receiving national press for its work on the Ventura burglary ring and the SoCal freeway killer. If Jimmy came to

Louisiana as a representative of Sterling, he'd be dealing with authorities who knew nothing of their reputation or expertise. In other words, Jimmy would likely get no help. "Protect yourself, Anna. You'll do more covertly for this case than overtly. Stay low, but I'm sending Jimmy anyway."

"What's he going to do that I can't?"

"Hard to ask questions when you're with the kid. Jimmy will have mobility."

Annie closed her eyes. She hated being shackled by her undercover role, but Ace was right. She couldn't get around with a kid on her hip, something that left a bitter taste in her mouth. "Sucks for me."

"Well, if you can find an ally on the police force, you might do us some good. You're a babe. Use it."

"Are you talking about flirting?" Felt like a dirty word on her tongue. Playing femme fatale was so not her thing. Not just because it was deceitful but because deep down, locked in the basement of her heart, was the thought she wasn't feminine enough to attract a man at such a base level.

"Find the lead investigator and use that pretty smile to get a few leads out of him. Stroke his ego and get him to tell you all about how he's going to find the person doing this. Unless it's a woman, then you may have to switch tactics."

"Lead is Picou Dufrene's son."

"Perfect."

Annie felt a bit of dread unwind inside her. She couldn't use feminine wiles to manipulate men, undercover or not. "I don't think he's the type."

"We're all the type. I hired you for a good reason, crackerjack."

"I'll fall flat on my face." Even though she already knew Nate was interested. Yet, something told her to play straight with him as much as possible. Her playing dumb as he opened his kit earlier proved as much—suspicion had lurked in his eyes. "I'd rather be direct."

"Just do your job," Ace said, "and Jimmy will be in touch when he gets in town."

"Fine. Tell him to bring me some hardware."

Sterling confirmed her selection of weapon and then hung up. Jimmy would be in Louisiana within three days, bringing her piece with him. The heat would make it brutal to wear a jacket concealing the weapon, but she'd think of something. She'd been nearly crazy not having her gun.

She pocketed her phone and turned.

"Hardware?" Nate stood with arms crossed, leaning against the bookcase.

"Agh!" She jumped.

She hadn't heard him enter the library. The man must be part cat. His eyes crackled with intensity even though his posture suggested indifference. How long had he been there? She swallowed mild panic.

"You're ordering hardware?"

"Do you always listen in on people's conversations? I get you're a cop, but that's rude."

He made a face. "I'm not a cop."

"A technicality. This is still a violation of my rights."

"To what?"

"Uh, privacy." She did her best smart-ass.

"You're in a private home sneaking around after we found a dead bird along with a threat intended for the little boy you're minding. I think forgoing privacy is a non-issue at this juncture."

"I don't think violating someone's privacy is ever justi-fied. It's in the Bill of Rights. I think. Besides, I know your mother taught you good manners, so use them and stop eavesdropping on phone calls." She crossed her arms and gave him a hard stare. "But, if you must know, I was talking about my laptop. Mine's on the fritz and a guy I know in New Orleans is bringing me a new hard drive. Thanks for asking." She stomped toward the door, stepping past him.

His hand clamped down on her arm. "What friend?"

"Seriously?" She looked up at him. "What do you care?"

He dropped her arm, looking startled at his action. "I don't. Just trying to keep track of who comes and goes around here. We have an ongoing investigation and I don't know anything about you other than you're particularly defensive right now."

Annie could still feel the warmth of his touch on her arm. Somewhere in the recesses of her mind, she wanted his action to be about her, not the investigation. Which was alarming in a way she didn't want to admit, even to herself. "Don't worry. I'm as interested in protecting Spencer as you. Now I need to get upstairs."

"But first I have some questions for you."

"Fine, but can I get Spencer first?"

His mouth twisted. "We'll talk later. With this new threat, you need to keep tabs on him at all times. Nothing like yesterday can happen again."

Annie bristled, even though she'd have given the same advice in his shoes. Even though she'd told herself the same thing right after they found the bird and note. "It won't."

He nodded. "Good."

Annie started toward the door. "Oh, I meant to ask—what was in the note?"

He narrowed his beautiful eyes, kicking up one side of him mouth. "I can't disclose that information."

"So you watch *Law and Order,* too, huh?" She'd get the contents from Carter Keene later anyway. Besides, she reminded herself, she had to start being nice to Detective Dufrene. Gain his trust. Try to be friendly.

His brow furrowed. "What?"

"All that cop talk," she said, allowing the irritation left-over at his spying to melt away. She wasn't a former FBI agent. Or a current undercover investigator. She was a nanny. A single nanny. Dear Lord, he was about to see right through her. She couldn't flirt for shit. "I care for Spencer, so I'll help any way I can. We'll meet later?"

Something flickered in his eyes. Suspicion. Then interest.

"To do what?" he asked, his gaze dropping to her lips.

She sucked in her bottom lip before she could think about it. "Whatever you want. I mean, um, don't you have to ask me some questions about Spencer and stuff?"

He pulled out his phone. "Give me your number."

She quirked a brow. A surprised brow.

But his internal resolve seemed to slide back into place. "Never mind, I'll interview you here."

Hmm. The feminine-wiles thing almost worked.

"Fine. I've got to shower then give Spencer his break-fast. I'll be around." Annie nearly choked on the last line as she shut the door.

Okay, she knew she couldn't proceed in this man-ner, mostly because attempting to flirt with Nate felt dangerous—career-crusher dangerous. Ace hired her with a probationary clause. Even an old FBI associate couldn't disregard the foolishness of tossing over a career for the temporary insanity that had seized Annie, leading her to quit her job, play mommy to a girl who despised her and fiancée to a man who only wanted to use her as a babysitter.

Yeah, when it had come to Seth and Mallory, Annie's skills as an investigator had failed her.

All because she thought she'd found something she'd secretly dreamed about in the small darkness of her bed-room in the apartment she'd leased in Philly.

A man.

A child.

A family.

To feel as though her heart could actually work like a normal person's.

But she'd been wrong.

So she couldn't fail in this quest. And she couldn't risk feeling any sort of interest in Nate Dufrene. Her assignment was to use whatever he could give her on the case. Not pin some deep-buried hope to feel something for a man who lived almost a thousand miles away from where she needed to be.

Annie had to play things smart.

She climbed the elegant stairway, which was deserving of more grand dress than running shorts and shirt, and went to her room. Spencer wasn't there, but she heard him and Tawny laughing down the hall. After a quick shower, she went to the room where Spencer was supposed to sleep, pushed open the door and found Tawny tucking pajamas in a lovely maple dresser. Annie nearly keeled over in shock.

"Hey, Annie. Spencer's ready for breakfast. I told him maybe you'd take him for a walk afterward." She turned to a sulky Spencer. "Sorry, birdie, I want to take you, but I've got to get on set."

Spencer buried his head in the fluffy pillows of the antique rice bed and said nothing.

"Come on, baby. At least you're here with mommy this time."

He lifted a tragic face to his mother but said nothing. His lower lip poked out a good inch.

Annie walked toward the boy. "Spencer, sometimes moms have to work. Mine did when I was little, and I went to day care. I had to share my toys with a mean boy named Kyle."

"You did?" He tipped his face to her. "Why was he mean?"

Annie sank onto the bed. "I don't know, but he bit me once."

"He did?"

She tugged him so he sat up. "Yep. But your mom loves you so much she hired me to be your nanny. And I won't bite you. I promise. I'll even share my toys."

Spencer grinned. "You don't have toys. You're a grown-up."

"Oh, yeah," Annie said, scratching her head. "I guess I need some toys."

Spencer laughed. "You're silly, Annie."

Was she? Silly was as foreign to her as flirty. She looked at Tawny, who watched them from the open doorway. The actress nodded and mouthed "thank you" before disappearing.

Annie felt a flash of pleasure at the woman's acknowledgment. Odd, she didn't usually seek approval from anyone other than her boss. Of course, some would say Tawny was her boss.

"Let's get some cereal and then we'll take that walk. You want a bath first?"

He shook his head. "I want Fruity O's."

"Of course, monsieur. Coming right up."

Spencer slid off the bed and pulled on his Crocs. Much to his mother's dismay, the rubber shoe was Spencer's choice of footwear. Didn't really go with the hundred-dollar ripped jeans and trendy boutique shirt, but Annie had to give the boy props for choosing something easy to clean. "Annie, you're good at fixing cereal. I think that's kinda cooking, huh?"

"I'm no Rachel Ray, but you won't starve."

CHAPTER SIX

NATE SAT FEET CROSSED at the ankle, taking up space in his mother's sitting room. Picou sat at her desk regarding him with solemn eyes as he traced the pattern on the brocade armchair. The air felt tight as a guitar string, but still he remained silent, waiting for Picou to find her footing after having been told about the woman asking questions about the past.

She cleared her throat. "We've had false alarms before."

"I read the report. This deputy is a friend of the woman's and he provided a physical description along with a description of a stuffed animal she said she'd had since she could remember—a pink blanket with a stuffed poodle attached to it. The woman said she called it Dobby."

"But that's not what Della called it. She called it her baby."

Nate quirked a brow. "I know, Mom. But think about what 'Dobby' is similar to."

"Darby," Picou whispered. "Why are you telling me this time?" his mother asked from her position at the old cherry rolltop desk she'd inherited from a maiden great-aunt. Her hands shook as she twisted one of the loose brass knobs.

"Because last time I didn't tell you, you refused to speak to me for over a month. That meant I didn't get any of Lucille's pound cake. Can't take that again."

"The pound cake?"

"Well, that, too."

His mother gave a quasi smile and turned toward the open window of the small room she preferred to visit every morning to drink her tea and read her devotionals. Birds flitted in the bushes outside, and he thought he heard Annie and Spencer in the breakfast room down the hall.

"I promised I would tell you any new information that surfaced in regards to Della. This may come to nothing more than a new piece of evidence in her murder. We might reopen the case and find out what really happened."

"Was her name on the tag?"

Nate sighed. This was it. The game changer. "Yeah."

Picou raised her hands and covered her face. Her shoulders shook as a choking noise joined the songs of the birds. He allowed her to wade through the emotion before saying, "May not mean anything, Mom."

She wiped her cheeks. "It means something."

"Could have been picked up at a yard sale. Found in a car. Anything."

"How old is the girl?"

"Twenty-seven."

His mother picked up a pen and clicked the top over and over again. "Birth date?"

"February 28th."

"About the time she went missing."

"Yeah, but that's all circumstantial. Imagine how many twenty-seven-year-olds are out there. This girl may not be Della."

"But she might be. It's the best lead we've had since they found Sal's body in that stolen truck in the bayou. Della wasn't with him."

"But they found her hair ribbon wedged in the backseat."

"Stop it." Picou's violet eyes flashed determination. Outside of color, they were eyes he knew well. He looked at them in the mirror every day before he walked out the door. "What's her name? Where does she live? Who raised her?"

"Sally Cheramie, and she was raised in the flats off Bayou Lafourche by a fisherwoman. She graduated from University of Louisiana Lafayette and teaches second grade," he said, gripping the arms of the chair. He didn't want to give her too much, but the woman's intensity had him blurting out more than he wanted to reveal. "Look, I wanted you to know, but I don't want you to count on this panning out. I still believe Della's dead, Mom. Everything points to it. I've seen the evidence. Read the reports."

"Don't say that." Picou slammed a hand flat on the polished wood. "There was no body. Billy Priest said Sal shot her and fed her to the gators, but there was no proof. They searched the area Sal hunted."

"But they found fresh tire tracks and cigarette butts, Mom. Sal had been there." The name Sal Comeaux brought anger surging through his body. Damn betrayer. His plot had amounted to naught—not a damn penny. And his cohort Billy rotted in Angola, swearing Sal was the mastermind. Nate hated both men.

But there was more. More about the girl he wouldn't tell his mother. He didn't want her to come crashing down if it amounted to nothing. Of course, he knew it was too late for that. Her hopes sailed high.

"Don't take away my hope, Nate." Picou's eyes were fierce. Damn, he shouldn't have told her, no matter what he'd promised. He should have followed his instinct and checked things out before he mentioned it, but it was too late. He'd screwed up.

"Listen, I'll go down to Galliano and talk to this girl and get some answers. Maybe talk to the woman who raised her as her granddaughter, but it will have to wait a day or two. With the threat to the boy, I'll be busy for the next few days. Blaine's getting pressure from the father, and we don't need bad publicity."

"I can go—"

"No, Mom." He gave her the look—the one he saved for a collar. The one that said, *don't mess with me on this.*

Picou closed her mouth and glared back. "I just—"

"No."

"Don't talk to me like that. I'm your mother."

He ran a hand through his hair. "I know and that's why I won't let you run around chasing a dream. This could break your heart."

"My heart was broken long ago, Nathan."

He fell silent. What was there to say to something like that? All their hearts had been broken the day Della disappeared and each family member dealt with it in a different manner. His mother had sought out every divine intervention from the parish priest to whatever crackpot psychic she could round up in New Orleans—and every other discipline in between. Anything to buy her a little hope.

"You want to protect me." Picou thumbed the worn pages of her grandmother's Bible.

He jerked his head up. "Yeah."

"Well, I'm a big girl and, here's the deal, I've known Della was alive for a long time. Deep down in my heart, I knew. When Zelda Trosclair came last week, she saw our family's future. The past will be restored by a dark stranger, one who comes from far. At first I thought it was Annie, but maybe—"

The door creaked and a small hand grasped the door frame, followed by a round face covered with what looked to be jam. Spencer's eyes grew wide when he saw Nate.

"Hey," the boy said.

Picou's attitude transformed. "Well, good morning, handsome."

Spencer pushed the door open. "Mornin'. Me and Annie's going for a walk. We're gonna look for animals and stuff."

"Well, that sounds lovely," Picou said, rising from the desk, her hands now steady, her gaze resolved. Didn't matter what Nate told her. She believed the girl asking questions was Della and she believed the crazy prophecy the mambo had given her.

"Annie said you might come, too. You wanna come, too?"

Picou glanced at him. "Well, I don't know. My son Nate is here."

"There's other po-lice here. I saw 'em." Spencer said, his eyes sliding to Nate. "Are you a police? You don't have a hat."

Annie poked her head in. "Spencer, come with me. You were supposed to wash your hands and face. Come back to the kitchen."

"You said Miss Peekaboo could come with us." The boy inched away from Annie's insistent outstretched hand toward Nate's mother.

"Miss Peekaboo?" Picou's smile was like the sliver of sunshine creeping in through the drapes. "Now, that's a new one."

"Sounds like a lounge act," Nate muttered.

Annie's lips twitched and sudden heat flared low in his belly. Damn, but her mouth was delectable. Pink, plump and out of place below those no-nonsense gray eyes. Just like yesterday. She'd totally distracted him when he was supposed to be questioning her.

"What's a wounge act?" Spencer looked up at Annie.

"I'm not touching that one," she muttered, grabbing the

boy's hand and pulling him toward the open door. "Excuse us. Spencer needs to wash up before we go for a stroll."

"I'll meet you in the kitchen in a few minutes," Picou called.

Annie's glanced back. "You're coming with us?"

"I'll show you where to find arrowheads and paint rocks. And I know where a fox lives."

Annie and Spencer disappeared. He heard the child chattering about the fox and it made him feel better somehow. Picou pushed a curtain back, securing it so the sunshine streamed fully into the library. It illuminated—as if seeking to prevent Nate from hiding the one piece of information he hadn't revealed to his mother—the fact the woman who'd raised Sally, Enola Cheramie, was Sal Comeaux's grandmother. It was an unturned stone because the old woman had sworn she'd known nothing of Sal or his whereabouts. When asked about the child, she told them the girl was one of her granddaughter's children. The Lafourche investigators never followed up on her statement.

Telling Picou about Enola would pull the nail out of Della's coffin. He wasn't ready to do that yet. Mostly because he wasn't ready to admit he had the same hope shelved on the highest shelf in the closet of his soul. Because to fail again would hurt too much. But maybe Sal Comeaux had rectified the wrong done to the Dufrene family before drowning in the bayou.

And maybe Nate wasn't truly responsible for his sister's death.

DAYS LATER, ON THE NOW-established morning walk, Annie allowed herself to lag behind Picou and Spencer as they scoured trees and bushes for wildlife. Every snail, bug and squirrel intrigued the child, whose experience with nature thus far had been at a petting zoo. He seemed to especially enjoy the dirt and rocks on the path.

"Look at this!" he cried for the fifth time in ten minutes. Picou patiently stopped to peer at a…rock?

"That's a sedimentary rock," Picou said, lifting the large stone. "See the little pieces of stone?"

The boy nodded. "What's this one?"

Annie zoned out because geology was boring. She glanced around the woods that encircled the large house. The production company filmed on the other side, leaving the large stretch to the right of the house unoccupied. Birds twittered overhead and some unknown animal scrabbled up and down the trees. It was empty and peaceful.

And a perfect place to meet Jimmy and get her gun.

She'd tried to keep busy with the boy, thankful for the morning walks where Picou regaled Spencer with stories and simple things like birds' nests, beehives and graveyard ghost stories. The boy loved it, and Annie actually found it restorative.

Jimmy had texted her when he arrived in town last night. Ace had gotten him hired on with the catering company providing craft service to the crew. They'd decided having him embedded within the area of actual production might be beneficial in tracking down whoever was responsible for the threats.

Outside of the dead bird and note, which had been sent to the nearest FBI lab, no other attempt at mischief had been made—or if it had, she didn't know anything because Nate and his partner had not been around. She assumed whoever played games with the family had been eerily silent, which could mean several things: no actual escalation, as Sterling suggested, no opportunity, or a patience belying a calculating coldness. It was the last one that bothered Annie.

The first threat received by the Keene family had been

in the mail. The nondescript white copy paper along with generic envelope held no trace evidence and was post-marked in Malibu.

You can't fix what you have done
Too bad I have to break the wrong one
Poor Spencer pays for another's sins

The writing gave little away, other than the perp was decently educated and bore a grudge. At first Carter had disregarded the note as a crackpot fan, turning it over to the police who pretty much thought the same thing, but when a brick crashed through the production-office window one night, Carter decided to call Ace Sterling, a man he'd used before. Since Annie had just hired on, Ace had suggested an additional bodyguard who could provide for the needs of the child while protecting him. So Annie went on her first undercover case.

Spencer's laughter brought her back to the task at hand. She didn't need to daydream.

Picou tugged Spencer toward a thin trail hidden in the underbrush. "Let me show you something really special."

Spencer skipped ahead of her, his little head swiveling clockwise as he took in the ancient oaks spreading above him. "Can I climb one of those trees?"

Picou contemplated the trees. "If the tree goddess gives you permission."

"Tree goddess?" Annie snorted. "Really?"

Picou turned her head. "Do you doubt the woods are filled with spirits?"

"Depends on how much liquor the high school kids left behind," Annie said, picking up an empty vodka bottle from where it lay near a huge felled tree.

Picou gave her an exasperated look before turning back to the boy. "And I had hopes for you."

Annie tossed the bottle toward the base of the tree. She'd pick it up on the way back. "I believe in what I see. With my own two eyes. I don't do unexplained."

Picou tsked as they forged ahead, finally emerging into a clearing holding three huge mounds measuring almost thirty-five feet in height.

"Cool," Spencer shouted, breaking into a run.

"Stop," Picou said, lunging ahead and grabbing Spencer by the T-shirt.

"Hey," he said, trying to wriggle away. "I want to climb them."

Picou pulled the boy toward her and crouched down. "These are Indian mounds."

Annie shaded her eyes against the brightness of the sun and studied the three mounds. She'd never seen anything like it. "Are they sacred?"

"Yes, and they are very old. Built even before the pyramids," Picou said.

"Really?" Annie moved beside them, slightly in awe that such an odd structure existed on the land owned by the Dufrenes.

"What's in them?" Spencer asked. "Is there a way to go inside?"

Picou shook her head. "Nothing inside. No one knows why they were built. Maybe as a marker for territory. Whatever they were it's unexplained." She glanced at Annie before looking back at Spencer. "They're very old and built long, long ago by the people who first lived in Louisiana. Isn't that interesting?"

Spencer nodded. "I guess. I wish I could climb on them."

"Just like my boys. Well, I suppose it wouldn't hurt. They might have well been a playground for little native boys and girls anyhow. Over at the ULB campus, the kids used to slide down them every home game. Grab some cardboard and your kid will be occupied for hours, leaving you to booze it up." Picou gave a wry laugh. "They finally stopped it several years ago. Didn't want them damaged, but I supposed one wee boy won't hurt these."

Annie grinned. "The power of a pile of dirt."

Picou allowed a smile, giving Spencer a little push.

He needed no further urging. His feet flew as he scampered up the mound. Annie pulled her phone from her pocket and pretended to check messages. In actuality she added a marker to her GPS. Perfect spot to meet Jimmy— easy to get to, far from prying eyes. Later she would meet Jane at the hotel bar for two-dollar longnecks and a zydeco band, but first she wanted to get her gun and see if Jimmy had learned anything. She quickly texted him and gave the coordinates to the mounds.

"Your phone might not work out here," Picou said, moving so she stood in the shade.

"You're right. No bars," Annie said, pocketing her phone. "Wanted to make sure my dad hadn't called."

Picou nodded. "Is he back in California? Is that where you're from?"

"Little north of San Diego. You ever been there?"

Picou shook her head. "Nope. Born and bred a Louisiana girl. This land has been in my family for 158 years."

"That's quite a past," Annie commented, keeping an eye on the child as he lay down, folded his arms across his body and rolled down the hill. His shrieks made her smile. Who needed twisted-iron play equipment when the Native Americans of the past had given them the perfect playground?

"I'm the only one left. This land has been held by a

Laborde son for generations. Would still be true if my brother Benny hadn't died in 'Nam."

"I'm sorry," Annie murmured.

"Me, too." Picou's eyes turned misty. "He was something else. Darby looks like him. Square jaw and thick blondish hair. Good lookin' like none other. He died in '69. I was twenty-five and had just married Martin. My mama looked at me and said, 'No more Labordes, *cherie*,' to which I said, 'The hell there aren't. I'm a Laborde. That hasn't changed just 'cause I married Martin.'"

Annie nodded. She understood. Picou's identity wasn't rooted in her husband; it was in the land, in her family's legacy. She rather liked that about Picou.

"So Beau Soleil is still held by the Labordes. We won it off the Duplessis family in a card game, who themselves took it from the Chickamauga Indians. Guess their ancestors built these mounds."

"Must be nice to have a history like that. Mine's not nearly as interesting. Do your boys feel that same closeness to this place?"

Picou snorted. "Maybe Nate, but he's always been hard to read. Abram is wrapped in his own world—one of pigskin, off-season workouts and recruiting, and Darby's been running from Beau Soleil ever since he was a boy. And Della, well, I haven't found her again…yet."

"I thought—" Annie closed her mouth. Who was she to prick a pin in the inflated hope of the older woman?

"You thought she was dead?"

Annie nodded.

"She's not. She's alive. And she's close." Picou stared out into the woods as if she might part them and find the treasure she sought.

"How do you know?"

"I've always known, but Darby made me certain. He's

her twin; and when he was small, he dreamed of her, cried out to go get her and bring her back. It's something you feel in your bones, you know. Deep down inside, throbbing, waiting." Picou paused as if weary from revealing something so personal. "And then there is the powerful mambo who gave me a prophecy."

Mambo? More like mumbo jumbo. Must be a Louisiana thing. People wanted to believe in something. Always had. Even Tawny flirted with the kabbalah and other mysticisms. But not Annie. The only thing she believed in was herself and the power of hard work. She hadn't been to Mass since her mother's funeral. Funny how what drove some people toward unflinching faith destroyed it in others.

"I hope you find her." Annie walked toward the mounds, uncomfortable at the turn of conversation. "Come on, Spencer, we need to get back for worksheets, PB&J and a nap."

"I don't want a nap," Spencer called, ducking on the other side of the mound.

"Here we go," Annie grumped to herself, trudging toward the first mound. "I'm not messing around, Spence. When I say jump, you say?"

"I don't want a nap," Spencer called.

"Wrong answer," Annie called.

Picou laughed as Annie chased Spencer around the mounds. She even encouraged him by telling him to yell out "Marco." Annie went along, being a good sport with her successive call of "Polo." Finally she caught him.

"The answer is 'how high?'"

Spencer giggled then latched his arms around her neck, giving her a sloppy kiss.

"Blech," she said, swiping off the wetness, but deep down inside her heart throbbed, much like Picou's hope. She didn't want to love Spencer, because he was a job, but there was something so utterly sweet and innocent in him, something she wanted to touch as if it might heal her, help her capture a piece of the innocence trampled long ago.

She'd tried to use Seth and Mallory to do that. To heal herself and pretend she was like any other woman. She'd wanted to love Seth quite desperately, hoped to find in him and Mallory what she'd lost the day she buried her mother. The day her prayers had failed. The day her father drank too much and lost himself in the liquor and later still when her sister had run away and fallen into trouble. Life had slapped her in the face, knocked her down and dragged her by her heels. Loving her father, sister, even her grandmother who passed away soon after her mother, had left her heartsick and battle weary…and very lonely.

By the time Annie had graduated from high school, she'd stopped feeling as if she cared for anything or anyone. She was an empty shell inside—one she'd filled with ambition. Her life had been her career, first in the Air Force and then in the FBI. Everything had been about protecting herself—financially and professionally.

Until Christmas Eve last year.

When she sat in her spartan apartment in Philly with no Christmas tree, no holiday ham, no presents, and watched that damned movie. At that moment she'd realized she didn't matter to anyone. And she hadn't wanted to live that way.

One month later she met Seth, a widower accountant testifying in a case. He'd dogged her footsteps, repeatedly asking her out. Finally, she agreed. He brought his eleven-year-old daughter on their date and for some reason, still unknown to Annie, she'd gotten in her head that if she had a family, she could be whole again. She could be like the women who brought their toddlers to Starbucks and read self-help books with other women. She could serve on PTA boards and they could take Christmas-card pictures with the golden retriever Seth would buy her on their first wedding anniversary.

Yeah, she'd snapped.

And it had been a disaster.

So she didn't want to love a boy who couldn't be hers. Who might disappear like poor Della Dufrene had. What if Annie couldn't stop whoever wanted to harm Spencer? What if caring for him made her blind? Made him more vulnerable?

No.

She couldn't let that happen.

She set Spencer away from her. "Let's get something to eat. You have a worksheet on numbers to do then we'll have a story before nap time."

"Mr. Bader and his Ghost Town Gator?"

"Sure."

Her phone binged and she slid it out of her front jean pocket. Good. Jimmy could meet her. While Spencer napped under the watchful eye of Brick the bodyguard, she'd slip out and meet him. With her gun in hand, no one would get to Spencer unless he or she could get through a bullet first.

Annie wouldn't fail in this task.

CHAPTER SEVEN

AFTER SEVERAL DAYS of interviewing the production crew and anyone who might have seen anything out of the ordinary, Nate concluded the whole dead-bird threat was more challenging than he'd originally thought. Whoever poked a stick at the Keenes was savvy enough to hide any cracks in his or her composure—a happenstance not typical in Nate's realm of experience.

The most effective method of investigation other than an out-and-out eyewitness was the interview of a suspect. For Nate, interrogation was his bread and butter. In most cases, from petty theft to possession to murder, the suspect sang like the sweetest of birds when confronted with the evidence and prosecution. And if the suspect didn't squeal, he or she at least gave him angle to work. But with this case, nothing. He hadn't felt the slightest waver in any of the people he'd interviewed over the past few days, perhaps because many were actors accustomed to hiding their true emotions behind a façade. And that presented a stubborn wrinkle in the case.

The one person he hadn't spoken to in-depth was Annie. Since their odd exchange in the library, he'd avoided questioning her on her background and on her impressions of the Keene family. Maybe because he was afraid of the desire that uncoiled when he was around her.

Damn it. She was a suspect. A viable one. She'd been

hired around the time of the threat and he knew she was a liar.

So why hadn't he already done his job?

He'd find out that afternoon, as soon as he finished the reports on those he'd taken statements from that morning. Time to interview the nanny.

He stared down at the forms and then shoved them toward where his cold coffee sat.

"You going to the Stumpwater Inn tonight?" Kelli asked, propping a hip on his metal desk.

"Is there ever a good reason to go there?"

The flirty detective ran a long red fingernail on top of the only photo sitting on his desk—the softball league championship pic—and gave him a barracuda smile. "There is tonight."

He rolled his eyes.

"What?" she said.

"You're eight months pregnant. You can't go to the Stump."

Kelli raised a perfectly waxed eyebrow. "So? What are you saying? I'm not hot enough for action down there?"

Nate shook his head, picked up the hand still tapping the photo and bestowed a gentlemanly kiss. "Never."

"Hey," Wynn said, "get your lips off my wife."

"Get your wife off my desk."

Wynn's mouth twisted into a grin. "I couldn't pick her up if I tried."

Kelli lifted a half-full coffee mug. "You wanna say that again, big boy?"

Wynn strolled over and took the coffee mug from his wife's hand. "I couldn't pick you up if—"

A quick kiss silenced him.

"Ugh, we're in the office," Nate complained, rolling his chair back.

Wynn broke off the tame kiss and smiled sweetly at his very rounded wife. She grinned back, before smoothing her maternity uniform shirt over her growing belly. "At least there's no chance of knocking her up."

"You hit it the first time, didn't you, sugar?" Kelli giggled. They'd been married for less than a year, so Nate let their inappropriate behavior slide, but soon he'd have to tell them to knock it off. Kelli redirected her attention back to him. "So, I'm trying to get Nate to go down to Gerry's Lounge at the Stumpwater. David Reneau and the Murky Water Boys are playing tonight, and I hear a lot of the *Magic Man* crew will be there. Might get lucky, Nate."

Nate shook his head. "The only lucky I want is a break in this case. Blaine's on my back, and he ain't easy to carry around."

"I meant on the case," Kelli said, allowing her voice to drop down to serious business mode. Under her artfully streaked blond hair, stacked bod and big mouth beat the heart of a talented investigator. "Liquor loosens lips."

"Among other things," Wynn sniped.

Nate glanced up. "I'd rather put on a dress and heels and stroll down Main Street than go to Gerry's tonight."

Kelli got that look, the one married women got around their husband's single friends. "You need to go. Not just for the case, but for social reasons. You need a woman in your life. You can't remain an island forever. A sexless island, cold, hard and lonely when the sun sets."

"Has she been reading poetry again or just listening to Simon and Garfunkel?" Nate rose and shuffled papers into one of the accordion files. He'd come in early tomorrow to complete the report and then get a summary to Blaine before noon. Not that there'd be much to summarize. He needed to catch a break. Soon. Before another threat. Or worse.

"Kelli's right, you know. You should go."

Kelli smiled and latched an arm through her husband's. "I love when you say I'm right."

Wynn ignored his wife and looked at Nate. "For the case."

Nate sighed. Both Wynn and Kelli had a point, but damn if he wanted to shower, shave and head out to the meat market of Bayou Bridge. The last time he'd been there, he'd spent twelve dollars for three beers and ended up driving an old high school friend home praying she didn't vomit in his new car. In Bayou Bridge, a single man with a steady income and all his teeth had a bull's eye on his back. Made a man twitchy.

"Fine. I'll go."

Wynn snorted. "Maybe I should come with you."

Kelli's elbow caught him. "You've got a nursery to paint."

Nate shook his head. "I'll be fine. I'll wear an ugly shirt or something. Maybe paint a tooth black."

Kelli rolled her eyes. "Please. You act like it's torture to go out and have fun. Women aren't that desperate to nab you, Nate Dufrene."

He ignored Kelli's bait, instead grabbing his piece from the top desk drawer, checking the safety and sliding it into his harness. He'd grab lunch at the Wing Shack then head out to Beau Soleil. He wanted to talk to the nanny before he went to Gerry's that night. Part of him wanted to see her because he wanted to see her; the other part hoped she might give him some needed insight. "Later. Have fun painting."

Wynn gave him a blank stare. "Have fun drinking beer, listening to good music and prying hot women off your lap."

Kelli whispered something in Wynn's ear and smiled.

Nate thought he'd rather be doing what they had planned that evening rather than what had been planned for him.

Gerry's.

Hell.

He left the station, climbed in his car and tried to enjoy the scenery on the way to the place where'd he'd grown into a man, but enjoying the effects the heat had had on the surroundings was hard to accomplish in September. Everything looked plain worn-out, waving a white flag of surrender.

Annie wasn't at Beau Soleil when Nate arrived at the house. That much was obvious from the moment he'd pulled into the drive and killed the engine. His mother looked exhausted. Her five-year-old guest looked enthused.

"Hey," Spencer crowed as Nate climbed out and slammed the door. The little boy ran to him, grabbed his hand and gave it a tug. "We're playing tag. Come play with us."

Nate looked down at their linked hands and then at his mother who nodded. Vehemently.

"Sorry, I'm not here to play," he said, untangling his hand, stepping over some yellow flowers and curving an arm around his mother's shoulders. Perspiration ran down her lined face. He couldn't remember the last time he'd seen his mother sweat.

"It's fun. Peekaboo's good at it. Almost as good as Annie," Spencer declared, kicking at the stones lining the flower bed before hopping past him and scrabbling up the steps. "Can I have another popsicle, Peekaboo?"

His mother slumped against him. In relief? Exhaustion? "Sure, sweetheart. I need to take a break."

"You still want grandkids?" Nate muttered.

Picou slid her gaze to his. "Of course. Did you think I'd let a five-year-old beat me? I won at tag."

Nate climbed the steps. "I need to talk to the nanny. Why isn't she here?"

"She's out running," Picou said, pushing through the screen door into the cool house. Nate and Spencer followed her. "Spencer woke up early from his nap, so we decided to play outside, but it's too hot."

"Yeah," Spencer agreed. The boy's brown hair was plastered to his head and he greedily yanked free the paper on the popsicle, shoving the red frozen confection in his mouth. He pulled the treat out again leaving a ring around his mouth. "Too hot."

Nate hadn't been around many kids, but this one was cute. Annoying, but cute. "So why's she running? It's nearly ninety-two degrees with eighty percent humidity."

"That's what I said, but she said she had to run whenever she can get it in. Spencer napped, so I told her I'd keep an ear out for him while I worked on my tatting." Picou offered Nate a wrapped treat. He waved it aside. "Fitness seems important to the girl, though I can't say it's particularly smart to go out in this heat. I'm not her mother, so…"

Nate changed his mind and took the popsicle and unwrapped it. He took a bite. It was blue raspberry. "Where does she run?"

Picou shrugged. "Usually runs on the highway, but she had trail shoes on this time. Maybe the woods?"

"I'll walk around and see if I can find her."

"Needle in haystack," Picou murmured, swiping the granite countertop with a worn dishtowel. "Why don't you wait around until she gets back?"

"Yeah, I'm good at tag," Spencer added.

Nate shivered. The last thing he wanted to do was waste time chasing Spencer around in the stifling heat. "Nah, I fancy a walk."

"'Kay." Spencer nodded. "I wanna go to the Invian mounds again."

He looked down at the kid, knowing horror was etched on his face. It wasn't as if he didn't like children, he just didn't know what to do with them. "You better stay here, Spencer. Mom will read you a story or turn on the television."

Nate glanced at his mother who wore a knowing grin. She nodded. "Or we can do a puzzle."

Spencer stuck out his chin. "I don't wanna do a puzzle. I wanna go on a nature walk with him." He pointed a sticky finger at Nate.

"No. I need to talk to Annie about some—"

Tears trembled on the boys lashed. "You don't like me?"

Nate blinked. How had the boy made tears so fast? He looked at his mother. She wore a secret smile, very Mona Lisa-like in nature. "You're crying?"

Spencer turned weepy brown eyes upward. "Why don't you like me? I'm good. I won't step on any bugs or get my shoes dirty. I promise. And I can help you find Annie, too."

Nate didn't know what to do—and he always knew what to do. But this had him beat. "Um, well, I guess it will be okay."

"Cool. I'm not supposed to go off with anyone except Peekaboo, Annie, my mom and dad, and Brick. He's our bodyguard. But you're a po-lice, so that's okay."

Picou shook her head in amusement.

Nate tossed the half-eaten popsicle in the sink, not bothering to hide his disgust. He had business to conduct and he wasn't into babysitting. "Fine. Let's go."

Picou turned with a bottle of something in hand. "Let me put some bug spray on his arms and legs. Oh, and sunscreen, I may need to reapply."

Spencer made a face and sprinted toward the back door. Picou caught him.

"I'll wait outside," Nate said, heading through the mudroom and toward the back door where they'd found the dead bird three days before. He didn't want his mother trying to coat him up with all that junk. And he needed to think. About questions for the feisty nanny.

About why she led him to believe she sold real estate in California. About why she had a phony website for a real-estate agency in Nevada. About who she was and why she was lying.

"Nate?" He turned to find his mother standing next to the boy. "About that thing down in Lafourche?"

"I'm going tomorrow, Mom."

Picou pressed her lips together. "Always tomorrow, huh?"

He nodded. "But it will come."

He beckoned the boy and set off to find the nanny.

ANNIE JOGGED DOWN THE path she, Picou and Spencer had tramped down earlier that morning, glad to be away if only for an hour. Thankfully, Picou had agreed to keep an ear out for Spencer. The boy would probably take a long nap since he'd stayed up late with Tawny and Carter watching some animated feature film they'd gotten their hands on three weeks before it hit theaters. He'd been hard to wake that morning, but she'd cajoled him out with the promise of a Ring Pop after breakfast. The parenting books had stressed the importance of a schedule for young children. She ignored the chapter about limiting sugar. A nanny had to do what a nanny had to do. Sugar was like crack for kids.

For a minute or two, she savored the absolute stillness around her, enjoying the sound of her breath and soft footfalls on the leaf-strewn trail.

Of course, she wouldn't be alone for long.

Jimmy waited at the mounds.

She increased her pace through the quiet woods, determined to make short work of getting the info and gun, returning in plenty of time to get dressed for the evening at Gerry's Lounge. She'd cleared having the time off with Tawny and Carter. Her employment contract gave her weekends off, but over the past four weeks, she'd elected to stay on for overtime pay. Any time she'd spent away from the Keenes had been utilized meeting with Ace and his team or checking on her father in the nursing facility in Palo Alto.

She slowed as she approached the mound. Old habits die hard. She didn't see Jimmy, but the former Secret Service agent was good at fading into the background. She surveyed the open area surrounding the mounds, noting that it wasn't perhaps the best meeting place after all since it left them somewhat vulnerable.

"Hey," Jimmy said, tossing a cigarette toward the pine straw at her feet.

She stomped on the lit cigarette. "How long have you been standing there?"

"A few minutes. You're losing your skills, peach."

"Bullshit. I knew you were there," she lied.

He grinned. "Right."

She jabbed her hands on her hips. "You come from an agency of glorified babysitters."

"Well, ain't you the pot?" Jimmy sauntered toward her, giving one of her sweaty curls a tug. "Good to see you, peach."

Annie pushed his hand away. From the time she'd met him, Jimmy struck her as the kind of guy who flirted with any gal age eighteen to one foot in the grave. He was average in every way with light brown hair, nondescript hazel eyes, slight build, nonthreatening nature—all perfect for getting folks to spill their guts. But for someone so Average Joe, Jimmy was convinced he was irresistible.

"Good to see you, too," she said, brushing her hair back, wishing she'd had the foresight to bring a hair clip. The sultry air had her hair corkscrewing into her eyes. "So how're things at base-op?"

"Not much to go on yet, but I've got some hot spots I'm pushing."

"Care to share?"

Jimmy looked around and stepped closer. "Mick bothers me. He's been screwing around with half the girls on production but has an eye on Tawny. Could be because they knocked boots at one time, but I'm getting strange vibes from those two."

"That explains the way Carter's acting—he thinks she's fooling around, but I'm not convinced. I think she may be using Mick to push Carter's buttons. Some strong undercurrents there. Anything else?"

Jimmy scratched the goatee on his sharp chin. "A few gals, extras mostly, have their eye on Carter, but it seems harmless. Goo-goo ga-ga over the Hollywood actor, and all. One chick follows him around a good deal and she's got a mouth on her, but who knows?"

"Too many possibilities to wade through," she said, swiping her gaze across the area where they stood. The woods were still. "I'm meeting Jane McEvoy tonight at the hotel bar. Maybe I can find a string for us to pull."

"Ah, Jane." Jimmy smiled. "Wouldn't mind a taste of her, but she's a bit of a cool customer. Some think she's got it bad for old Mick, but he doesn't pay her any attention."

"She's only hanging out with me because she's bored, but it's a good opportunity to snoop around without the kid at my hip." Annie held out a hand. "My gun, please."

Jimmy withdrew the 9 mm from the waistband of his jeans and handed it to her along with a small box of ammunition. She pulled the small backpack she carried off her back and unzipped the pocket, double-checking the safety, before sliding the gun and ammunition inside. The zip of the bag was the only sound in the woods, that and the call of some bird she couldn't identify.

Jimmy watched with eyes that missed nothing. "I'm doing my best to be one of the guys. Feels like I'm wasting time. Tonight we're going to Baton Rouge."

"So we're both going clubbing? Can we charge our drinks to Ace?"

"A hot chick like you can work it hard enough to get 'em free, *cher*."

"You're a Cajun now?"

"Nope. A chameleon."

Annie's snort coincided with a stick cracking on the path behind them. Jimmy took two steps back into the shadows, pulling her with him, curving one arm around her waist.

"Let go," she whispered, wiggling in his grasp.

Jimmy tightened his hold "Cover, *cher*."

She heard Spencer chattering. What the hell? She glanced down at her sports watch. Two-fifteen. He should still be sleeping. Had Picou brought him out again? Then she heard the low muffled voice of a man.

Adrenaline shot through her veins, and she pushed at Jimmy's chest.

More breaking sticks and muffled words.

Someone had Spencer.

She allowed the strap of the backpack to fall from her shoulder while simultaneously unzipping the front pocket where she'd stowed the gun. Her hand hit metal at the same time Jimmy's lips covered hers.

"Mff," she sputtered as his other arm came around her,

pulling her tightly to him. She jerked back, trying to break the contact because he tasted like an ashtray, because she didn't like guys with goatees kissing her, and because Spencer might be in grave danger. But Jimmy held fast and even increased the pressure against her lips.

She wrapped her hand around the gun's grip and prepared to do battle with whoever had the boy she'd been hired to protect.

CHAPTER EIGHT

ANNIE STRUGGLED TO REMOVE herself from Jimmy's arms while ripping her mouth from his—before he tried some tongue action or something equally disgusting.

"A little afternoon delight?" The voice came from behind them and held little amusement.

She allowed the gun to fall back into the pocket of the backpack and spun toward the wry voice. Nate stood in the path of the woods, holding Spencer's hand. Her heart froze, and for a moment, she felt as if she'd been caught cheating on him. Maybe it had something to do with his eyes flinging poisonous darts their way.

"Nate," she said, removing Jimmy's hands from her hips and stepping away. She shifted the backpack on her shoulders and prayed the gun wouldn't fall out of the still-unzipped pocket. "What—what are you doing here?"

"I woked up already. Why you wrestling with that guy? Who's he? Is he marrying you?" Spencer said, dropping Nate's hand. For once Annie was glad of Spencer's inane questions.

"No, he's not my husband. We're just friends."

"Oh," Spencer said, seemingly satisfied with her answer. He shifted his attention to the mounds behind her before stomping through the high grass surrounding the clearing, heading for his best chance at getting dirty.

She watched to make sure he reached them safely then turned back to the person who wouldn't be as satisfied with her answer. Nate's voice had said it all. He wasn't a happy camper. But why should he care if she sneaked around the woods to meet up with strange guys? None of his damn business.

Jimmy stepped forward. "Guess you caught us, man. I'm Howie, her little sugar daddy." He extended a hand to Nate, but the detective ignored it.

Annie faked brittle laughter. "Oh, Howie's an old friend...not my sugar daddy."

"So I see," Nate said, stepping past Jimmy and walking toward her. He dismissed Jimmy. "So Howie can't come to the door like a regular person?"

Annie swiped a hand across her mouth, trying to erase Jimmy's kiss. "Um, we needed—"

"—a little alone time," Jimmy said, moving to her side and curling an arm around her waist.

She wrenched herself from Jimmy's grasp. "No, we didn't."

She looked at Jimmy hard, trying to communicate her intent to him. Even if she'd vowed not to play the flirt with Nate, she didn't want him to think she was taken. She wasn't sure if that was out of interest for the case...or her own. "I told you we were over, Howie."

Jimmy hid his puzzlement well. "I don't—"

"So you're telling me you came out here to meet an ex-boyfriend? Here? In the woods away from everyone?" Nate's eyes communicated the simple thought that she was a dumbass.

"Yes," she said.

"No," Jimmy said at the same time.

She glared at Jimmy. Nate cocked an eyebrow. "So which is it?"

Annie zipped her backpack and threaded both arms through the straps. "Look, Howie and I used to date. A long time ago. When my hard drive screwed up, I called him to bring me a new one. He works for an electronics store and gets a discount. I was going to take him to lunch, but I haven't been able to get away. I knew he was heading up today, and since he likes history, I told him we'd meet here. I didn't want a bunch of questions from everyone, and I didn't think he'd take it as a sign I wanted mauling."

Jimmy faked disbelief then anger. "I thought you wanted to be alone. You're such a goddamned tease, Ann. You always pull this shit."

Annie blinked. Jimmy was a good actor. "Watch your language around the kid."

Jimmy narrowed his eyes. "All this way and used my damn discount for nothing. I only get to use it three times a year. Three times and I blew one on you."

"You thought I'd trade sex for a hard drive? Please. I have standards."

Nate watched them carefully. Annie felt his hard perusal. She glanced at him and noted he didn't look convinced. Just disgusted. And that made her feel rotten.

"Always thought you were too good for me, didn't you? But not too good to use for your own gain. I hope the damn drive doesn't work. It's a refurbished one anyway." Jimmy huffed, shoving his hands into his pockets. "You're welcome to her. She wasn't so good in the sack noways."

Now, that was going a little too far.

Jimmy gave her a hateful glance before stomping back down the path. He may or may not have thrown her the bird. She didn't know because she watched Nate who thankfully took to studying the canopy of branches overhead.

"Sorry, that was a bit awkward," Annie said, breaking the silence.

"Yeah."

Silence fell again, only interrupted with an occasional "whee" from Spencer.

As she watched the boy roll down the hill, she berated herself for getting caught in the first place. Now Jimmy would be unable to go back to the catering gig. His cover was blown and he was useless. Second, somehow she'd lost her mojo to control situations. Maybe leaving the Bureau and playing soccer mom had scrabbled her brain and addled her ability to canvas a situation and play it to her advantage. Had she lost what made her Anna? Control, intelligence and good reaction? And if so, how the devil would she make herself indispensable to her new boss?

"Look, he's not anything to me."

Nate slid his gaze to hers. "Why should it matter to me who you screw in the woods?"

"It doesn't. And I wasn't. I haven't seen him in years. Don't know why he thought this was something other than a favor between old friends." She patted the backpack for good measure, praying it threw off any suspicions Nate had about her being involved in anything wonky. She wanted him to open up to her, to talk about the case. If he thought she was involved, she could kiss those chances goodbye. "He owed me, you know?"

"Were you using him?"

"Of course not," she said, licking her lips. "He volunteered to get a drive for me when I said something about being down here in Louisiana and having trouble with my laptop. We're Facebook—"

"Look, I'm not interested."

"In me?"

A little pulse ticked in his jaw. She wanted to reach out and trace it with a fingertip, but that would be nuts.

He finally looked at her. "I'm not starting anything with you. You're a suspect."

"I am?"

"And even if you weren't a suspect, I wouldn't be interested in anything more than a little fun."

Her heart felt as if it had snagged on something and she involuntarily lifted a hand to her chest. Why would his words hurt? Sure, she thought he was hot and her stomach flip-flopped around him at times, but he was nothing more than a pawn to be used. Nothing more than her ticket to helping crack the case so she could get a better foothold in a career path. "Who said I want you?"

His mouth tightened. "Just being straight with you. I'm not interested in a relationship."

She couldn't stop the anger welling inside her. "Well, good. I'm not either. I'm only nice to you because of Picou. She's a decent person who doesn't deserve such a jackass for a son…a jackass who presumes I'd drop my panties for any guy who comes along."

"You call what you've been nice? Hate to hear what you consider down and dirty."

"Good luck seeing anything down and dirty with me, bucko."

His mouth kicked into a little smile. "I like you pissed off."

"Oh, yeah? Well, stick around. I'm about to turn into a frickin' amusement park." She crossed her arms. She rarely got her panties in a wad, but this man irritated the hell out of her. How dare he issue a warning about a nonexistent relationship? Whatever. He was hot but not that hot. "And you're not invited for a ride."

At her words something flared. Like spontaneous combustion. Spark. Ignite. Burn. The air grew thick. Nate shifted, his posturing less defensive, more open. Maybe even inviting.

She could feel his heat and it her made want to sidestep

like a nervous mare. It also turned her on. How could a man go from irritating to smoldering in seconds?

Her gaze slid to his. Damn. His eyes had gone all half-lidded bedroomy. When had that happened? And why did it make the back of her knees feel sweaty?

"No pass no play, huh?"

She swallowed. Heat unwound in her belly, coating her in warm, liquid lust. Her eyes zeroed in on his mouth. Those lips were very tempting, daring her to kiss the smirk away. "Special passes are granted for good boys. I don't think you qualify."

Those delicious lips curved into the type of smile that plucked hidden strings in Annie's belly. "Don't you wish you knew if I were good?"

She opened her mouth just as Spencer yelled, "Cowabunga, dudes!" The childish jubilee ripped her from the hotness she contemplated, jarring her back to reality.

Mere minutes ago Nate wasn't interested, so why was he tempting her? "Okay, let's stop talking analogies here. You just said you don't want me, so stop flirting with me."

"I didn't say I didn't want you. You're beautiful, passionate and pretty damn smart, and that's something every man is interested in sampling." He brushed a finger over her bare shoulder and she flinched. "I said I wasn't interested in a relationship."

"So you mean straight-up, no-strings sex?"

He smiled.

"Are you the stupidest investigator in the county?"

He frowned. "It's a parish."

"Whatever." She glared at him. "You just said I'm a suspect. What about that, Einstein?"

His eyes narrowed and the amped-up heat between them dissolved. "Of course you're still a suspect."

"So why would you even contemplate trying to get in my pants?"

He looked confused. It almost made her want to smile. Almost. Part of her was peeved he wanted to treat her like a Guadalajara whore. Part of her thrilled to the idea of scorching the sheets with him.

"I don't know. I'm a man?"

"Seriously? That's your excuse for being a chauvinistic, incompetent asshole? That's the reason you're using for tossing away your career? You're horny?"

"Damn. You turned mean fast."

"Yeah. Because I don't like being treated like I'm easy. I'm not." She watched him shift back and forth in his loafers. She'd hit a nerve. "Somehow I thought you wouldn't treat me that way."

Her words were an arrow piercing his armor. She saw him deflate. "Ah, hell, I don't know why I'm doing this."

He grew still and his brown eyes got that vulnerable look in them, the one she'd glimpsed only fleetingly when he'd been around his mother several mornings ago. That softness drew her to him more than any heat.

He dropped his hands to his hips, sliding them into the pockets of his khaki trousers, and sighed. "Look, I'm not good at saying I'm sorry, but in this case, I'll be glad to grovel. That wasn't well done of me. Guess I'm rusty around women."

"Yeah, like I need a tetanus shot," she said, allowing lightness in her voice.

"Possibly." He glanced at her. "Sorry I overstepped… acted like an ass."

Annie nodded. "Okay."

"Okay?"

"Yeah," she said, pulling her gaze from his and searching for Spencer. She saw his head bob behind one of the mounds. A stick quickly followed, before being launched into the air like a crooked spear. Boys and sticks. What was with that? "People say and do stupid stuff all the time. I'm used to it, and frankly, I'm a testament to screwing things up, so I try not to hold grudges."

He nodded, but didn't say anything else. Again, silence sat between them, but this time it didn't feel so thick.

"Any chance we forget about my being an idiot?" he asked. His dark eyes didn't beg, but the velvet depths were steadfastly contrite. "Do a rewind?"

Spencer came bounding over, waving the stick. Annie's gaze met Nate's. "Sure."

Then she gave her attention to the boy, who professed to have found a "real live" Indian spear. "Of course it is. We'll have to show it to your mother. She's coming home early tonight and said you'd watch another movie and eat popcorn."

Spencer bounced and Annie caught Nate's smile at the boy's glee. "Cool! You going to watch it with us, Annie?"

"Nope, cowboy. Annie's off tonight."

She felt Nate's interest again, and knew she could have done what Ace had suggested. Hell, she could have gotten exactly what she wanted—a hot tumble with Nate and an opening to get primo info about the case from him. But she couldn't use herself like that. She'd have to find her leads the forthright way—snooping around.

She placed a hand on Spencer's sweaty neck and steered him back toward the path, but Nate's grasp on her elbow stopped her. "I still need to interview you for the record, Annie. That's the reason I'm out here."

His touch seared her, but she reminded herself of her conviction. "Sorry, I need to get back."

"Won't take long."

"Annie, I gotta go poop," Spencer called out.

"See? Spencer's got to make potty," she said.

Nate frowned. "I'll walk you back."

"Fine."

He didn't look happy, but, really, when did he ever look happy? Not much, in her limited experience. She plowed back toward Beau Soleil wondering what was so important he'd bothered to track her down in the woods. But, of course, she had an inkling.

Sterling had done a decent job of building her cover, but she knew any investigator worth his salt could poke a hole in her flimsy story. Nate fit the bill.

Last night she'd thought about tossing her undercover identity with the Cajun detective. Heaven knew she hadn't done a good job of earning his trust, and lies seemed to trip on her tongue where he was concerned. Honesty with Nate would be refreshing, but she needed to clear it with Ace first. She didn't want to screw up anything within her probationary period. She needed that steady paycheck.

Spencer was thankfully quiet. The crackle of the newly fallen leaves and the bustle of a hidden forest were the only accompaniment to their journey toward the large yellow-bricked house. When they emerged at the side of the property, she turned to Nate. "I'm not trying to hamper your investigation, but I'm meeting someone in an hour and I need to shower. Would it be okay to bring Spencer with me and meet you at the station tomorrow?"

Nate shook his head. "I'm out tomorrow. Just for the day."

"Oh." Curiosity nudged her, but she held her tongue.

"You and Spencer should come with me. What I have to do won't take long and then I can take Spencer on a swamp tour. Didn't he want to see alligators?"

"Yes!" Spencer shouted. "Yes! Yes!"

Annie placed a firm hand on Spencer's shoulder to prevent him from tromping her foot in his zestful jumping. "If it's work-related, we'd be in the way."

Nate shrugged. "Not really, and it would give me time to interview you. Two birds and all that."

Spencer stomped. "I want to go see the alligators, Annie. You promised."

She looked at Spencer then back at Nate. "I'm not sure we should allow this to get too personal…"

"That's up to you. I'm going down to Bayou Lafourche to a town called Galliano. I have a quick errand then we can do the airboat. It'll be educational, and you'll have Spencer safe with law enforcement—at least for a day."

Annie had no other recourse but to agree. Another day spent putting together puzzles and practicing Spencer's handwriting and numbers sounded mind-numbing anyway. And then there was Nate. Big, gorgeous Nate with his broad shoulders, dimple in his left cheek and quiet strength. So tempting to sit beside him as he drove, soaking in his aura, listening to his low gravelly voice, fantasizing she was just a girl hoping for something with a stand-up guy who wouldn't choose anything or anyone over her. "Okay. As long as his parents agree."

Spencer whooped and took off toward the porch where Picou stood in crane pose. Or that's what Annie called it.

"Tomorrow," Nate said, tossing his mother a wave and walking toward his car.

Annie watched him go. The view was nice, but it was more than that. More and more, she felt herself being pulled toward Nate. Not to mention, deep down she still wanted to believe in love, family and a pretty ribbon tied around a happily ever after.

Past mistakes didn't define people, but they damn sure made it hard to believe in fairy tales.

"Annie!" Spencer's voice carried across the lawn. "Hurry up. You gotta come wipe me!"

Lovely.

ANNIE STOOD IN FRONT of the three-way mirror Tawny had brought in and sighed. "I don't know, Mrs. Keene. I don't think I can walk in these heels."

The actress gave a much-put-upon sigh. "Tawny. And those are the newest Louboutins. They lift your ass. Practice walking in them."

It was a command.

Annie tottered across the bedroom, trying to maintain a steady stroll. She wore heels upon occasion, but never ones that were four inches with a sexy strap around the ankle. She turned, teetered and thrust her arms out for balance. She weebled, she wobbled, but she didn't fall down.

"Not bad," Tawny said, tossing the blouses she'd discarded onto a wingback chair in the corner. "Much better than the whole Mother Teresa thing you had going on. What were those shoes? Orthotics?"

"No. Serviceable flats."

At that, Tawny snorted. "You're funny when you want to be, Annie the Nanny."

Annie suppressed an eyeroll and studied herself in the mirror. She had to admit, she did look semihot. Thanks to leaving her fake ID on the dresser in her room. When Annie had slipped through the kitchen earlier to retrieve it, Tawny caught sight of her in the knee-length gray skirt and powder-blue sweater set and literally shrieked. Tawny had pointed one long red nail Annie's way and forbidden her to leave the house looking like Sister Agnes—whoever that was—and whisked her upstairs for a personal clothes consultation. She'd gone through Annie's closet in thirty seconds before insisting Annie borrow something from her fall collection.

Annie had had little say in the matter.

And for once, the actress reacted friendlier to her. Annie suspected it had something to do with her leaving for the night and Tawny having her family to herself, including the handsome husband. Annie had finally figured out Tawny's behavior—the woman wanted her husband, and anyone or thing that interfered was treated to instant dislike. His work and Annie included.

Annie turned the toe of the silver pump inward. "You sure these match? I think my flats would work."

"Of course they match. Metallic colors are neutral and patchwork is all the rage. Besides there's silver thread woven in the flower on the shirt."

Annie plucked at the clingy blouse and glanced down. So there was. She smoothed down the black-and-gray snakeskin-print skirt. Miraculously, it didn't grow another three inches. Instead it hit her midthigh just as it had when she'd first pulled it on. "I don't know, Tawny. The clothes are beautiful, but too expensive for a nanny to wear. I wouldn't want anything to happen to them."

Tawny frowned. "I'm loaning it to you. Not giving it to you. And I insist."

Annie nodded. "Well, then I thank you for being so generous."

"No problem. Now come on in the bathroom and let me do something to your hair. I have a fascinator that will look good against your curls. Your hair is so plain brown. Have you thought about highlights? I think a nice caramel would complement your complexion. It did wonders for my sister. She was plain brown, too, but I talked her into highlights and they made a world of difference. Now she has honey-blond highlights…or at least she did the last time I saw her. It's been a while."

What in the hell was a fascinator? And highlights? What was wrong with plain brown?

Tawny disappeared into the bathroom chattering about jewelry and a hot-pink lip gloss.

Annie stood stock-still and wondered if escape was an option. She took one step toward the door just as Tawny popped her head back out. "You coming?"

"Um, sure."

Thirty minutes later, Annie tottered down the front steps, climbed into the rental car and looked frantically for a napkin in the glove box. No way in hell was she wearing bright pink blusher or garish lipstick. Luckily, she found a McDonald's napkin wedged under the car manual.

She pulled down the sun visor to find the mirror and scrubbed away, praying she didn't look like a streetwalker. After a few seconds of rubbing, she felt as if she'd removed most of the heavy makeup. Big hoop earrings framed her face and the black silk rose looked frivolous nestled in her curls, but she was afraid to pull it out. It would have to stay.

She flipped the visor up and started the engine. She was late to meet Jane, but the past hour had given her better insight into Tawny. A fragile truce seemed to have developed between the two of them, especially since Annie faked being interested in one of the craft-service guys.

When she'd gotten back from the woods with her gun and a sinking feeling her undercover status was doomed, she'd put in a call to Ace and asked to come clean with Nate.

"Fine, but remember, it could backfire. Most local cops don't know our reputation, so they might horn you out altogether."

"I don't think this guy will do that."

"Just how close have you gotten to him?"

She cleared her throat. "Not that close. I've tried to be his friend, so I can catch crumbs, but I think he'll trust me more if I tell him I work for you."

"Why?"

"Because he caught me and Jimmy in the woods. He's suspicious."

Ace blew out a breath. "How the hell did that happen? Jimmy said the drop-off was secluded. You let the cop see you get your gun? Shoddy work, Anna."

Her stomach sank. "Of course not. We covered it up, but the idea of me out in the woods meeting someone looks suspicious."

Ace remained silent.

"I'm looking at it from his point of view, and if I were him, I'd be wary giving out information to someone like me." Ace finally grunted, but not in an encouraging way. "Look, I trust him. He's a good guy and the son of the lady we're staying with. I think it would be the right move."

She had rolled the dice, but she stood by her assessment. Tomorrow on the way to wherever it was Nate was taking her and Spencer, she'd test the waters. She hoped her perception of Nate wasn't colored by the fact she longed to run her tongue over his stomach and devour him like a Godiva chocolate. She shook the thought from her head. *Watch it, chica. You'll end up writing parking tickets if you keep thinking like that.*

"Fine," Sterling conceded, "but on a need-to-know basis, when you think the time is right. Hopefully, he'll be discreet and not blow your cover."

"Yeah," Annie said, before hanging up. An uneasy feeling had settled in the pit of her stomach, but she leaned more toward trusting Nate than she did trying to go it alone. At this point, she'd take the gamble.

She withdrew a tube of creamy pink lipstick from the Fendi patchwork bag Tawny had insisted she carry and swiped it over her lips. Then she slid the tube next to her gun. She'd debated over taking her weapon, but it made her feel stronger. More like the Annie she wanted to be. Not like a probationary member of a security firm.

She put the car in Reverse and backed out of the drive, praying she'd be able to suffer through drinks at the Stumpwater Inn and hoping tonight would bring her some luck in finding a clue to who might be toying with the Keene family.

She had to stop thinking so much about Nate and start thinking about the job.

Put Nate Out of Your Mind was her new motto.

At least for the night.

CHAPTER NINE

SET OFF I-10, THE Stumpwater Inn wasn't a dump, but it wasn't exactly the Ritz. Nate smelled the local hot spot as soon as the door whooshed open. Nothing like cigarettes and booze to compliment the scent of sanitized lobby with hunter-green carpet faded to match the couches by the coffee bar. Behind the oak reservation desk was Rosie Chatelaine, who waved at him with a quizzical smile.

Yeah, it had been a while since he'd been here.

He didn't bother to stop and chat. Wanted to get this over with as soon as he could, so he veered toward Gerry's. During the day, the club served a country-style buffet, but at night it offered live music and ladies' night specials. Nate went a couple of times when he first moved back to Bayou Bridge, before he stopped drinking whiskey, before he realized Gerry's was filled with people looking to get filled up on something other than booze, before the club scene depressed him.

He pulled open the door and was immediately assaulted by music and the stronger smell of cigarette smoke, though smoking was prohibited. Dave Reneau warmed up his fiddle over the Def Leppard blaring through the bar speakers as the bartender and a buxom redhead slid longnecks along the worn bar to men wearing too much cologne and women wearing not enough clothing. Nothing unusual for a Thursday night.

"Yo, Nate Dufrene. My eyes lyin', or what?"

A hand slammed onto his shoulder, and he turned to find his old high school baseball coach standing at the end of the bar wearing a leather jacket two sizes too small and washed-out jeans that had seen better days if the ripped knees were any indication.

"Coach Bell." Nate nodded.

"Aw, hell. Don't call me Coach in here. Call me Greg." The man looked around as if some of the barfly broads might catch wind he was twenty years too old to be bar hopping. "How's Abram? What's ULB looking like for the Auburn game? The line is tight and I don't wanna lose my shirt."

Nate shrugged. "No clue."

He didn't want to talk about football. He did that every day, thanks to having a brother who was a University of Louisiana Baton Rouge tight-ends coach. He glanced around and that's when he saw the nanny.

Annie Perez perched on a bar stool looking like an ad for naughty.

He actually did a double take.

It was her, and yet it wasn't.

She wore a short skirt of silvery gray and a tight sleeveless shirt that had flower on it. Her hair curled around a black rose and she wore lipstick.

His groined tightened at the sight of those plump lips covered in silky-looking lipstick. It wasn't bright and whorish. Just subtle light pink, beckoning light pink, gotta taste them light pink.

"Excuse me, Coach. I see someone I need to talk to," Nate said, stepping in Annie's direction.

"Oh, I see that," the man said, his eyes following Nate's line of sight.

Annie held on to a martini glass filled with something pink, girly and wrong for her. Annie had too much bite to suck down something with a cherry bobbing in it. The blonde next to her was pleasantly pretty, but the dress she wore was a size too small and her tan a little too faux. She had dimples and blue eyes, and he'd talked to her for exactly fourteen minutes on Tuesday. Jane McEvoy. Tawny's former roommate and current best friend.

"Ladies," he murmured, lightly touching Annie on her elbow. She started and the pink bubbly martini sloshed onto the bar.

"Ah, Detective," Jane purred, lifting her own fruity cocktail in toast. "You don't seem the type to frequent places such as this."

He quirked an eyebrow. "I don't seem the type who'd enjoy zydeco and a beer?"

Jane's mouth curved at the corners. "Of course, but it seems too bourgeois for you."

"I like bourgeois. I take a pass on the finer things in life. They're always more trouble than they're worth."

"Too bad," Jane purred, running one finger down his forearm. He met the invitation in her eyes with a blank stare then turned toward Annie.

"Night off?"

Her eyes shuttered. "Yeah. Well-deserved night off."

"Didn't know you two were chums."

Jane's hand moved in a caress. "We're not, but we're getting to know one another. Always room for one more. Pull up a stool."

He needed to canvas the bar. He'd seen a few familiar faces from the brief interviews he and Wynn had conducted, but there was no way he could step away from Annie. Not when he'd seen the high heels she wore...and the way they made her legs look.

"Don't mind if I do."

He grabbed a stool from a table holding an extra one and

slid beside Annie. Jane's eyes flashed momentary irritation but she recovered.

"What are you drinking?" Jane asked, jerking her head toward the female bartender. "I'll buy the first round."

"Abita Amber." Hell, might as well let her buy him a beer. She'd push until he rolled over one way or another. She had that bulldogged look about her. Sweet-looking on the outside, controlling on the inside. But that was a guess.

Jane beckoned the woman over. Nate caught Annie's gaze and tried to discern her mood. She didn't seem comfortable, but neither did she seem ill-at-ease. Frankly, he was surprised she'd spend her off night at a bar. If someone had made him guess, he'd say she was the type to head to the gym on her off nights or maybe catch a classic movie— if they had a movie theater in Bayou Bridge.

"Is this band any good?" Annie asked, fiddling with the chain of the handbag hanging off her shoulder. Seeing the feminine accessory only heightened his awareness of Annie as a woman. Again, heat flared in his nether regions.

"Pretty good. I've known ol' Dave since he starting taking violin lessons in town. He's good 'cause he loves the music. You ever hear zydeco?"

She shook her head. "Not really."

Jane passed him a beer as Dave and the Murky Water Boys launched into a cover of a Buckwheat Zydeco song, "Boogaloo, Ma 'Tite Fille." Nothing left to do but tap his feet at the sounds of the accordion, fiddle and guitars. The dance floor came to life with couples whirling, stomping feet and clapping hands. Even though he dreaded the club scene, people knew how to pass a good time in Louisiana... and it was infectious.

"Teach me to dance," Jane shouted over the music, and because his mama had raised him to be a gentleman, he held out his hand. He felt Annie's eyes on the hands clasped in front of her. He met her gaze.

"You're next," he called as he followed the blonde actress to the writhing dance floor.

Jane caught on fast as he led her in a two-step around the dance floor Gerry Boudreaux had redone to look like the old cypress one in Mulates. At every turn he saw a smiling face and he let Jane pull him closer. Though she was perfectly pretty, he felt nothing as her breasts brushed the front of his polo shirt. He spun her, complicating the dance, but she followed him step for step.

The song ended and the bar erupted in applause. Dave grinned and launched into another up-tempo song. Jane tugged his elbow. "Let's do another."

He shook his head and looked over at the bar for Annie. She wasn't where he'd left her. Maybe someone had coaxed her onto the dance floor. He spun Jane around and glanced at the couples moving around them.

Jane looped her arms around his neck. "Come on, cowboy. Take me for another spin."

He looked down at the actress. Her green eyes were glazed, indicating she'd not been on her first martini when he'd arrived. More like her third. This was a woman ready for some real fun, and if he'd been into her, that tight dress would hit the floor easily later on. But she wasn't the woman he wanted to get naked with.

You shouldn't be wantin' to get naked with any woman right now. You have a job to do.

He jerked his head toward the bar. "Let's go back."

"Party pooper." She laughed, linking her arm through his. The crowd had gotten rowdy and he still didn't see Annie. Not that he had to keep tabs on her. He merely wanted to, even though he was supposed to be keeping his eyes and ears on the people from the *Magic Man* production.

"Where did Annie go?" he asked when they reached the bar. No one had nabbed their stools and their half-finished drinks remained.

"I don't know," Jane said, downing the rest of the martini and snapping her fingers at the bartender. "Why should I care? She's a big girl."

He scanned the crowd, his gaze lighting on Mick Manners, the dashing ne'er-do-well from the *Magic Man* production. He sat at a table with four women, one of which was Annie.

"Be right back," he said to Jane.

He slipped through the crowd, heading for the table. Annie hadn't seen him and she looked engrossed in whatever Mick was saying. The other women talked to each other, but Mick's arm rested casually around Annie's shoulders as he murmured into her ear. The nanny's head bobbed in agreement as he told her something obviously fascinating.

Nate felt like someone had sucker punched him.

His fist tightened even as he reminded himself he had no claim on her. The brief thought of getting more time to grill Mick clicked in his brain, along with questions about why Annie was hanging out with Jane McEvory, but none of them superseded the jealousy that bit down on him and gave him a good, hard shake.

"So here's where you went," Nate shouted over the lively music. "Always finding you with a new man."

Aggravation flashed in Mick's eyes, but he caught a glimpse of relief in Annie's eyes before she shuttered them. "You stalking me, Detective?"

"Nope. You promised me the next dance, remember?" He grabbed her hand and pulled her from the bar stool. She opened her mouth, but he didn't give her time to protest. Instead, he led her to the dance floor, ignoring her yelp. He could feel her struggle with keeping her balance in the high heels and felt the chain of her purse hit his wrist, but he refused to let her get away.

Instead of pulling her into his arms when he reached the designated dancing area, he skirted the couples flying around in rhythm with the music and slipped out the door to the smokers' patio. Several throngs of smokers clumped together, huffing, puffing and drawing on beers, so he pushed through an iron gate on the path to the darkened pool area. He pushed through a second gate, stopped and dropped her hand. She tripped on the uneven concrete, but regained her footing before he could reach out to her. She jerked her arm away and tugged the chain of her purse higher on her shoulder. "What in the hell do you think you're doing?"

Good question.

He stared at her as she glared at him. "Getting you away from STD boy in there. Do you know how much he sleeps around? He's not your kind of guy, Annie."

As soon as he uttered the words, he knew he sounded like a dumbass.

Annie crossed her arms over her chest and glared at him. "Who made you my daddy?"

"No one, but if he were here, he'd probably thank me for rescuing you."

She snorted, pushing a hand through her hair. The motion was innately feminine as was the whole look she had going on. Her legs looked longer in the heeled sandals, and the skirt flared nicely over her toned thighs while the clingy shirt hugged small breasts he could no longer ogle since her arms were crossed. "Don't count on it. Besides, you're a detective, not the morality police."

He shrugged and shoved his hands in his pockets. He couldn't explain what he'd done. Well, not to her. How could he explain away the jealousy that had ripped through him at the sight of her with Mick Manners?

"Nate, I'm a big girl. I know you're this Southern gentleman with protective instincts, but if I want to wrap my ankles around Mick, I will."

"Wrap your ankles around… You want to sleep with him?"

"I didn't say that. We were talking. He bought me a drink, not a hotel room."

She shook her head in disgust, but her eyes were limpid and there was a hint of pleasure around her glossy lips. The moon's reflection glittered in the water of the pool and somewhere in the stand of trees and palmettos that flanked the back patio of the hotel, a bird called out. And Nate felt his heart make a funny skip, something that had never happened. Something that scared the devil out of him.

He ripped his gaze away from her. "Fine. I'm sorry I messed up your little tête-à-tête. Go on back."

She didn't say anything. He crossed his arms and stared at a planter with a dying palm tree in it. He felt stupid. Childish. Unprofessional. Embarrassed.

He felt her hand move on his forearm. "Nate?"

"Go. I shouldn't have interfered."

Her hand flattened, stroking up his arm. "You're jealous."

"No, I merely thought someone should look out for you."

Her soft chuckle told him she thought differently, and it made him feel naked. "You're jealous."

He looked down at her. Her lips curved into a smile, but it wasn't deprecating, merely satisfied. Her gray eyes looked sliver in the pale light, and her touch invited. Nate had been tempted by many women over the years, but none tugged at him like this brash woman—even if she were a liar.

He lowered his head. "What if I was?"

She sucked her breath in. Her eyes dilated and he swore he could hear her pulse gallop. She licked her lips and whispered, "Was what?"

"Jealous," he said before lowering his mouth to hers. He caught her slight gasp with his lips before sliding a hand around her waist and pulling her to him in a kiss that curled his own toes.

And then and there, he knew he'd borrowed trouble.

ANNIE KNEW NATE WOULD kiss her. She didn't know when or where, but she knew it was inevitable.

She didn't, however, expect the absolute torrent of desire that swept through her belly, flooded her insides and enveloped her in liquid want.

Nate tasted like yeasty Louisiana beer and turned-on man, so she opened her mouth to him, twined her arms around his strong neck and gave in to the wave of desire crashing over her. He tasted her, all the while sliding his big hands over her bottom, up her waist and then back down again. His hands awakened need so intense all deliberate thought flew from her mind. There was nothing but Nate, the moon and the need to get naked with him.

"Mmm," she moaned against his mouth, melting against him, hungry for the feel of hard male against soft female.

"Mmm," he returned, deepening the kiss, cupping her ass, amping her pulse to out-of-control.

Like a firecracker igniting, she spun out into the darkness, alive and burning, seeking explosion.

Annie tugged Nate's shirttail from his pants, noting the heat of his naked skin. At the same time, his hands ran underneath her skirt, clasping her ass, lifting against his erection. He pulled her upward and she twined her arms around his neck just before she wrapped her legs around his waist.

"Over there," she murmured, ripping her mouth from his.

"Hmm?" He slid his mouth down to the pulse in her neck. She couldn't stop her head from falling back nor could she stop the squeal of pleasure as one of his hands slid beneath her panties and stroked her.

"Sweet mother of—"

"Don't say Nate," he said against her breastbone.

She almost giggled but couldn't manage it. His fingers had established a rhythm that took her breath away.

Frenzied heat engulfed them.

"Annie," he groaned, nibbling his way down to where her breasts strained against the top.

"Take me over there," she ordered, pointing to a chaise longue by a shabby tiki bar. It stood in the shadows, and if they slid the chair behind the bar, no one would see them.

Nate didn't release her. Instead he held her hips as he strolled to the lounge chair and kicked it so it slid behind the bar. Ah, they thought alike.

He lowered her to the plastic-strapped lounge and covered her with hot, hard body. It was absolutely forbidden and delicious, and Annie couldn't have stopped her hand from reaching for Nate's belt buckle if a storm had ripped through striking her with a bolt of lightning.

Hell, that's what it felt like anyway. A storm of absolute lust, and Annie played in the onslaught.

Nate's mouth reclaimed hers, and for a second go around, her thoughts flew away to be replaced only by the dark deliciousness of Nate Dufrene. By the way his lips moved over her stomach, up to her breasts. By the way his hands quickly divested her of the silk thong before expertly exploring her yielding and very much ready-for-him flesh.

She heard the scrape of his belt buckle hit the ground and the sound of his breath panting against her skin.

She felt like she was burning up.

About to explode.

She pulled his head up and then down, so his lips met hers. Their mouths hit hard and she tasted blood, but she didn't care. She wrapped her legs about his waist and lifted her bottom. "Please."

Nate slid into her, like a man coming home, and the moment he sheathed himself fully within her, she came apart.

"Ah," she cried. He caught her scream with his mouth as his hips started moving. She wrapped her legs and arms around the man whose deep, hard thrusts kept her spinning, peaking over and over again. Annie held hard to Nate as he drove into her. The top half of the chaise longue dropped level with the pavement beneath them, but Nate didn't stop. Annie felt the grass skirt of the tiki bar cover her forehead, but Nate didn't stop.

"Oh, yes, that's it. That's—" Nate whispered into her ear before biting her neck. His murmured encouragements weren't needed. Annie pushed against his shoulders, and he allowed himself to be maneuvered to the side. He sat up to prevent himself from smacking the pavement, pulling her with him. His back hit the curve of the bar, so they were totally ensconced in the cradle of dried grass and empty beer bottles. Annie vaguely registered the smell of mildew, but even that didn't faze her. She had one mission. Absolute completion. She rose above Nate, shoved him back and took over, moving fast and hard above him.

He tilted his head forward and tugged her shirt so he

could cradle both her breasts in his big hands, nipping them, sucking her nipples into his mouth.

"Nate!" she screeched as she tumbled yet again over the edge of sanity. This time he joined her, his groan of release stifled by her breasts pressed against his mouth.

For a moment, they simply held each other, their ragged breaths the only sound in the night air. That and the pool filter.

Then Annie opened her eyes.

Nate did, too.

"Oh, shit," he said, his head snapping back. He pulled her shirt down.

Reality slammed her.

"Oh, my God." She pulled herself off him, sitting down hard and drawing her legs together. She covered her face with both hands. "What have we done?"

She pulled her hands away and looked at Nate who tried to tug his pants up. His wadded-up boxer shorts prevented him from zipping his pants, but at least he was covered. She glanced around and saw her panties hanging drunkenly on the arm of the broken chaise longue.

Nate shook his head. "I don't know. I've never done something like this before."

"Shit, shit, shit. We didn't use a condom. Oh, my—" Annie covered her mouth with her hand. She felt vomit perch at the back of her mouth. How could she one minute be leaping into the sun, her body thrumming with more pleasure than she'd ever experienced, and the next minute be ready to toss up her Cosmopolitan?

Nate bolted upright. "No condom. Oh, shit."

Annie looked up at him. He looked as horrified as she felt. "Yeah. That seems to be the word to describe it."

Silence fell between them. Annie closed her eyes and tried to pretend what had happened had been a dream. A delusion of epic proportions. She opened her eyes. Nope. She was still sitting bare-assed on the concrete surrounding a second-rate hotel swimming pool with the Cajun detective she'd had unprotected sex with. Advertisements about STD prevention and unplanned pregnancy flitted through her mind. How had she done what she just did? "What do we do? I've never had unprotected sex before."

"Me, neither. I mean, I don't have diseases or anything like that." Nate buttoned his pants then ran a hand through his hair.

"Yeah, but the other."

He glanced up with a panicked look. "Okay. Where are you on your cycle?"

Annie stiffened. "That's kind of personal."

"Not after what we just did."

"Um, let's see. Let me think." Annie couldn't keep the panic out of her voice. She not only felt sick, but she thought she might cry. She'd never lost her head like that before, and she couldn't even blame the liquor. She'd had only one martini. Okay, one and a half, but she wasn't even close to drunk. "I had my period last week. Um, it ended about six days ago."

Nate lowered his head. "You're ovulating. Great. Just great."

Annie felt tears press the back of her eyes. She never cried. But then again, she never mistakenly made a baby either. Not that she had. Just because she was ovulating didn't mean Nate had pollinated her. No, not the right term, but something like that. And how did he know about ovulation anyway? He was a man. "How do you know about ovulation?"

"I went to med school. Didn't finish because I had to come home when Dad died, but I studied anatomy."

Annie blinked. Of course he had. Why not? The man

seemed to know everything. Have it all together. Except he'd screwed up, too. "Well, why didn't you stop us?"

His head jerked up. "What?"

"Why didn't you stop? You're the cop."

"Detective."

"Whatever. Where's your control?"

His laughter was bitter. "You're blaming me?"

Annie shook her head and then dropped her chin to her chest. "No. Sorry."

Nate took her hand. "Hey. It'll be okay. It's likely nothing will happen. Okay?"

She shook her head, but didn't look up. "Not with my luck."

"It's hard to get pregnant. Think about the people who try all the time but don't. Tons. Thousands. Probably millions."

Annie nodded, but his voice hadn't been convincing. Both she and the most responsible guy she'd ever met had just effed up on a monstrous level. Only morons had unprotected sex. That and teenagers. And even most teens were smart enough to pull out. "Yeah, sure."

"Don't cry." He tugged her to him, wrapping an arm around her.

"I don't cry," she said against his shirt, trying like hell to clamp down on the raw emotion choking her. She wouldn't cry. She wouldn't. But a few tears escaped anyway. "I'm a screwup."

"No, you aren't."

"You don't know what it's been like for me. I messed up a perfectly good career. My last relationship was a disaster. I suck at being a nanny. And to top it all off, I just had unprotected sex with a virtual stranger and possibly created a new life. One I'll be responsible for and as before mentioned, I suck at being a nanny so being a mother ought to work out real well for me. And you should know I'm Catholic."

Nate laughed.

"Don't laugh. This isn't a laughing matter."

"I didn't want to. Trust me. But we can't undo what's been done. Everyone has regrets, Annie."

"Yeah, but we may have to feed and diaper ours."

That sobered him.

"Besides I have more regrets than most," she said, swiping her arm across her nose. "It shouldn't be this way. I'm a deliberate person. I make lists, Nate. Pro-and-con lists to make sure I'm making the right decision."

He had to understand she wasn't stupid. When she took risks, they were calculated risks. She thought things out, thoroughly, carefully. "But nothing ever works out. It's as if I should do the opposite of what it seems like I should do. All my decisions backfire on me."

He didn't say anything.

"And this time, there was no thinking, Nate. None at all. And I still effed up. Don't you see? I'm destined to live a crappy life full of dead ends, wrong turns and flat tires."

He sighed and drew her back for another hug. He dropped a kiss on her temple. "Take a deep breath."

"No."

"Ann, this will be a wait-and-see thing. If it ends with you being pregnant, we'll deal with it then. Let's not borrow trouble. Okay?"

"I won't marry you."

His chuckle was dry. "I didn't ask you to."

Annie felt her cheeks heat. Of course, this had nothing to do with marriage. They were just two people who liked each other enough to let horniness take hold and put them in a tight spot. She struggled to her feet and Nate followed suit, snagging her panties and handing them to her.

"Thanks," she said, tucking her hair behind her ears. She had dropped her purse with the gun inside on another chair when Nate had kissed her. She saw it glittering in the moonlight, snatched it up and shoved her panties inside. She needed to find a bathroom and then she'd go back to Beau Soleil. To hell with picking Mick's brain or listening in on other people's conversations. To hell with telling Nate she was undercover and not a suspect in this stupid threat case. To hell with everything.

Her thoughts bounced around hysterically.

It was the clothes she'd borrowed. Tawny had trussed her up like a goose and made her look easy, giving Nate the wrong impression. Allowing her to fulfill the flirty promises she'd made to him several days ago in the library. She'd seen the way he'd looked at her, had embraced it and reveled in the power. She'd been headtripping and had allowed her herself give in.

God, why was she here in the first place?

She should have stayed with the Bureau. Should have stayed the same old Anna—driven, pragmatic and…lonely. But wasn't lonely better than standing here now, sans panties, working as a nanny, trying to solve a dead-bird case?

She was an incredibly stupid, weak woman. Raw disgust throbbed in her belly.

"Go home, take a bath and we'll start over tomorrow," Nate said, brushing her arm in what should have been a soothing caress.

She jerked away. "Tomorrow?"

"We're going down to Galliano."

"You think that's a good idea? After what we did a few minutes ago?"

Nate shoved his shirttail into his jeans and shrugged. "It won't happen again. I'm working a case. Nothing about that has changed."

"You're thinking about your case? Really?"

He studied her. "Nothing has changed."

"Bullshit," she said, pulling her eyes from him and studying a lone floatie bobbing in the deep end of the pool.

"I haven't been able to figure you out yet, Annie Perez."

She frowned. "Well, those were some nice investigative skills you used under the tiki bar."

He jerked his head toward the tiki bar and collapsed chair. "That had nothing to do with Spencer or this case or the fact you're not what you seem. That over there was two people forgetting about the world and finding pleasure in being a man and a woman."

Oddly, his words soothed her. He made their ripping each other's clothes off in the back of a roadside motel in plain sight sound not so sordid. "Fine. We'll talk tomorrow. I can't go back on my word to Spencer anyhow. Not without war breaking out."

Nate nodded, took four steps and kissed her. "Thanks."

And then he disappeared like some phantom lover, leaving her with a handbag holding a gun, extra lip gloss and her panties.

And perhaps a child.

Her stomach burned at the thought. Annie lifted her face to the full moon and whispered a fervent prayer that she hadn't screwed up her life even more.

She hoped the man in the moon was listening. Hoped He still knew she prayed to Him. Hoped He'd throw her a bone on this one.

But the moon just stared back blankly at her.

NATE PUSHED THROUGH THE rusting gate onto the smoker's porch and took a deep breath. Which was a bad decision. More people had convened outside while he had practiced bad behavior under the tiki bar, so the breath he took had been in a cloud of smoke.

After nearly coughing up a lung and drawing viperous looks from the smokers, he went back inside Gerry's and headed for the men's room. He was pretty sure he'd zipped his boxers in his fly, and he needed to stop and think about what had transpired moments ago. About the total disregard for discipline he'd spent his life creating.

Talk about screwing the pooch.

He entered the men's room, which was thankfully empty, and avoided his own eyes in the mirror while he tucked his boxers and shirt into his jeans and washed his hands. When he looked up for something to dry his hands on, he caught sight of himself.

Shit.

His hair stuck up and pink shimmery lipstick smeared his neck. He looked like a man who'd been well laid.

Which he had.

But that was the problem, wasn't it?

The passion between him and Annie had risen up and grabbed him by the throat, giving him little choice in following through. It was as if he'd been under a spell, one that rendered him senseless and stupid.

He scrubbed the lipstick off his neck, smoothed his hair, braced both hands on the sink and sighed. What if he'd gotten Annie pregnant? Bile scalded his stomach and he swallowed, tasting the smoke again.

A kid.

He drew in anther deep breath. It wasn't as if he didn't want kids, it's that he'd never thought much about it. And to bring one into the world that way…the result of two people being wholly irresponsible under the light of a full moon. Wasn't ideal. Wasn't good.

God, he hoped she wasn't pregnant. He would never live

that down with his coworkers, his friends…his mother. Everyone knew him to be dependable, steadfast and intelligent, but the combustible sex he'd had with Annie out at the pool had been nothing close to those things. It had been the most intense and fulfilling sex he'd had. Ever.

The bathroom door opened and a drunk kid tumbled in, falling into Nate without an apology.

Nate felt on the verge of losing control, this time in a whole new way—plowing his fist into the rude-ass drunk unzipping his fly. For whatever reason, Nate itched for a fight, for some way to deal with the disappointment he felt at himself. Some way to beat down the fear thumping in his chest. Fear over a sperm finding its way to an egg and multiplying over and over until a child was formed. His child.

But he wouldn't beat the hell out of a random stranger. Because he was Nate Dufrene. A man who didn't stoop to infantile levels of behavior merely because he messed up. No, Nate was a man who accepted his failures and mistakes, swallowing them, allowing them to become a fire in his belly. A fire that kept him searching for justice.

Nate moved back, shaking water from his hands, regretting so much about tonight. If only he'd found the same strength of character earlier.

With that thought, he left, refusing to look back. Something was wrong with him and he didn't know whether it was because the next day would dredge up old hurts and hopes or because the feelings he had for Annie were murky as the Louisiana swamp. But it was something.

Perhaps it was the guilt he'd held on to over his sister—both his guilt for leaving her alone and vestiges his father had taken to his grave. Nate was like his father in many ways. He was tough and ambitious. Driven. That same hard-assed approach had led to Della being taken. Martin Dufrene had fired Billy Priest, one of the kidnappers, setting him out of the mill in front of all the other workers. Called him a good-for-nothin' who didn't deserve the woman and child who'd run off weeks before. Nate's father had set everything in motion by an unforgiving nature.

Maybe it was a Dufrene curse, to spoil everything innocent around them, like weeds choking out beauty.

Maybe Nate was too much like his father.

He'd certainly lost his control like him.

And that was something he didn't like at all.

CHAPTER TEN

THE NEXT DAY WAS sunshiny and happy.

Unlike Annie.

Of course, Spencer found this out early when he pitched a fit for a certain cereal he'd never before mentioned, but it became obvious to Annie the boy didn't care about her grumpiness. His world consisted of Spencer and what made him happy.

So she pasted on a tolerant face and took him outside fifteen minutes before the appointed time Nate would pick them up, mostly so she wouldn't do or say something she regretted.

"So are we going to see boats? Are we going to ride on one?"

The questions made her head throb...or maybe the throb was leftover alcohol and regret from last night's escapade.

Picou glanced over from her place in a rocking chair. She wore yoga pants and bandana—this time purple— and her bare feet sported yellow polish on her toenails. "Yes, dear boy. Nate has already talked to a friend about a boat ride."

Picou's words were tinged in...hope? Happiness? Something about the way she spoke, the spark in her odd violet eyes made Annie wonder the source of the woman's contentment.

Just to prove the point, Picou turned to the morning sun peeking through the oaks and took a deep breath.

"And gators, too?" Spencer hopped up and down the front porch steps rattling the glass in the front door.

"Stop," Annie said.

"Maybe," Picou said.

"Spencer, why don't you color a page in your coloring book?" Annie wanted the boy to stop hopping around. It made her already queasy stomach rock harder. She'd packed several activity books, crayons and the iPod touch in the bag she carried. Nate said it would take at least an hour and a half if not longer to reach their destination.

"'Kay." The boy nodded, trudging up the steps.

"Or you could kick the ball in the yard," Picou suggested, sipping from the teacup she balanced on the arm of the chair.

"Yes!" Spencer shouted, tripping back down the steps and lambasting the ball he'd forgotten earlier into the waxy bushes of the side of the yard.

"That should take some piss and vinegar out of him," Picou said. "And if that doesn't work, you can always try Benadryl."

"What?"

"Dear, you don't want him to settle down and focus until you're in the car. Let him expound some energy. Run, gallop and frolic the wiggles out."

"Oh," Annie responded, drinking the chicory coffee Picou made each morning. At first she'd been appalled at how different the coffee tasted, but after a couple of cups, she found the flavor addictive.

"You don't know much about children, so why did you take up nannying?"

Understatement of the Year.

"I like to eat," Annie said.

The older woman laughed. "I don't mean to say you're

not good with the boy. I can certainly see the affection, but you don't, ahem, always seem to—"

"—know what I'm doing?"

Annie swallowed the strong brew, fleetingly thinking about caffeine and pregnancy. Her stomach lurched, and she struck the whole preposterous idea of being pregnant out of her mind and gathered her thoughts. "You're right. I'm not the most skilled caregiver, but I'm not terrible. Don't share your thoughts with the Keenes. I need to make a house note next month."

Picou shook her head. "You're not bad. Not at all. You'll make a fine mother someday, my dear."

Annie choked on the coffee. Some went up and out her nose.

Picou leaped up and clocked her in the center of her shoulder blades—which hurt.

"Ow." Annie threw up a hand, coughing, but managing breath. "Okay, okay. I'm fine."

Picou eyed her for a moment before settling back into the rocking chair. "Goodness, child, I personally hate when things go down the wrong pipe. Didn't mean to spook you."

After a final clearing of her throat, Annie waved the older woman's words off. Too late for spooking. "I've never wanted children."

Picou raised her brows. "It's not for some, I suppose, but I loved most of the moments."

Annie remained quiet, fervently hoping for a change in topic.

"You never know what a child means until you lose one. I know better than most. And that's what Tawny fears. I can see it in her eyes. Feel it in her words. These threats to her child have shaken her to her core."

"I know."

For a moment the two women sat in companionable

silence. The only sounds were the whap, whap, whap of Spencer kicking the soccer ball.

"Nate likes you, Annie," Picou said.

Annie flinched. The older woman had the uncanny ability of yanking rugs out from beneath people with cutting candor. "I— Well, that's—"

Picou laughed. "Yes, I know my boys. Each of them is different as the grains of sand on a beach. Or is it snowflakes? I forget which, but I know that boy, and he is very attracted to you."

"I know," Annie said, taking another sip of coffee out of sheer nervousness.

"That's what I like about you. You're direct and say what is on your mind. You suit him well."

"Mrs. Dufrene, I mean Picou, I'm honest." Annie had to swallow after the statement, mostly because that was a bald-faced lie. She'd lied since the moment she met Picou, and she wouldn't stop. Not until Spencer was safe from harm. "But I'm not looking for a relationship. Once filming wraps, I'll be heading back to California."

"Mmm" was all the older woman said. It was an unconvinced response and Annie wanted to tell her to tuck her dreams for anything between Annie and her son away. Not going to happen. Unless...

Annie clamped down on that thought. Then she looked down at her flat stomach. Acid sizzled in her gut and the blueberry muffin she'd choked down moments before threatened to make a curtain call. Even if she got pregnant from the results of losing her mind last night, allowing thoughts of her and Nate going somewhere more permanent felt way premature.

The sound of a car crunching down the drive announced the arrival of the man who'd haunted her dreams, occupied her waking thoughts and, perhaps, trampled on all she had planned for her life—or rather not planned since she'd chucked that away on the last man who'd come along. Her mother's old adage came to mind. *There's many a slip betwixt the cup and the lip.* Yeah, her newest slipup came rolling to a stop in the horseshoe drive.

Spencer abandoned the ball and ran to the shiny crossover BMW that was very different from Nate's patrol car.

"Hey, Spencer, ready to roll?"

"Yeah!" Spencer gave a fist pump and yanked on the backseat handle, before being swallowed by the depths of the sporty car.

Annie stood with a sigh and grabbed the bag at her feet.

"Come, now. It won't be all that bad," Picou said, kicking her chair into motion and pulling her bare feet onto the seat. "I've never been on an airboat, but I believe people enjoy skimming at breakneck speed over the swampland."

If it were only the thought of being launched out of a speeding boat. More like the thought of being in too close quarters with a man who'd shut down and overridden any common sense she proclaimed to have. "Yeah, I'm sure it'll be awesome."

Annie's gaze was drawn to Nate as he climbed out of the car with an easy elegance, grabbed the booster sitting on the hood of the rental car parked several yards away, and helped the wriggling puppy of a boy fasten himself into the backseat. Then he turned and walked toward where she sat with Picou on the wide porch. She tried to smile and failed.

"Morning, Mama." He looked at his mother, before his dark eyes came to rest on her. "Annie."

"Morning," she mumbled, glancing away from the intensity present in the mahogany depths. "I'll go pack this stuff and get Spencer set up."

He'd already done her job for her, but whatever. She didn't want to stand beneath his scrutiny, didn't want Picou to use her extraperceptive powers and figure out there was actually something pretty crazy going on between the two of them.

She moved down the steps past Nate and headed toward his car. She heard Nate lower his voice as he talked to his mother, but she didn't dare risk a look back for fear of revealing how much he'd affected her in the bright light of morning.

She wanted him even more. With a gut-jerking need that shocked her. And there was no excuse for it. No vodka. No full moon. She tried to stamp down on the desire spiraling through her. She had to stop her passions from flaring out of control around that man.

She shouldered the bag and walked to the passenger side and slid inside a car that smelled new. Vastly different from her ancient Altima parked inside the collapsing garage of her *abuela's* bungalow in California. A girl could get used to plush leather and air-conditioning.

"Ready?" Nate asked as he slid into the seat and started the car.

"Sure," she said, making herself small in the seat. The whole car felt filled with his presence, which would have been fine if she didn't have that whole wanting-him thing going…and if they hadn't accidently had sex the night before.

"Are we almost there?" Spencer asked.

Nate laughed, breaking the tension. He looked over at Annie. "He does realize we're not moving yet?"

"Instant gratification is his middle name." Annie glanced over her shoulder. "First we have to actually drive, Spence."

"Oh, yeah. I know," he said, waving to Picou as Nate backed out of the drive.

Annie pointed to the dashboard clock, which read 8:58. "See this number?"

Spencer nodded.

"When it gets to..." She glanced over at Nate.

"10:35," he said.

She quirked an eyebrow. "When it gets to 11:00, we'll be there. Now here are your crayons, activity book and iTouch. Make yourself busy."

She passed the bag back to the child and watched as he pulled the iPod touch out, put on the headphones and started flinging birds at pigs on the small screen.

She faced forward and adjusted the seat belt as Nate turned onto the highway. They drove for several minutes, reaching the quaint town of Bayou Bridge with its plethora of antiques stores, coffee shops and occasional Acadian restaurants. Five minutes later they were heading south down Highway 31 toward the interstate. The landscape along the road changed constantly from wooded swampland to sweeping pastureland, giving way to periodic moss-draped marshes. Once they hit the interstate, the scenery blurred and the smoothness of the ride briefly lulled Annie into sleepy contemplation.

"I shouldn't be long in Galliano," Nate said, pulling her from watching the horizon.

"Okay," she said, wanting to ask his purpose for going to wherever it was they were heading.

"I have to do a quick interview with someone and get a DNA sample then we can take Spencer on the airboat ride."

"Fine."

He pulled his gaze from the broken yellow line and looked at her. "You okay?"

She shrugged. "Sure."

She felt the doubt in his eyes even though she stared out at the rushing scenery. The air thickened and she tugged at the top buttons of the cotton blouse she wore. She didn't want to talk about what happened last night. Maybe if they didn't talk about it, they could pretend it away.

"This doesn't feel okay."

She turned toward him. "What do you want me to say?"

One hand dangled over the steering wheel and she couldn't see his eyes behind the sunglasses he wore. He looked exactly what he was—smart, sexy and unreadable. "I don't know. Something besides 'sure' and 'okay.' I'm feeling like a dentist here."

"A dentist?"

"Pulling teeth."

She shook her head and glanced back at Spencer before lowering her voice. "What we did was crazy and I don't want to talk about it. I don't want that bit of lunacy to define everything between us now."

"But it does."

"But it doesn't have to. We're both professionals who lost all good sense last night along with a few choice pieces of clothing. We screwed up. It won't happen again. End of story."

"But—"

She threw a hand up. "No buts. I don't want to feel like a damn ticking time bomb. Please."

He nodded. "Fine."

She crossed her arms. "Good."

Annie angled the vents away and tried to find some inner peace deep inside herself. Her *abuela* had once told her she could find calm in the middle of a storm merely by snatching a piece of stillness from her soul, but at that moment, Annie could find nothing to make things better.

"So tell me about this case. Why do you have to go so far? Shouldn't the authorities there be able to do the sample for you?"

She didn't miss the tightening in his shoulders. "Nothing much to tell. This is an old case and more of a personal issue."

Personal issue? DNA testing? Questions tumbled around in her mind, but she remained silent.

He glanced her way. "So you want to tell me about your case?"

She straightened. He knew. Well, of course he did. He wasn't stupid. "I think you already know about my case."

Nate's lips curved north. Good Lord, the man was sexy when he smiled. Her libido did a little dance, but she kicked it back into the closet. She knew he'd suspected her as something more than a generic caregiver since the moment he'd met her. Time to come totally clean…and hopefully get some help with the threat to the child.

Annie sighed. "You're not stupid. I know you went digging for info on me the night after we met, and you didn't find anything. But that was the problem, wasn't it? Annie Perez should have had a trail a mile long. You probably blew right past that phony Nevada real-estate site."

Nate glanced her way. "Yeah, something like that."

"Well, I hope you don't think I'm in on a kidnapping plot."

"That's not what I'm thinking," he said, gliding into the fast lane, passing a line of eighteen-wheelers laden with pipes and industrial tools. The signs around them told her they were close to Morgan City. The travel book she'd read on Louisiana several weeks ago had told her the small city was the hub of the oil industry in the state.

She tore her gaze from the evidence that proved the guide true—heliports, shipyards and tool yards—lining either side of the interstate and looked at him. "So what are you thinking?"

"You could be someone running away from an abusive

boyfriend, a crime you committed, or debt, but I don't think that's the reason you're hiding who you are."

He looked at her again, the pause an invitation for her to spill, but she didn't take the bait. She wanted to know his thoughts.

"You remain calm when others don't. You're logical, assertive when needed, but good at fading into the background and observing. Extremely fit, highly analytical and you know the lingo, so I'm betting on one of two things. Either you're a federal officer and this is far more serious than what I've been led to believe or you're a P.I."

Annie raised her eyebrows. The man was good, at many things, but it was obvious he made the grade as an investigator. He was young for a detective, especially one who'd attended medical school. She still wanted to find out about that little tidbit, but she had enough on her plate with the current topic. "Whatever I tell you needs to remain confidential."

"Of course."

"I mean 'between you and me' confidential."

He slid his eyes over to her. "Lots between you and me that will remain confidential, *cherie*."

"Touché," Annie murmured, getting a slight tingle at the traditional Cajun endearment on his lips. She glanced back to make sure Spencer still wore his earphones. He did, but they weren't necessary, not if his bobbing head and soft snoring were any indication. "I'm both. Kind of."

She paused, unwilling to reveal she'd left the bureau because she'd taken a chance on love. Sounded, well, stupid. "My name is Anna Mendes, but my mother called me Annie. I'm formerly with the FBI. Recently employed by Sterling Investigations and Security in Los Angeles. Actually, protecting Spencer is my first assignment for the firm."

"FBI, huh?" Nate said, crossing a large bay-like canal and continuing farther south. "I can see that. Why'd you leave?"

"Personal reasons. But that doesn't matter. What does matter is I'm working on this case, same as you."

"So why not tell me in the first place? Why all the subterfuge? We could have saved a lot of time." His voice held a tinge of irritation.

She sighed. "Why do you think? I'm supposed to be undercover, Nate."

"But why not tell me?"

She glanced over at him. Okay, he seemed peeved. "I didn't know you. Didn't know how you would react. You do know how law enforcement treats private investigators?"

He shrugged. "Like conspiracy theorists."

"That well?" Her laugh was bitter. But she understood. Most private investigators were overweight guys who couldn't hack it in law enforcement. Their chief bread and butter came from peeping out from behind bushes catching cheating spouses for divorce attorneys. Most law-enforcement agencies avoided them like week-old liverwurst. But the standard P.I. was very, very far away from the sophisticated powerhouse that was Sterling Investigations.

"Yeah, I get it, but if you would have told me earlier we'd have already compared notes and made better progress."

"I didn't trust you."

"And you do now?"

"Yes." She nodded. "Now I do."

She didn't want to explain why she trusted him. Didn't understand it herself since it usually took months before she'd even tell a coworker her coffee preference. But something about Nate—the way he handled everything carefully, dependably and intelligently—had her blindly placing her faith in his hands. Of course, he'd tossed away last night…just as she had.

Last night had been out of character.

And a grave mistake.

She felt Nate's eyes on her, so turned and met his gaze. "I hope you can trust me, too, Nate. This isn't about me or anything that's happened between us. This is about that little boy. I have to keep him safe and find out who's playing these games with the Keene family."

Nate nodded, his emotions shuttered, his game face in place. "Is that what you think? Merely someone playing games?"

"That's what it feels like, but people who use a child like Spencer as a tool of fear can be capable of more than threatening letters. Hollywood division was dismissive, but Carter felt it was more than some random freak show and hired us to protect Spencer. The college student who took care of Spencer had been let go, rightfully so—she got caught sexting with her boyfriend when she was supposed to be minding Spencer. It was the perfect opportunity to slip me in and give me a cloak of cover to poke around."

She almost laughed as he silently muttered, "Sexting?" before shaking his head. "So what have you found?"

"Not much."

Spencer yawned and kicked the seat. "Annie, are we there?"

Annie turned back to Spencer. "Almost. Not far now."

The boy rubbed his eyes and yawned again. A seldom-used "aww" button inside her beeped. The boy was super-cute, especially when he was sleepy, still and very quiet.

"I'm thirsty."

The "aww" button shut down. "You want a juice pack?"

He shook his head. "No. I want chocolate milk."

Flashbacks of vomit and roadside gas stations hit her. "Apple juice or water. Which do you want?"

"I don't. I want chocolate milk."

Annie sighed and counted to ten. "You're not having milk. We're not stopping. Juice or water."

"No!" Spencer screamed. "No, no, no!"

Nate's hands tightened on the wheel, but he didn't look over at her. She quickly flipped through the latest parenting book in her head. How to handle a meltdown in public. Was this public? Not really. And she couldn't leave the area. No place for a time out. She was on her own.

"You're acting like a baby," Annie said.

Spencer kicked. "I'm not a baby. I want chocolate milk! Gimme it!"

Another deep breath. Another count to…almost ten.

"If you don't stop pitching a fit, we're not going on the boat ride."

Annie's words stopped the fit-pitching cold. Legs stopped, screeching stopped and Spencer's mouth fell open. "No, no, Annie. I want to go on the boat. Please."

"Then stop acting like a baby."

"I'm not a baby. I'm five."

Annie saw Nate smile. "You're acting like you're two."

"Okay," Spencer said. "Gimme the juice."

She leaned over the console, rummaged around in the bag and pulled a juice from the small insulated bag. She looked at Nate. "Is this okay? I don't think he can spill it."

The man eyed the box and punch-through straw and finally nodded his head. "He spills, you clean."

"Fair enough," she muttered, handing the drink to the child and turning back around. "I'm starting to think those parenting books are full of shit."

"You've got game," Nate said with a smile. "I would

have rather picked through garbage than masquerade as a nanny."

"Says the man who could be the father of my child," Annie said before realizing the implication of her words. Nate actually swerved across the yellow line before correcting.

"Hell, don't say things like that," he said, throwing her a desperate look.

"Sorry, it slipped," she said, turning and looking out at the flat yellow grasses reaching as far as the eye could see. The only elevation came when they rose above industrial canals cutting a swath through the delicate ecosystem. "I—I think we shouldn't think about that little possible mistake."

"I thought so, too," he drawled. "So don't. Today we're going to enjoy the land—"

"—and see some alligators!" Spencer finished for him.

"And see some real, live alligators," Nate repeated, closing the subject and setting the tone for the day. "But we need to talk later."

He gave her a purposeful look, and though Annie felt mixed-up crazy about Nate, she knew she'd done the right thing telling him the truth. Perhaps together they could pull a suspect and get some closure for the Keene family.

CHAPTER ELEVEN

NATE HADN'T BEEN DOWN Lafourche Bayou in many years. Not since the redfish trip he took with Abram and a few other coaches when his brother first took the job at ULB. Shrimp boats bobbed on the side of the bayou where two highways hugged the banks. Businesses and modest houses clung to the highway in an unusual pattern of living. Periodic lock bridges invited residents to cross over to the other side to visit friends or other businesses. They passed bakeries, gas stations and the occasional warehouse. Spencer squealed in delight at each boat.

"Here comes a tug boat," Nate commented as they sat waiting on one of the lock bridges that had opened for the boat to pass.

"I know what tug boats do," Spencer said, craning his head and watching the boat. "They push barges."

"Very good," Nate said, enjoying the joy the child took in the simple pleasure of watching boats work. Annie didn't look as thrilled, but she nodded in agreement.

After the bridge closed, he rolled over to the other side of the bayou and started looking for Galliano Elementary School, where Sally Cheramie taught second grade. His heart thumped a little harder in his chest despite his mind telling him this was no big deal, that the woman who had started asking questions was likely not Della, but someone who'd come across a similar blankie when she was small, someone who had two parents who were not Picou and Martin. But his heart didn't listen to his head, mostly because the hope that had nestled deep inside for so long had awoken and climbed out of its hiding place.

"Why are you going to a school? Is this where your witness is?" Annie asked.

"I'm going to school next year," Spencer said. "Kindergarten."

Nate didn't answer because his mind was too busy working out how he'd do this. He hadn't called the woman to tell her he was coming. He wanted to catch her unaware, perhaps even study her for a few moments. He'd learned early on to not give suspects time to prepare. But this wasn't a suspect. Not really.

"Do you mind waiting?" he asked Annie as he pulled into a visitor parking space and scanned the area. He hadn't formed much of a plan on the way down. Hard to with Annie sitting next to him and Spencer chattering in the backseat. He felt off-balanced.

She shook her head, her gray eyes questioning. "No problem."

"I gotta go potty, Annie," Spencer said, wriggling in his booster while grabbing the crotch of his shorts. "Hurry."

Annie unbuckled, looking at Nate. "We'll go inside and find a restroom while you take care of your business. Mind leaving me your keys?"

He sighed. "Sure."

After passing the keys to Annie, he climbed out and pressed the map on his iPhone where he'd uploaded the plans of the school—which was so easy to do it was scary. Sally Cheramie's room sat in the back, near the playground. Normally, he'd check in, but he didn't want the front office to alert her to a visitor.

Annie took Spencer's hand and tugged him toward the front of the school, and he watched for a moment before ducking around the corner and heading toward the back of the building. He kept an eye out for security, feeling a little creepy sneaking around like a common criminal.

The double doors at the end of the building were propped open with a rubber door stop, something that made the school vulnerable—but for the moment he was relieved a custodian had forgotten to remove the appliance. He entered the building, which smelled of paint, crayons and Lysol. Vibrant artwork hung on bulletin boards lining the hall and the tiled floor glinted from a recent waxing. No one traveled the second-grade annex, but plenty of activity took place behind the classroom doors he passed on his way to Cheramie's Cowpokes room.

Outside Room 103 he paused. A half window in the door revealed a cheerful classroom painted in bright yellow and green. Twenty-some-odd kids sat in desks working on an activity, as their teacher circled the room, peering over shoulders, making suggestions and smiling in encouragement.

Sally Cheramie.

She was tall and willowy, with dark hair that brushed her shoulders. She wore a simple sleeveless dress and a wide gold bangle bracelet that looked nice against her tan skin. Practical flat sandals adorned her slim feet. She looked nothing like a shyster. More of an elegant, warm-hearted elementary school teacher…who happened to be fairly attractive.

Nate felt the presence of the man before he spoke.

"Excuse me. You got business with Miss Cheramie?"

Nate turned to find a custodian clad in a chambray shirt and tan trousers clasping a rolling trash can in one hand and a broom in the other. He was big, black and suspicious. And he looked ready to wield the broomstick against any intruder.

The door opened at his back.

"Clarence?" Sally's voice floated over his shoulder, rich, mellow and very much of the bayou. "Is there a problem?"

Nate spun around. "No problem."

The woman stood with one hand on the doorknob, the door half-open. She hit Nate with eyes that were exact replicas of Darby's. Nate felt the floor actually shift beneath him.

He swallowed, but said nothing. He didn't think he could.

"Sir?" Sally said. "Are you okay? Have you checked in as a visitor in our office?"

He shook his head, unable to take his eyes off her. He never thought it could happen—that he could simply look at a person's eyes and identify him or her. But he knew beyond a shadow of a doubt he was looking into the eyes of Della Dufrene. Not to mention, she looked too similar to the woman standing next to Martin Dufrene in the wedding photograph sitting on the mantel at Beau Soleil.

He'd found his sister.

ANNIE FROWNED AT THE secretary. "I need to use the facilities for only a moment. It's an emergency."

"Sorry, ma'am but we can't let people come in off the streets to use the restroom. It's not safe for our children."

Spencer wiggled. "I gotta go! Hurry!"

A woman stepped out from an inner office. "Is there a problem, Lacy?"

The younger woman shook her head. "This woman wants to let her kid use the toilet."

The older woman, who wore a pressed suit, looked at Annie.

"Are you a parent? I don't think we've met. I'm Iris Guidry, the counselor."

Annie shook her head. "No, I'm with someone who is visiting, and Spencer—" she looked down at the squirming five-year-old "—has to use the restroom."

"Oh, well, let the child go to the toilet," Mrs. Guidry said, gesturing to the restroom located off the office.

Spencer tore loose and ran to the bathroom. The door slammed shut and everyone in the office jumped including Annie.

"Well," Mrs. Guidry said, crossing her arms with a smile. "Guess he did have to go. Now, who did you say you were with?"

Annie felt something niggle at the nape of her neck. Nate hadn't wanted to reveal what he was up to, so what did that mean? Should she tell Mrs. Guidry the counselor the truth? Or make something up? The latter. "We had to drop lunch off for one of the teachers. I'm actually heading out right now."

Mrs. Guidry frowned. "Which teacher?"

Jeez, elementary teachers could teach FBI investigators questioning technique. They could probably sweat an ax murderer. "I don't know her name. I'm with my boyfriend, and it's his sister or something."

The bathroom door opened behind her. She didn't care whether Spencer had washed his hands or not, she wanted out of there. "Okay, so thanks for letting us use the facilities. Come on, Spencer."

"Where's Nate, Annie?" Spencer asked, drying his hands on his shorts.

"He's dropping off lunch, sport. Let's go."

"Who's he dropping off lunch to? I didn't know he had lunch. I'm hungry," Spencer rambled as she grabbed his arm and tugged him out the office door. Nate hadn't come in the front door. Had he gone around back?

She should go back to the car, but some weird curiosity

pushed her to turn right instead of left. She walked swiftly down the hallway, ducking her eyes when a teacher leading a group of rowdy kids passed her. She glanced down the branches off the main hall, but didn't see Nate. When she reached the end, she looked right and saw him standing in the hall in front of an open doorway with an attractive woman and a janitor.

She glanced behind her. Mrs. Guidry headed toward her, her heels clacking against the polished floor. Uh-oh.

She dragged Spencer with her as she headed toward Nate. "Hey."

He turned to look at her. The other two standing with him did also. Spencer slid in the Crocs he wore, but she pulled him behind her anyhow.

"Look it, Annie!" he cried. "Will I get to do that when I go to school?"

He pointed as something on the wall. "Sure, bud."

She reached Nate and stopped. Spencer slammed into the back of her thighs. For a moment all four adults stood looking at each other.

"What's going on here?" the lady in the white sundress asked, studying Nate then Annie.

Annie glanced at Nate who looked as if he'd swallowed a bug, before meeting the woman's equally confused gazed. The janitor held his broom in attack mode, and the clack of Mrs. Guidry's shoes grew nearer.

"Nate?"

The woman brought a thin hand to her chest. "Nate?"

He looked at the woman then at Annie. "This is, um, this is—"

"What the devil's going on here?" Mrs. Guidry demanded, pushing the janitor back and glaring at Nate. "I've called security. You're not allowed to be on this campus without checking in to our office with a valid driver's license."

Nate reached into his back pocket. Annie felt the janitor's body tighten. Nate drew out his credentials. "I'm Nate Dufrene, an investigator for the St. Martin Parish's Sherriff's office."

The young woman in the white sundress had grown pale. She shut the door behind her with a click as Mrs. Guidry took Nate's badge and looked it over.

"Fine," the counselor said, handing it back to him. "Now, what business do you have at Galliano Elementary and why didn't you bother to check in in the office? This woman here said you were bringing lunch to your sister."

She didn't give Nate time to answer. Instead she spun to the teacher. "Sally, is this your brother?"

Sally licked her lips, shifting her blue eyes from Mrs. Guidry to Nate and then back again to the counselor. "I don't know. Maybe."

Mrs. Guidry crossed her arms and shook her head. "You're telling me you don't know if this is your brother or not?" she muttered.

Nate interrupted. "I'm her brother."

Annie didn't say anything, mostly because it was the oddest situation she'd ever been in and she wasn't quite sure she understood what was happening. Spencer wiggled like a fish on a hook so she let go of his hand. He flew to the bulletin board nearest them and studied the artwork.

The young teacher shook her head. "You don't know that. Not for sure."

Nate's brow furrowed as he watched the woman he'd declared his sister.

Everyone else stood still as mud, the tension so thick it held them in place, riveted, waiting. Nate clasped the woman's elbow and she flinched. He held tight, turned her slightly, while reaching for the shoulder strap of her dress. "You have a strawberry birthmark—" he tugged the linen material aside "—right here."

Annie's mouth fell open as she stared at the mark on the right shoulder blade of the woman and realized the implications.

Sally jerked, stepping backward, colliding with the door at her back. For a moment, she stared at Nate before her blue eyes filled with tears. She shook her head. "No. I can't deal with this. Not here."

Nate's own eyes looked damp. "Della."

The woman vehemently shook her head. "No."

Nate closed his eyes and a soft laugh escaped him. "I told you to stay on the patio. You never listened to anyone."

At his words, the young woman fell against the wall and slid down until her bottom hit the tile. A soft sob shook her shoulders as she covered her face with her hands.

"I remember your eyes," she said, in between her hands. "I can't believe it, but I remember you."

Nate bent down and lifted his sister from the floor of the hallway, wrapping his arms around her, drawing her close. He breathed in deeply as he rocked her, eyes closed as he squeezed her tight. Then he said something that nearly broke Annie's heart in two pieces. "You didn't die."

Annie looked around the group standing frozen in the hallway of Galliano Elementary. Mrs. Guidry swiped at the dampness on her cheeks and the janitor's mouth hung open. Spencer skipped from bulletin board to bulletin board, and a face peeped over the edge of the glass in the classroom behind them.

Finally the janitor broke the silence. "Are we being filmed on TV or something?" He periscoped his broad head side to side. "'Cause this feels like something I've seen on *Maury Povitch*."

NATE CLIMBED INTO THE car and looked at Annie. "Well, I didn't exactly plan that well."

"And you seemed the type to have a plan," she said as they backed out of the lot. He belatedly glanced back at Spencer to make sure he was secured properly, but Annie had proven she hadn't allowed the strange moment to affect her. Spencer was harnessed snugly in his seat. She may think she wasn't good at taking care of Spencer, but she was.

"I actually had a plan. To observe then confront." But it hadn't been a good one. Too many unforeseen complications like janitors, kids and nosy school counselors. Not to mention, Annie had distracted him with the way she moved, smelled and laughed. Every moment on the way down had been bittersweet, remembering the feel of her skin against his, the way she moaned when he moved inside her, then knowing he could never feel that again. That thought had his head cloudy. He shouldn't have insisted she come with him. If she'd stayed—

"It went very well." She interrupted his thoughts. "What happened back there was a miracle."

He felt her gaze on him. His emotions still thrashed inside him. It all felt too much. Too intense. Too gut-wrenching. Too euphoric... Too guilty. He hadn't believed it could ever happen. He'd convinced himself his sister was dead. If he hadn't believed that, maybe he would have found her sooner. There were so many questions to be answered, but for the moment all that reverberated inside him was he'd found Della.

"A miracle," he repeated, his voice breaking with the words. Something washed over him again, turning him soft, but he couldn't stop it.

He braked at a red light. He didn't want to look at Annie, didn't want her to see the raw emotion, but he couldn't help himself. He glanced over and their eyes met. Something happened. Something as profound as the moment he'd shared moments ago with the sister he'd last touched when he shoved her to the ground and told her to get lost over twenty-four years ago. The moment between Annie and him wasn't combustible as it had been the night before, more like an invisible hand brushing over them, smoothing, uniting, bonding them into something more than what they'd been before.

Annie's lips curved and she laughed.

He'd never seen her laugh like that. Joyous. She felt what he felt and it caused something to expand inside of him, growing, filling places that had been hollow for so long.

Then it overflowed and he joined her in the laughter. "Holy cow, I found my sister, Annie. She's alive."

She wiped tears from her cheeks. "I know. I can't believe I witnessed that. And that janitor—" She dissolved into giggles. He wiped his tears and allowed himself to enjoy the normally serious woman chortling over how amazed Clarence was. "He kept looking for cameras."

A horn sounded behind them indicating that light change, and he pressed the accelerator, heading north.

Picou.

He sobered. How would he tell her? It would be shocking—but maybe not to Picou. She'd always professed to know Della was alive. And what about Sally Cheramie… or was it now Della? He'd left her shaken, conflicted and about as upside down as a person could be. He'd told her he'd be in touch later that evening, but where would they all go from here?

So many questions. So many things to think through.

But for the next few hours, he didn't want to think. He wanted to celebrate the chains that had finally fallen off him. He wanted to feel free and there was no better thing to do than climb onto an airboat, strap in and feel the wind in his hair.

And no better person to do that with than Annie. And Spencer, too, of course.

He wouldn't think about anything else—not Della, not the mistake they'd made the night before nor any case he worked. Just Annie, Spencer and the Louisiana marsh.

"What're you going to do now?" Annie asked.

"Huh?"

"About your sister? And Picou? And your brothers? How are—"

"I'll text Mom. Other than that, I'm not doing anything. Right now we're going to take a break from the heaviness of life. I need that. I need to live in the moment for the next few hours."

She looked hard at him, but said nothing.

"You understand?" he asked, glancing over briefly before refocusing on the narrow, curving highway following the curve of the bayou. "For a moment. That's what I need. A moment to feel—"

He fell off because he didn't know how to finish.

"Free," Anne finished for him. "Actually, that sounds better than terrific."

He nodded before glancing at Spencer in the rearview mirror. "Good. Ready to look for gators, Spence?"

"Yes!" the boy shrieked.

Both he and Annie smiled.

Yes, for the next few hours, he wanted to be a different Nate, the Nate he'd left behind when Della had disappeared, the boy who laughed easily, loved hard and grabbed ahold of life.

If only for a few hours.

Then he'd figure everything else out.

CHAPTER TWELVE

THE BOAT SCARED THE crap out of her and she didn't want to climb up onto the high seats and strap herself in, especially when she saw the driver.

Caleb Lyles looked about sixteen.

Of course, he had a sort of swagger and knowledge of the environment surrounding them that told her he'd likely been doing this sort of tour for years. But that didn't comfort her when he placed one muddy boot on the deck of the flat-bottom barge-looking boat, turned the cap he wore backward, looked at the eight paying customers on his tour and said, "Everybody ready to rock?"

Unfortunately, the huge propeller engines revving drowned out her resounding "no!"

He didn't hear her because he floored the engine, leaving the launch and her breath behind as he careened down the tree-lined bayou. Before she could scream, they headed out into the vast yellow grassland. The boat skimmed the marsh as huge flocks of birds rose into flight, fleeing the deranged Cajun ransacking their world.

"Gators!" Caleb shouted.

Annie clutched her seat, peered around Spencer's head and saw things rolling to the side as they shot through the waters. She couldn't tell if they were gators, not in their panic to get out of the way.

"Where?" Spencer shouted.

"Up there," she shouted back, refusing to relinquish the grip she had on the vinyl seat.

Annie's hair whipped behind her, and she prayed her sunglasses wouldn't be ripped from her face. They were hauling ass. She glanced over to Nate who sat across from her.

He looked so different.

The wind pushed at him, and it looked good on him. His T-shirt flapped behind him, pulled tight across his chest and stomach. His thick hair slicked back and the grin on his face warmed places inside her. Places she didn't want to acknowledge at that moment. This man had gotten to her, no matter what she'd told herself.

Nate glanced over at her, and though she couldn't see his eyes behind the sunglasses, she felt his smile. He looked ten years younger, as if the weight of the world had slid from his shoulders.

And she guessed it had.

She carried burdens with her—worry over selling the condo, carving a new career, oh, and a possible pregnancy—but never had she carried around the thought she'd been responsible for someone's death. Obviously, Nate had. As silly as it seemed, he'd believed he'd contributed to Della's death. And it must have sat on him like a stone.

But it had created the man he was.

A man she knew to be driven, burning with the need to right wrongs in a world all too often sideways.

So it pleased her to see him throw away his cares and revel in the simplicity of a boat, some water and a beautiful state spread before them in unique splendor.

And it was splendid. So different from anything she'd ever seen before. They carved a swath in the fabric of the marshland, hurtling toward a thick grove of trees.

Annie gasped and drew back as they flew into the

wooded area. The light disappeared as branches grasped at the boat, lacy moss catching on the tarp serving as a canopy. She had no clue how Caleb knew where to turn. There were moments she was certain they'd crash into a tree, but he wove in and out as if he were a water moccasin navigating the bayou. And then suddenly they broke into a meadow full of water lilies.

Caleb cut the motor and the craft stopped among yards of floating flowers.

"Wow," said one of the women sitting up front.

"Yeah," someone echoed.

"But where are the gators?" Spencer asked.

Caleb laughed. "You didn't see 'em scatterin' outta our way, little man?"

Spencer shook his head.

Caleb stood and studied the plants trying to swallow the boat. No one paid much attention to him, but Annie tightened when he grabbed a net and scooped up something.

"Here we are," he said, pulling something from the net. In his hand he held the tiniest alligator she'd ever seen.

"Aww" was the collective response.

Spencer held out his little hands and Caleb moved his way.

"He's a tiny fellow, but he still has teeth," the teen said, holding the reptile in front of him. The small creature's head bobbed, almost too big for its slender body, and somehow it was endearing.

Nate leaned over and studied it. "Can he hold it?"

Caleb eyed Spencer, and Annie could almost see the thought of lawsuit flip through the kid's mind. Finally he nodded. "As long as I hold the mouth."

Annie helped Spencer put both hands together and watched as Caleb placed the alligator on Spencer's hands.

"Ooh," Spencer said, his eyes alight. "He's so cute, isn't he, Annie?"

She nodded and even ran a finger down the creature's back—to show her support for Spencer's absolute fascination with the thing. It was surprisingly soft.

"Let me take a picture," she said, rooting around in her bag. She withdrew her iPhone and snapped a photo. Spencer grinned bigger than a gator as she took several more. Then everyone wanted a picture.

And the whole time Nate smiled, making Annie's heart thump crazily.

Later, after they docked at the Black Bayou launch, Annie combed her fingers through her hair, squirted some hand sanitizer into Spencer's hands and thanked Caleb for such an adventure. Surprisingly, it had been one of the better activities she'd engaged in. She'd always liked nature, but rarely played in it. This little zip through the swamp had inspired her.

Nate unclicked the locks on the door and they climbed inside, Spencer chattering the entire time about the boat, the gator and his new best friend, Caleb Lyles.

Sweet contentment settled over her for the first time since she'd set foot in Louisiana, which was odd considering all she had on her plate, but it had felt good to live in the moment she'd shared with Nate and Spencer—almost like a commercial break from true life drama.

She glanced at Nate who stood outside the car calling his thanks to the Lyles family, looking windblown, broad-shouldered and mouthwatering. Her fingers itched to touch him again, even if she'd convinced herself last night had been a mistake—a never-to-be-repeated mistake. At that moment, it didn't seem to matter.

She wanted him.

Nate slid into the car, slammed the door and looked at her. As if sensing her hunger, he obliged by leaning over and kissing her.

Annie didn't pull back, but instead slid her hand to his jaw and kissed him back. It felt wonderful, toe-curling wonderful, and against her better conviction, she drank him in.

He sighed against her mouth and pulled back. "Guess I shouldn't have done that."

"Probably not."

"Couldn't seem to help myself."

"Understandable."

Spencer's head appeared between them. "Ooooh, I saw you kissin'."

Then he laughed as if he'd told a joke—a very funny joke—before clicking himself into his booster and jamming his earphones on his head.

Nate ignored the kid and eyed Annie's lips, which she unconsciously rubbed together. Hunger glinted in his gaze, but he didn't kiss her again. "This has been the most unusual twenty-four hours of my life."

"You think?" she said, pulling the seat belt across her lap.

Nate cranked the engine, backed out from the Cajun cabin and boat launch and set back down the road they'd traveled hours before. Yeah, the past twenty-four hours had come at her too fast, making all that had occurred hard to process. What she did know was that certain parts had made her inordinately happy. Maybe even joyful, but she couldn't be sure because it had been a while since something so pure and good had welled inside her.

Not even Seth on his knee with a diamond ring had done the job.

Nor had passing the FBI exam.

Or getting the acceptance letter for the Academy.

Or—

Well, that was it for exciting things in her life. The rest of it had been kind of…boring.

Nate remained silent as he drove toward Beau Soleil, but

contentment radiated off him. Soft snores from the back-seat assured Spencer had dropped off to sleep, so she settled into the delicious softness of the leather and relaxed.

Nate's hand crept over the console to capture hers, and she didn't bother protesting. Mainly because she knew this was a moment that couldn't last—a slice of time taken from the crappy reality of life, to be savored like fine chocolate. Wonderful but fleeting. Nate wouldn't leave any trace of himself on her hips, but he might leave a piece embedded in her heart.

Regret for what couldn't be sliced her heart as Tom Petty crooned on the radio and the sun dropped toward the flat horizon.

"Beautiful, huh?" Nate said, nodding toward the sinking sun.

"Yeah, but it won't last."

"No?"

She looked at him. "Last night, today, all this was—"

"—not a beginning?"

"No." She shook her head, trying to stave away the sadness. Soon, she'd leave and he'd go on. Looking at Louisiana sunsets all by himself, or worse, with some other woman.

He released her hand. She looked down at her lonely hand and felt the emptiness. "Guess I forgot myself."

"Me, too. But I will treasure this little piece of whatever it was we had. Sweet madness. A vacation from the shitty reality of life."

"That's how you see life? As shitty?"

"Sound bitter?" She felt his nod. "Yeah, I guess, but my life hasn't ended up the way I wanted."

"You're a control freak."

She stiffened.

"Hey, don't be offended. I'm one, too. I can be an unbending bastard. It's my worst fault, but life taught me a lesson today. Or maybe it was God."

She nodded. Maybe God or karma or whatever had taught her something, too. Maybe she'd learned what it felt like to let go and embrace the wind, the water and the possibility of life rampaging out of her grasp…and it turning out okay. Perhaps she'd learned to hope for something more than putting all her eggs in the career basket. Maybe there was something more for Anna Mendes…

She looked at the man who'd turned her upside down in less than a week. "What did it teach you?"

"I can be dead wrong. Makes me wonder how many times I've stubbornly refused to see what was right before me? How many times have I whacked out a path in a direction I wasn't meant to head and so lost my way in the process?"

She studied her hands. Mostly because she didn't want to look at him, didn't want him to see how his words scraped her raw. Wasn't she the same? Forcing things. Seth and Mallory came to mind. Hadn't she pushed and pushed in a direction she thought she wanted until she hated everything about who she was?

Where had it left her?

Right where she sat.

"I don't have the luxury of wandering down a path right now, Nate." Deep down, she wanted to lace up her hiking boots and see where a relationship with Nate would go, but she couldn't get distracted from the road she was on. "We both have a case to solve, and that must take precedence."

He nodded. "True, but once we solve this—and we will solve it—then we owe it to ourselves to talk about this thing between us."

She felt a finger of uncertainty trace her spine. She

shouldn't entertain thoughts of something more lasting with Nate. But… "Maybe."

He studied her before putting his attention on the road. He didn't say anything else for the next twenty miles.

The music changed from rock to zydeco. Annie leaned forward and turned it off. Nate didn't react. Merely turned off the highway and onto the long, winding drive that would take them to Beau Soleil. The mood shifted again, and Annie knew the sojourn was over. Time to go back to Beau Soleil, her job and the unsteady agreement of "business only" between her and the man sitting next to her.

Spencer yawned. "Are we home, Annie?"

Not hardly. "Well, we're back at Beau Soleil."

"Is my mom here? Can I show her the picture of the baby gator?"

"Of course."

The house appeared and with it a lone woman standing vigil on the front porch. Annie had been so wrapped up in her thoughts and fears she'd almost forgotten Della and the mother waiting for word, hoping for the impossible.

Nate pulled into the graveled parking lot next to the horseshoe drive, shut off the engine, took a deep breath.

Picou appeared like an eagle swooping upon prey. "Why didn't you answer your phone? I've called half a dozen times. You know I waited to hear from you. A text that says 'everything is okay' is all I get? It's been hours. Hours, son."

Annie climbed out and watched as Nate took his mother by the shoulders and gave her a smile.

Picou lay her hands on her son's forearms as if she might not be able to stand. Her eyes filled with something Annie could only describe as wonderful. "Really?"

Nate smiled wider.

Annie felt her heart flutter, and thanked the good Lord

she got to witness this moment. She knew she'd replay it in her mind over and over for years to come.

"Oh, my," Picou clasped her hands to her face. "I can't— Truly? You're sure?"

Nate nodded. "I didn't believe, Mom. I never believed."

Tears coursed down the cheeks of the older woman. She shook her head, but didn't say a word. Her violet-blue eyes said it all. Annie swallowed the emotion clogging her throat as Spencer whined and struggled with the seat belt strapping him in his seat.

"You were right, Mama. All this time. You knew."

Picou smiled. "Oh, my sweet Jesus, Della is alive."

"She is."

Picou slapped Nate in the head. "Next time you find my daughter alive, you better damn well call me!"

Nate ducked, but laughed.

"I'm serious. I'm mad as hell at— Aah!" Picou shrieked as Nate lifted her in a bear hug. She smacked his back before wrapping both her arms around him.

"Thank you," Annie heard her whisper.

CHAPTER THIRTEEN

ANNIE SHOULD HAVE SLEPT soundly because the day had been exhausting, but sleep wouldn't come. Too much on her mind. Not to mention Spencer had crawled into the bed with her around one o'clock and started practicing for the World Cup while drooling on her pillow.

The shadows stretched long against the frostinglike molding edging the room and she watched them, begging for the monotony to lull her to sleep.

Didn't work.

Maybe it was the fact she'd had three messages waiting on her when she'd finally chanced a look at her phone. The first one had been from Seth reminding her that her half of the mortgage was due by the end of the week and suggesting they once again lower the price of the condo they'd unwisely bought together. The second had been from her father's nursing home seeking new insurance info, and the third call had been from Jimmy, who'd stayed buried within the catering company. He'd been cryptic but said he'd found out some info on Jane McEvoy that might be worth checking in to.

Though those things were certainly enough to keep her from dreamland, she knew the main reason had to do with the way Nate made her feel.

Like none other.

Surely she had lost her mind. No one fell for a guy she'd known for such a short time. Especially not Anna Mendes.

She didn't have a romantic bone in her body. Okay, well, maybe one or two romantic bones, but she couldn't believe what she felt for Nate was love. More of a fascination. Or a gravitational pull. But she really should stop thinking—

Something bumped downstairs.

Annie tensed before dismissing the noise as someone in the house in the same predicament as she. Failure to sleep. Most likely Picou. The woman had been ecstatic upon learning her daughter was alive. Nate had to do some fancy talking to keep her from loading up and heading south. Once he'd convinced her to give Sally some time, Picou had focused her pent-up energy on cooking a Louisiana feast of epic proportions. Fried meat pies, crawfish étouffée, and decadent French bread had filled their bellies as Picou regaled them with tales of her children. Annie was certain nothing could diminish the spark burning in the woman's eyes.

So it could be a too-happy-to-sleep Picou.

But Annie had not heard anyone on the stairs. There was a certain step that creaked no matter where one tread.

No one had gone downstairs.

Annie cast a glance at Spencer. He lay flat on his back, mouth open, tummy rising with each breath. She slid out of bed and soundlessly padded across the room to her closet, hoping the hinges didn't protest when she opened it. They didn't. She rose to her toes, searched with her hand for the gun hidden in a small handbag beneath a stack of linen and pulled it down, automatically double-checking the safety latch.

She crossed the room and inched open the door, praying for the same soundlessness as the closet. Luck smiled on her. She crept down the hallway toward the stairs where she descended, pausing midway to check her surroundings and listen for any sound to give away the position of the person below her.

Weak fluorescent light from the kitchen sink made a beam on the wooden floor below. There was no other light on anywhere else in the house. A shadow broke across the light, making it evident that person was in the kitchen.

Annie slipped as quickly as she could down the remainder of the polished steps of the main stairway, wincing when the creaky step groaned with her weight. She wondered briefly if she should have stayed with Spencer, protecting him. But if she'd done so, she'd be defensive rather than offensive. No sense in second-guessing herself.

Act with force. Without doubt.

She swung around and tiptoed toward the swinging door leading into the kitchen. She dropped the gun to her side, but flipped the safety latch. She knew a round was in the chamber.

Annie was locked and loaded.

She raised her hand and pressed it against the kitchen door, but she felt the movement too late. The door flew open with intentional force and smacked her in the head, driving her backward and down. Her bare feet fought for traction, but didn't find it. She fell backward, cracking her head on the antique sideboard behind her, hitting hard. Something fell and broke as she fell. Her elbow hit a knob on the drawer and her gun flew from her fingers. She heard it clatter to the floor and slide away from her as she hit the hard oak.

She registered a blur above her as darkness crept into her vision. She tried to move, to reach toward the shadowy figure moving toward her, but she couldn't manage to fight the dark circles widening, sucking her into them.

Her last conscious thought was that she'd left Spencer alone in her bed.

Then darkness claimed her.

NATE DIDN'T FEAR MUCH in life. Nothing outside of his family ever held much weight with him. Possessions could be replaced. Careers rebuilt. Reputations righted and restored. But when he'd seen Annie lying on the stretcher in the foyer of his childhood home, he'd felt the same cold fingers of fear he'd felt some many years ago on the night Della had disappeared. He remembered that feeling of hopelessness well, lying in the bed one floor above him, scared witless at faceless people who could do horrific things to people he loved.

Feeling that way about Annie should have sent a lesser man packing, heading for the hills, afraid of losing once again. But Nate wasn't the sort of man to tuck tail and run, even if he didn't understand exactly what it was he felt.

Annie lay still on the stretcher as the paramedics took vitals and tapped data into their handheld computers, but her eyes shone with fury. They reminded him of a stormy sea, promising vengeance on whoever stood in her way.

A goose egg popped out above her right eye and the gash on the back of her head likely needed stitches. Blood matted the dark tresses surrounding the cut and some still smeared her neck.

He glanced over to the floor. A pool of blood lay at the clawed foot of the sideboard, peppered with the crystal slivers of the decanter that had plunged to the floor and shattered.

"Don't ask," she said, waving a hand at him. "I didn't get a look at the guy."

"Nothing?"

She closed her eyes, before opening them again. She

glanced around, at Picou nervously twisting the belt of her robe and Carter hulking near the stairs, before glancing back at him. Her eyes told him she had something to say that could not be said in front of those present.

"Her vitals are good," the paramedic said, still tapping into his handheld. Nate knew Ross Sandifer well, but the female partnering with him was new. "She needs a couple of stitches, so we'll transport her to Lafayette. Needs a CT scan, too."

"No," Annie said, sitting up. She swayed slightly before swinging her feet around and setting them on the floor. "I'll be fine. Can you do the stitches here? Or use liquid bandage to bind it?"

"I don't think that's a good idea," the female paramedic said, trying to press Annie back onto the stretcher. "You need to be checked by a doctor."

Annie looked up at him. "He's a doctor. Sort of."

Nate shook his head. "Not technically. I passed med school and boards, but I never completed my residency, which was in pathology, by the way. No live patients."

"But you—"

"I have to agree with Ms.—" he glanced at the paramedic's name tag "—Brunet here. You need to get checked out."

"I'm not going anywhere. I didn't hit my head that hard."

She was being stubborn, but he wasn't going to argue. He had no right to demand anything from her. She was a grown woman and if she wanted to disregard common sense, then she damn well could. "Fine."

The paramedics looked at one another. Ross shrugged. "Okay. I'll see what I can do with the back of her head. Get the forms, Tina, and make sure she signs them. I ain't losing my job over this."

Fifteen minutes later, Annie was sutured and sitting on a wingback chair in the study. He'd persuaded his mother into going back to bed, and Carter disappeared back up the stairs with a promise to move Spencer to his bed so Annie could get some rest. His bodyguard rumbled behind him.

Annie glanced up as he closed the library door. "The bastard got my gun."

"You have a gun?"

"Had a gun."

"Hell." He ran a hand through his hair and sighed. Not good. If the perp wasn't armed before, now he was. "You didn't see anything? No impressions of the person who did this?"

"No, but the way whoever it was came out of that kitchen, he or she knew I was there. It was intentional. Damn, I should have known."

He lifted an eyebrow.

"It's that step, eleven down from the top."

Of course. That eleventh step had gotten him punished many a time. No way to sneak up and down past curfew without a telltale squeak. "So what did this person want?"

Annie shrugged. "Pretty bold to waltz in and take a kid from his bed."

"Been done plenty times before, though," he said, mulling over the possibilities. It would be audacious, but perhaps the perp hadn't wanted to take Spencer. Maybe this was about another threat. "Did anyone check the kitchen? Look for a note or message?"

Annie nodded. "Carter looked around after Picou called you. He said he didn't see anything."

"I'm going to take a look. Will you be okay?"

She nodded. The knot on her forehead had subsided a bit, though it was still an angry red, and her eyes clouded with fatigue and pain. He hated seeing his feisty Annie so vulnerable.

Nate left the library wondering when in the hell he'd started thinking of Annie as his.

He flipping the switch and the huge fluorescent lights flickered before casting steadfast light onto the counters and tiled floor below. He took a stroll around the room that still smelled of seafood and fried meat pies. The back door had been jimmied open. White splinters of wood littered the swept floor right at the jamb. It hadn't taken much effort to force the old lock to give.

Guilt socked him. He should have seen to reoutfitting the old house long ago. With his mother living so far out with only Lucille as an infrequent companion, the place needed to be shored up security-wise. Locks should work correctly, fire alarms tested and safeguards put into place. His mother wasn't getting any younger and he hadn't done a good enough job at looking after her. Maybe he should list his small cottage in town and move back to Beau Soleil.

That would really put him full circle.

Living with his mother.

He shoved that thought away, unable and unwilling to even think about giving up what little he still had left of himself, and examined the lock and door facing. It was unlikely there would be any fingerprints. The lab report he'd found in his in-box that evening had revealed no trace evidence on the previous note nor on the dead bird. Another big, fat dead end.

He'd need to check for prints anyway, but first he wanted to figure out the motive for breaking into the house. What was the purpose? It could be to take Spencer with Annie foiling the attempt, causing the perp to flee out the front door. But that didn't seem logical unless whoever had broken into the house had intimate knowledge of the surroundings and the occupants within. Otherwise, grabbing a kid, not knowing the configuration of the darkened house or the location of the subject, would be dog-assed stupid.

He didn't feel as though the perpetrator was stupid.

So either the perp knew the layout well enough to feel secure or there was another reason.

Nate stood at the door, staring into the bowels of the kitchen. The new granite his mother had installed gleamed as did the black-and-white old-timey tiled floor. The new stainless-steel Sub-Zero drew his eye. He walked to the appliance, grabbed a paper towel and opened the door.

Bingo.

Sitting on the shelf in the middle of storage containers and yogurt cups was a chicken carcass with a note attached.

You want what you want
Throw away what you don't
selfish bitches don't get
to keep what they don't deserve.

Nate closed the door, careful to maintain the paper towel between his naked hand and the steel door handle.

The kitchen door swung open and Annie walked in. "You found something?"

He nodded. "A note and a chicken carcass. Whoever is doing this is done with rhyming."

Annie hugged herself. "Crap, we need to catch a break."

He looked at his watch. 3:19 a.m. "But not now. I'll get my bag out of the car and give Wynn a call. I know you want to help, but this is official and I need to treat it as such."

She opened her mouth to argue, but he held up a finger. "Don't. You need rest."

"I might have a concussion and shouldn't sleep as a precaution."

"Then you should have gone with the paramedics. Your job is to protect Spencer. You need rest so you have your wits about you."

She frowned and it struck him that though this private investigator was sexy as hell, there was something attractive about her stubborn demeanor. God, but he'd always loved a woman who dug in and refused to surrender. A challenge. That was definitely Annie.

He watched her as her mind clicked through pros and cons of doing what he suggested and almost smiled as she sighed. "Fine, but tomorrow we need to meet. Jimmy called and—"

"Who's Jimmy?"

"Howie."

"Oh. So that was a ruse. I mean, of course it was a ruse." He felt a little dense for not realizing the whole kiss in the woods thing was a total sham. Oh, he'd seen something shady about it, but jealousy had colored his response. "I'll be here tomorrow so we'll meet then. See what Jimmy's got, we'll compare notes and see what we can come up with."

She nodded.

He couldn't stop himself from taking the six steps necessary to reach her. She looked up at him and he felt his heart beat harder. He traced the bruise forming around her bump. "You scared me."

Her eyes looked bigger than normal. "I did?"

"Yeah," he breathed before gently brushing his lips over hers. He added a soft kiss on her forehead, mindful of her injury. "That's something new for me. To feel the way I did when I saw you hurt. When I thought about what could have happened to you."

Annie swallowed and then licked her lips. "This shouldn't be happening. It doesn't make sense to—"

He silenced her with another quick kiss. "I know, but that doesn't change the fact there's something between us. It's not going away because we want it to."

She brushed his jaw with her hand. "I'm scared."

"That makes two of us."

He delivered another kiss on her forehead, breathing deeply the essence of Annie. She smelled clean, like shampoo and baby powder. Not necessarily a turn-on, but he could grow to love the soft scent. He gave her a small shove toward the kitchen door. "Go. We'll talk in the morning."

For once she didn't argue. She disappeared through the swinging door with a resigned look.

Nate turned toward the refrigerator and took out his phone. Every cell in his body screamed for him to follow Annie, to watch over her, to hold her, but he had a job to do.

He'd asked her to think about something more after they solved the case, but did he want to go there? Was he ready for a serious relationship? Was any guy?

His phone rang.

Wynn.

No more thinking about relationships. Time to work. The faster he caught the scum slipping chicken bones in people's refrigerators, the sooner he could find peace.

Maybe.

"Get your ass to Beau Soleil. Someone left a chicken in the fridge and it ain't for dinner."

CHAPTER FOURTEEN

"I'M STILL SCARED." Tawny looked up from the patio where she perched in a teeny bikini on a chaise longue. She looked fantastic, except for the fear in her eyes.

Tawny, Jane and Annie had been sitting outside on the back patio in companionable silence, sipping drinks. Neither Tawny nor Jane had been needed on set that day and so had spent the morning sleeping in, then the afternoon sunning, reading tabloids and gossiping about the celebrities they knew in tinsel town. Annie now knew who was still in the closet, who'd gotten a little work done and who was addicted to pain meds. She could give a flying fig about insider information. She'd have rather had the day off so she could meet with Nate and check developments. It had been almost five days since she'd lost her gun.

"This detective will figure it out," Jane said, fanning herself with the *US* magazine Tawny had asked Annie to pick up when she'd visited town that morning. "He looks so capable."

At this Tawny smiled. "Oh, so that's what you call it. I'd say he's emphatically bedable."

"Do you even know what 'emphatic' means?" Jane asked, lowering the magazine to slap at a mosquito.

"Exclamation point, dot, dot, dot," Tawny said, pointing a finger after each dot.

Annie tried to pretend she wasn't bothered by their talk. Of course women found Nate attractive. He was subtly hot, extremely masculine and emphatically intelligent. Exclamation point, dot, dot, dot. And though she'd slept with him, or rather not slept while having sex with him, she had no claim on the man. Not really.

But maybe.

"Spencer's safe," Annie said, taking another sip of the lemonade Picou had made. Spencer played in the shade of a broad-limbed oak, kicking the new ball she'd bought him a few hours earlier. They had gone into Bayou Bridge to buy a present for his cousin Braden, but Annie had learned the hard way children accustomed to getting whatever they want often demanded whatever they wanted. Loudly. The ball had been a compromise—one she knew she shouldn't have made. But when people turned, stared and tsked, it kicked a gal into survival mode.

Spencer had gotten the stupid ball no matter what the damned parenting books had warned. The smug family psychologists who'd penned them hadn't faced the power of Spencer Keene and his overly dramatic tantrums.

Annie, who had once faced the snub-nosed end of a loaded pistol and not even broken a sweat, had been beaten down by a five-year-old.

"Well, he's safe for now, but what if that person had succeeded the other night? Look at Annie's face. That could have been my birdie." Tawny took another swig from her Bud Light and swiped her arm across her mouth.

Both women turned toward Annie and her fading bruise. "I got this because I wanted some water. That person wasn't trying to hurt Spencer. Just leave that note."

Tawny didn't look convinced and Annie couldn't blame her. The blood, ambulance and rotting chicken carcass seemed to foreshadow what could happen if the potential kidnapper wasn't nabbed soon.

Tawny adjusted her nearly nonexistent bikini top and

said, "What kind of freak leaves dead birds and chicken bones all over the place?"

"Mambos," Picou said, entering the patio and setting a plate of fruit on the glass-topped table. "Voodoo priests and priestesses often use chicken blood in their prophecies."

"Seriously?" Jane asked, tying her bikini top behind her neck and pulling on a light cotton cover-up. "Sounds like some churches I've been to."

Picou launched into a lecture on ancient voodoo culture and its place in the modern world. Annie listened with one ear as she mulled over a few tidbits she'd heard over the course of the afternoon. It might not be much, but it had given credence to Jimmy's idea Jane didn't like Tawny as much as the actress thought she did.

Nothing about Jane seemed significant to the case until she had started ribbing Tawny about Carter, a bar and a mixed-up drink order.

Tawny had laughed about Carter ditching Jane at the bar to do the limbo with her on the dance floor, but Annie had sensed an edge to Jane's words. Oh, she'd laughed, but not with her eyes. Annie knew how to connect dots and tried to put together a picture of what had happened.

She guessed Jane had been snaked. Tawny had been unemployed and passed over for more roles than she cared to mention, but grabbed the brass ring when she'd seduced Carter away from where Jane had him pinned at the bar. Then Jane had watched from the bar, nursing her own drink, as the blonde bombshell regaled Carter with her Arkansas accent, baby-blue eyes and double Ds. Two months later, Tawny was in production for a sitcom on Fox and wearing a five-carat diamond. Jane had ended up in the shower selling feminine-hygiene wash in a commercial.

Annie tapped a finger on the lip of the glass, wondering if man stealing was enough motivation to send threats and leave dead birds all over the place. She briefly touched the bruise covering her cheek and eye and winced. Then she thought about the movie with the boiled rabbit. Yeah, crazy people used whatever they could to exact revenge.

She hated sitting by doing nothing. She felt useless and wanted to be in on the investigation, doing something more active than playing nanny. But Ace hadn't been happy with the developments, especially the stolen gun, and had insisted she stay put.

Spencer sprinted over to the patio. "Hey, guys, look at what I can do."

He backed up, held the ball in front of him and kicked it. The line drive went right toward Jane's upturned nose.

"Son of a bitch!" Jane screamed, cupping her hand over her nose as blood spurted between her fingers.

"Oh, my gosh," Tawny cried, grabbing a napkin from beneath her beer and thrusting it at her friend. "Here."

"Great," Jane said, grabbing the napkin and holding it over her nose. Blood dripped over her fingers. Annie extracted several ice cubes from her glass, wrapped them in a napkin and handed it to the woman, who took it and replaced the blood-soaked one Tawny had given her.

"I'm sorry," Spencer said, his face twisting into tearful grimace. "I didn't mean to—"

"Well, you should be," Jane hissed. "Look what you did to my nose."

She removed the tissue, revealing a throbbing, Rudolph-worthy nose. Tears unwillingly slid down her checks, mingling with the blood still trickling from her nostrils. Annie couldn't stop the *Brady Bunch* episode where Marsha got hammered with the football from playing in her mind. Jane's sorta looked like Marsha's…except real.

"He said he didn't mean it," Tawny said, reaching out

and gathering her son into her arms. "It's okay, birdie. You didn't mean it."

"Of course it's okay. Nothing wrong with him ruining my nose. I only have to shoot two scenes tomorrow," Jane said, rising and shoving the chair in which she'd spent the past few hours across the patio. "Spencer can do no wrong. You coddle him and let him get away with everything. He's a spoiled brat and you're going to regret it someday!"

Jane stalked toward the front of the house, passing Picou who'd gone inside to replenish the lemonade. The older woman spun and took in a sobbing Spencer, a bloody napkin and the ensuing squeal of tires. "What the—"

"An accident," Annie said.

"She's such a drama queen," Tawny huffed, cradling her son and dropping kisses atop his sweaty head. "She pretends to like Spencer to get on my good side."

Something prickled on Annie's neck. "She doesn't like Spencer?"

"She doesn't like any kids. Thank goodness she can't have any of her own. They'd be the saddest things ever."

"Can't have any?" Annie leaned forward. "As in physically can't have any?"

"Is there another way to have them?" Tawny asked with a roll of her eyes. "Well, I guess people can adopt, but Jane had a hysterectomy when she was in her early twenties. Something about an abortion that went bad. Or maybe it was a tubal pregnancy. I'm not sure because it happened before I knew her. Guess she forgot to take her hormones today because she's in full-on bitch mode."

Annie stood. Jane McEvoy had officially become a person of interest. "Did you tell the detectives investigating the case?"

Tawny frowned. "Why? What does her not having periods have to do with what's going on with Spencer?"

Annie glanced at Picou. The older woman's brow furrowed and she looked contemplative. She looked back at Tawny who looked as she always did. Clueless. "Well, maybe not, but who knows what drives people?"

Spencer's sobs subsided into a sniffle as Picou sank down into the cushioned chair Jane had abandoned. The older woman tapped her chin. "Was Jane in California when you received the threats?"

"Yes," Tawny and Annie said in unison.

Picou nodded. "And the threats didn't start here until Spencer got here. Whoever's making those threats is here. In Louisiana. So anyone who was in California who is now in Louisiana is a suspect."

Tawny shook her head. "There's no way the nutcase is Jane. I know Jane. She was my roommate for three years, not to mention my maid of honor and Spencer's godmother. She's high-maintenance and sometimes a pain in the ass, but she's not capable of doing something so mean."

Annie wasn't so sure. She held no idealized notion of friendship, maybe because she hadn't had many true friends, but she'd seen cases where the most trusted turned out to be crooked and capable of atrocity. Perhaps Jane had nursed the anger against Tawny until it turned into something akin to hatred, something that had driven her to act criminally. "Still, you need to mention this to Picou's son. Or that FBI guy."

Picou nodded. "I sensed anxiety around that woman. Her aura is yellow. Something's going on in her life that's displeasing."

Tawny shrugged. "It doesn't have to do with me or Spencer. It has to do with Mick. I don't feel comfortable telling on her. Her medical history is none of anyone's business. In fact, I shouldn't have told you."

Tawny wasn't going to throw a friend under the bus.

Annie knew she could tell Nate, but Tawny needed to see withholding information held up investigations, including the one Annie did for Sterling Investigations. "Mrs. Keene, um, Tawny, I respect your loyalty. It's an admirable trait in a friend, but Spencer is more important, don't you think?"

The woman looked down at the boy resting his head on her stomach. The child wasn't asleep, but he was soaking in his mother's love. "Yeah. He's the most important thing in my life."

And that was why he was being used against her.

Picou cleared her throat. "So maybe it wouldn't hurt to mention it to Nate. He's a good guy. He wouldn't let anything leak out about Jane that wasn't necessary."

Tawny nodded. "Okay. I'll say something to him when I see him. He said he'd come by and give us a briefing on what they've found so far. Carter insisted."

Picou nodded. "Sensible."

Tawny chuckled. "I don't think anyone has ever called me that before."

Annie needed some time to meet with Nate herself. "I haven't had a day off, Tawny, and I know—"

"You can take tomorrow off. I'm taking Spence to the water park and Brick will come with me." She feathered her son's hair.

"Do I have to wear my floaties?" Spencer asked, his voice muffled by the cushions. He lay flat on his mother in sweet contentment.

"No, it's not a pool. Just fun things to splash in."

Annie rose and stretched, waggling a hand toward Spencer. "Let's go up and set your things out before we have supper. Miss Lucille's back from visiting her family and Picou told me she made her famous gumbo for supper. I can't wait to try it." And hopefully have time to call Ace and let him know this new development. They needed better background on Jane and Annie needed to get inside the woman's hotel room and search it. But how?

Hmm. Maybe a shoulder to cry on…or rather rant on. Maybe she'd take some gumbo as a peace offering. The sooner the better. Like that very night.

NATE STARED AT THE preliminary lab report and frowned. Nothing.

That's all he'd gotten with this case. A big fat zero.

"It's time to get tough with these assholes," Wynn said, plucking a well-chewed toothpick from his mouth and tossing it in the metal trash can.

"We don't know what assholes to get tough with. No leads."

"Bullshit. There's something, somewhere, and we've been too dumb to find it. Or distracted."

Nate felt himself bristle. Yeah, he'd been distracted but no more so than any other case. Big gray eyes flitted into his mind. He loved the way her eyes looked dilated with pleasure.

Wynn slapped a file on top of several others, jarring him from his musings. Maybe Wynn was right. Maybe Nate couldn't handle the investigation properly because he was in lust with the nanny.

"Maybe, but it's hard to get excited over a decaying rotisserie chicken with no prints, no trace evidence, nothing. Annie didn't see anything before she got knocked out except a blur. So did you pick up knowledge on how to identify a printless, clean-as-a-whistle blur when I wasn't looking?"

Wynn tented his fingers and studied him. "Are you banging this nanny?"

Nate tossed the report on his recently cleaned-off desk. "That's none of your business."

"She's a suspect. A nice piece of ass, I'll give you that, and kudos for actually pulling yourself away from those boxes in your house, but she could be in on this."

"So she gave herself a concussion to cover up her involvement?"

His partner shrugged. "I've seen stranger things."

Nate shook his head. "No, she's not in on this."

Wynn played with the pencil cup on his desk. "Fine. Make sure you don't let getting tail color your judgment."

"I've never allowed a woman to color my judgment. Annie's not making these threats, and she's not a piece of ass. She's—" He stopped because he wasn't sure what she was.

Wynn glanced up. "Look. No problem. We've got bigger fish to fry than you and the nanny. We need to bust something loose, so I say we head over to that movie set and scare something up."

"With who?"

"Let's start with Mick. I've heard from too many people that the creep has the hots for Tawny. I say let's bring him down here. Make him jumpy. He's such an arrogant asshole, he's bound to give us reason."

Nate shrugged. "Worth a try. But first, we need to go by the Quick Mart and check out the alibi for our perp in that robbery case. If it doesn't check out, I'll give Harvey the green light to charge him so we can put that case away. Then Keene asked for a briefing."

Wynn stood. "Since when did you start kissing people's asses, Dufrene? You running for office next year?"

No. He wanted to check on Annie, and running down the leads with Keene was an excuse to see her. God, he really was starting to act like a pathetic schoolboy. Annie didn't need him to take care of her. She was more than capable of taking care of herself even if someone had knocked her black-and-blue and taken her gun… So maybe not. Maybe Annie needed him, if only a little bit.

He hadn't reported her gun stolen because he didn't want to blow her cover. No need for a nanny to tote a gun. If she stayed undercover, she stayed safe. She'd been an accidental target the other night. An incidental for someone who hadn't wanted to be discovered.

He hoped the stolen gun didn't come back to haunt him.

Nate grabbed his own piece from the desk drawer and told Wynn explicitly how he could kiss his own derrierre. The words weren't fit for polite society, but the bull pen had never offered anything remotely in the way of polite conversation.

Annie ladled gumbo into a plastic storage container and sealed it. She'd take Jane dinner while doing some active investigating. Spencer was in his jammies, happily making Play-Doh food with the gift that was supposed to be mailed to his cousin in Arkansas the next morning. But Annie didn't care that poor Braden wouldn't get his gift. Tawny and Carter were pretending to eat the food and looking much more agreeable to one another—and Annie was free for the evening.

"You think that's going to make her feel better about her nose?" Picou asked, when she pushed through the swinging door and caught Annie filching the gumbo.

She shrugged. "It was the best stuff I've ever tasted. Gotta do something for her."

"Why are you being nice to her?"

Annie turned around and set the container in a plastic bag along with several pieces of French bread and a slice of Lucille's famous buttermilk pie. "Because she was nice to me. Invited me for drinks several nights ago, and I ended up getting a headache and bailing on her after only an hour. I feel bad, I guess."

"Kinship?" Picou asked, folding some napkins and grabbing a bottle of tea. She placed them in the bag beside the gumbo.

"What do you mean?"

"She's a single gal. Doesn't seem to have a family or many close friends, working for the Keene family."

Annie cocked her head. "Do I seem pathetic to you?"

Picou's words had slammed her. She knew her life wasn't ideal. Did the older woman have to point that out?

"Not at all. I merely see similarities. Not physically, of course, but your aura is often bright yellow as if you're deeply stressed or insecure. Other times it's brown as if you are guarding yourself."

Annie almost snorted. "Well, thanks, but I'm not unhappy with my life."

The older woman arched a brow.

"Okay, so I'm not exactly jumping up and down thrilled with it, but I'm trying to get there. Maybe that includes doing something nice for someone." Or maybe it was snooping around so she could get this case solved and get her tail back to L.A. But even as she thought it, she knew she wasn't sure about going back. Part of her wanted to stay here under the lacy Spanish moss brushing the green grass. Under the Louisiana stars with the infernal mosquitos and unbearable heat. With Nate. With Picou. With an unnamed future child with brown eyes and corkscrew curls.

She was delusional. She shook her head and swallowed the craziness with a swig of water.

Picou didn't say anything. Instead she picked up a note pad. "I called Della today."

Annie looked up. "You did?"

"Nate has been so preoccupied. He was supposed to

call her again today, but didn't have time. I know he's busy and that this is about Spencer, but I just want to hold my little girl."

"What did you say? How did she take it?"

"I pretended to be a salesperson." The older woman smiled. "I had to at least hear her voice. She sounded so different. She has that bayou accent."

Annie watched as Picou scratched loops across the paper. She tied the handles of the plastic bag together and placed it in a larger handled paper bag. "She is from down there."

Picou looked up. "I think she knew it was me. She acted like she didn't know, but there was something fearful in her voice. She's scared of me."

Annie shook her head. "No, but her world has been turned upside down. You will have to give her time. That's what Nate's trying to do. Give her a little space."

"But I need to see her. Touch her." Picou dropped the pen and stared out at the night. It was nearly eight o'clock. The sun had run away leaving a blanket of darkness behind.

"You'll get there," Annie said, picking up the rental car keys from the counter by the back door.

Picou's voice was heavy with tears. "I hope."

Annie set the bag on the counter and did something so uncharacteristic she shocked herself. She walked to Picou and wrapped her arms around her. "You will."

Picou held tight to Annie. Her arms were bony and strong and the silver braided hair at her shoulder smelled like lemons. Annie couldn't remember the last time she'd hugged another woman, but she knew this was right. For both of them. Something sweet and warm invaded Annie's heart as she gave Picou a final squeeze. Something that reminded her she was innately human and needed the healing touch as much as Picou did.

"Thank you, sweet Annie," Picou said, using her index finger to wipe the dampness from beneath her haunting violet eyes. "I needed that."

"So did I," Annie said, picking up the keys and bag she'd abandoned. She lifted the shopping bag in toast. "Two good deeds in one night. I'm earning points somewhere."

Picou smiled and gave her a thumbs up. "You're earning your wings, kiddo."

Annie slipped out the door, feeling vaguely satisfied at having done something heartfelt. It had been a while since she'd tossed her reservations aside and acted on what her heart had urged.

She looked down at her flat stomach and remembered. Scratch that.

Five days ago, she'd listened to her heart. Or was that her libido?

She set the bag on the passenger seat and started the car. Time to put her emotions away and her thinking cap on. She needed to find out if Jane had been leaving the threats, and if she had, Annie would find out.

Nothing stopped Annie when she was ready to break a case, and as she gingerly touched the purple bruise on her cheek, she decided she was past ready.

CHAPTER FIFTEEN

MICK MANNERS WAS definitely an ass.

But Nate kind of liked him. Like recognized like, he guessed.

"So you're taking me in because I bought a chicken at the store? I'm doing a high-protein diet thing to slim down from my role on *Lost in Laos,* and my assistant had the stomach flu so I had to go myself. Look, I regret it. Do you know how many people wanted my autograph? One lady who looked about fifty years old asked if I would sign her bra."

"Can it," Wynn said, grabbing the man's arm and forcefully steering him toward the unmarked car.

"This is bullshit," Mick growled. "I'll have your asses handed to you on a silver plate."

"I'll make sure to shower. Wouldn't want anyone ogling my derriere on a silver plate if I hadn't cleaned up proper like," Wynn said, unlocking the car and opening the back door. "You can come quietly, like we're good friends taking a ride, or we can cuff you and book you for resisting arrest."

"Whatever," Mick said, sliding into the car and slamming the door.

"That went well, don't you think?" Wynn said, looking over top of the car at Nate.

Nate grunted and slid into the passenger's seat. Normally, he drove, but Wynn had sensed the deep anger brewing in him after their perp in the robbery case's alibi panned

out, and had insisted. He'd also requested Nate try playing good detective with Mick while he played the role of
bad cop extraordinaire. That had lasted for all of ten minutes. Nate hadn't lost it on Manners, but he'd come close
a few times.

"I want my attorney."

"I want you to shut the hell up," Nate responded, turning down the static on his handheld. "Then I want you to
think hard about what is about to happen. About what your
adoring fans will think when they hear you're threatening
a five-year-old boy just because his mother won't let you
play on her playground."

"What?" Mick rattled the cage between the seats. "You
guys are effin' crazy."

"No, that'd be you, bud. You're the one displaying dead
birds and writing freaky poetry."

Mick Manners reared back against the seat. "I can't
believe this shit. This is like—"

"—in the movies?" Nate finished for him.

"Yeah. Dirty cops looking to pin something on someone
so they can grab the limelight and say they solved a case."

Nate slid his gaze to Wynn. His partner smiled. He loved
this sort of drama. "We can keep that from happening if
you'll tell us why you did it."

"Why I did what? I didn't do anything."

Nate shrugged and flipped the lights on the dashboard.
They were out in the boondocks, but he felt Mick's panic.

"Okay, fine. I have a thing for Tawny. I always have. We
dated before either of us broke into the business, and I fell
for her. She's sweet and her ass is as tight as a schoolboy's."

"And you know about schoolboy backsides?" Wynn
tucked a toothpick in his mouth.

"No, man. I don't swing that way," Mick said with a

derisive laugh. "Sometimes I wish I did, then I could get Tawny and her amazing tits outta my mind."

"Right," Wynn said.

"So I've been flirting with her. Keene has been so wrapped up in business. I saw Tawny's sadness. Nothing easier to pluck than a lonely chick. And this was a chick I liked to pluck, so I gave her some attention. Tried to make it more than friendly, but she's stuck on Keene. She was just using me to make him jealous. I might have been okay with it if she'd given me some action, but I got nothing but blue balls."

"So did that drive you to write poetry? Threaten her son?"

"Hell, no. I ain't that damn desperate, man. I can bag chicks on the set to ease my pain, you know. I may be a shit sometimes but I don't mess with no kids. And I'm not screwed up in the head enough to kill birds. I ate a damn chicken, man. That's it. I threw the carcass out a few days ago."

Nate knew he told the truth. They'd stretched it when they grabbed hold of the fact he'd eaten a chicken a few days ago. Hell, half the department picked up chicken at Maggio's Supermarket—both fried and rotisserie. Nate made a loop with his finger. Wynn jerked the car hard to the left and spun around on the empty blacktop.

"Damn!" Mick yelled, banging against the bars separating them. Nate smiled because Wynn lived to pull stunts like that.

"Okay, we don't have to take you downtown."

"You call that crappy little one-stoplight town *downtown*?" Mick asked.

Nate laughed at that. "Yeah, you've been most accommodating, Mr. Manners, and we at the sheriff's department appreciate your cooperation as we investigate this case."

The actor snorted. "Figures all you have to do around here is chase phantoms. Chickens and threats against a kid…that's all y'all got to do? What? Did a cow get out of the pasture, too?"

"Maybe we better take him in. Resisting arrest?" Wynn glanced at Nate.

"Please," Mick said. "I gotta be up at six o'clock for a shoot. I cooperated, like he said."

Nate nodded. "Let's cut him loose. I'm tired of messing with the jackass."

"Back at you, buddy," Mick said, as Nate switched off the blue flashing lights.

"I knew you'd see in me what you see in yourself. I like that about you, Mick."

"Well, there's nothing I like about you."

Nate grinned. "I'll take myself off your Christmas list."

ANNIE SET THE BAG NEXT to the bureau strewn with dirty clothes. Jane wasn't the tidiest of persons.

"So why are you doing this?" the actress said from the vanity where she plucked her eyebrows. Her nose was no longer red even though it looked puffy. No black eye, unlike Annie. "I mean you got no stake in me getting pissed at Tawny. Hell, she could fire you for being nice to me after I acted like such a bitch."

"No, she wouldn't do that," Annie said, wandering around trying for nonchalance, but looking hard at the objects scattered around the room. She hated hotel rooms. Hard to feel at home in a place with Bibles in the drawer and switches at the base of cheap ceramic lamps. "I know how it feels to be on the receiving end of—"

"—stupidity?" Jane finished for her.

"Not exactly stupidity. More like someone being blind."

Jane spun around. "You've been taking care of the kid

for over a month, right? So you know he's a little turd and Tawny indulges him and makes excuses for him."

Annie didn't think Spencer was a turd. He was a little boy. Sure, he was slightly spoiled, but he also had a wonderful innocence, a lust for adventure and the sweetest sloppy kisses at bedtime. "It's easy for mothers to overlook faults."

"Then you don't have a mother like mine. She points out everything wrong with me. Nothing I do makes her happy. Ever. She complains about every part I don't get and the fact I'm not even considered B list."

"My mother died when I was twelve."

Jane's eyes met hers in the mirror. "Sorry. I guess I shouldn't complain about my mother, but they can all be like that. If yours was still around, you'd probably be complaining about how you're not good enough either."

Annie would gladly take her mother's censure if she could have her back. But her mother had never been critical. As an elementary teacher with curling auburn hair, crinkly blue eyes and a somewhat wide bottom, her mother had fit the image of a laughing Irishwoman who made everyone feel good about who they were. Her death had broken Annie's father, scattering their small, once-happy family into dark corners to grieve alone. Yeah, Annie could handle maternal criticism. Happily. "Maybe. I'm glad I'm not a mother myself. It's hard being around kids. Nothing easy."

"Better you than me," Jane muttered, stepping from the alcove bathroom and hovering over the bag Annie had set down. "I can't stand all the fawning she does over him. Makes me want to puke. The kid monopolizes all her time now. Can't even get her to go out for a drink with me anymore, and she used to be quite the party girl. What's this?"

"Chicken and andouille gumbo."

"Oh." Jane pulled the lid off and sniffed. "Mmm. Smells good. What's andouille?"

"A spicy sausage." Annie sank uninvited on the bed and crossed her legs. She hadn't seen anything in the room to arouse suspicion, just lots of clothes, a few Diet Coke cans and some torrid-looking romance books. Too bad Jane didn't have to go to the bathroom, so Annie could dig through drawers. "So, you're not a Spencer fan?"

Jane ladeled a spoonful of soup into her mouth. "Whoa. This is incredible."

Annie nodded.

"I don't dislike the kid. Just hate what he's done to Tawny. She was fun at one time. Now she's different."

Might be enough motive to threaten Tawny's child, but it still seemed weak. Who flirted with kidnapping as a way to make a best friend become the life of the party once again? If Jane were the person writing the threats, then she needed a better reason. But Annie had seen some strange things done in the name of some seemingly minor slight.

"We all grow up, I guess."

"Yeah, whatever," Jane said, slurping the gumbo. "Guess I'll apologize to Tawny tomorrow. I shouldn't have gotten so pissed. The swelling went down. By tomorrow, hopefully it will look normal."

"I meant to tell you it looked better."

Jane didn't say anything. Silence sat between them and Annie felt the nonverbal cue Jane wanted her to go. She needed to draw more from the woman, do some mental and physical digging around, but if she pushed too hard, Jane would grow suspicious and clam up.

"I've got an early call," Jane said.

"Oh, of course," Annie said, rising and starting toward the door. "I'll be on my way."

"It was decent of you to bring me dinner and check on me. Not many people would have been so nice."

Annie shrugged. "Trying to earn wings."

"Why? More fun to earn horns." Jane laughed at her own joke before setting the bowl on the faux-wood dresser and following Annie to the door. "Well, thanks again."

"Sure," Annie said, stepping out where the outside light hummed and bugs swarmed her head. She ducked and glanced back at Jane. "See you around."

Jane smiled. "Be careful. Crazy people running around, you know."

With a final wave, Annie walked to her car, pressing the button that made it beep to life. She was bummed about not accomplishing much. Okay, so Jane had a narcissistic mother who pressured her to succeed. A dime a dozen. The woman hadn't seemed jumpy, tense or remotely suspicious. Annie had struck out.

She started the car and pulled onto the highway off I-49. Since a few gas stations clustered around the highway, Annie pulled into one to refill the tank of the rental car. Not many people were out; in fact, there was only one car and a motorcycle at Arby's. Big eighteen-wheelers sat silent, parked in a dark lot behind the truckers' gas station, as their brothers in transport whooshed by on the overpass, stirring the night air.

As Annie capped the tank, she caught movement out of the corner of her eye. A woman in a baseball cap crossed the highway, carrying a paper bag from the one of the convenience stores. Normally, Annie wouldn't have noticed, but the woman moved quickly with evident nervousness. She headed toward one of the cheap motels, head down, steps brisk. The yellow halo of the motel lights caught her profile as she furtively glanced over her shoulder and entered a room at the back of the motel.

Tawny.

Annie glanced at her watch. 10:17. The woman had to

be visiting Mick or someone else involved in the production of the movie if her nervousness was any indicator.

Despite what Annie believed, Tawny was stepping out on her husband.

Disappointment struck her as she pocketed the credit card and got back in the car. When she'd left earlier, Tawny and Carter had seemed to be getting along, laughing and pretending to be fussy diners as Spencer served up Play-Doh spaghetti and hot dogs. They'd looked almost happy. So why would Tawny sneak out to hook up with Mick Manners? Sure, the guy was good-looking and somewhat darkly charming, but he had a worn look about him. Disillusioned, cynical and bored. Like a faded rock star who'd partied too hard. Like that John Malkovich character from *Dangerous Liasons*. Jaded.

Carter was arrogant, sure, but he loved his wife. Annie could see that.

Briefly she debated going to the hotel and snooping around to see who the actress might be meeting, but Tawny cheating wouldn't be related... Or would it? She needed to think about what this meant to her case.

Tomorrow.

Tomorrow she'd see Nate and maybe he could get someone to check out Mick—and hopefully get a firm lead. She needed to feel as if she mattered to the case, and wasn't just the bodyguard. She missed having an investigative partner—someone with whom to bounce ideas, to spout theories and have her back.

Tomorrow she'd tell Nate about Tawny. About Jane and her mother, her barren womb and her grudge against her best friend.

Tomorrow she'd catch a break. She felt it in her bones.

CHAPTER SIXTEEN

THE PHONE RANG EARLY in the morning, waking Nate from heavy sleep. He grabbed the cell phone from his nightstand and grumbled "This better be damned important" into the receiver.

"I can't do this," she said.

At first he'd thought it was Annie, but then the accent hit him. Sally Cheramie. Or Della. His sister.

"Sorry," he said, staring at the blinking red numbers on his alarm clock. The power had gone out sometime during the night. He sat up, allowing the sheet to fall on the floor, padded naked across the room and squinted at his watch. 7:08 a.m. Too damn early to deal with this even though he knew he'd have to take it off his backburner at some point. Picou had hounded him like a mockingbird after a cat. He'd dodged the pecking long enough. Della had come to him. "What can't you do?"

"This. This whole I-have-a-new-family thing. I can't. My *grandmere* is sick and she doesn't know about you. About the Dufrenes. She thinks I'm her real granddaughter. That's what Sal told her, and she had no reason not to believe him…or maybe she didn't want to. I don't know." Her voice shook and she sounded like a jumper he'd once talked down off an overpass. It had ended well, but had been dicey for a good ten minutes.

"Deep breath, okay?"

He heard her inhale then exhale. "She called me yesterday."

"Who?"

"Your mother. I mean, my mother. Picou."

Irritation flooded him. He'd told the infernal woman to give it time. "You have to understand how excited she is. She had you ripped from her and has been waiting over twenty years—"

"I know," Sally interrupted. Or was it Della? Either way, the woman on the other end was in tears. "My *grandmere's* in organ failure. She's dying and I can't do this to her. I can't tell her I'm not a Cheramie."

He closed his eyes and counted to ten. He had to choose his words carefully and not fly off the handle like his father would have done. "You don't have to tell her anything, okay?"

There was a long pause. He could hear her thinking. "Okay."

"But, you have to do what's right. You didn't ask for this to happen to you, but when the lab technician let it slip you weren't related to Enola Cheramie, things were set in motion. They can't be undone, Della."

"Don't call me that," she said, her voice stronger. Fierce. "My name is Sally, and I never should have called Dennis at the sheriff's office."

"But you did, and now even if it's hard, you have to move forward and be fair to our family. We loved you, we lost you and we've found you again."

Silence sat on the line. He studied the red flashing numbers on the alarm clock before picking it up and fiddling with it, resetting it so it would chirp the next morning and get him to the station on time.

"I know. I do. But it's complicated."

"Yeah, it is, and it's going to get worse. We haven't told

anyone beyond my, I mean our, brothers and Lucille. Once word gets out about you, people are going to talk. It will be a sensational news item, maybe even national press. We're going to deal with a lot of crap."

"Don't tell, Nate. Please. Not until my *grandmere* is stronger. She's not doing well, and I don't think she can take the idea I'm not hers."

He paused, weighing his words. "But you are hers, Della. And you're ours, too. She raised you and, I'm presuming, loved you. Even she can understand how you feel…and how we feel."

"Maybe," she whispered, "but please, I know it's hard and maybe it's wrong, but can I please have a bit more time? I'll come to Bayou Bridge soon. I promise."

He wanted to yell at her, but he knew her world had been rocked. He pictured his mother, the way her eyes had flooded with relief and joy, and knew Della couldn't wait much longer. "Yeah, we won't tell the world, but you need to come to Beau Soleil. For our mother's sake."

Again, there was a long pause. "Okay. I'll come, but I won't make any long-term promises. I'm not sure I want to—" She broke off. "I don't know if I can be called Della. Don't know if I'm ready to be the girl you lost. I'm me. Not her."

"None of us is asking you to give up who you are. We're asking you to give us a chance. We all have to go slowly." He congratulated himself on restraint. He really wanted to tell her to get her ass to Beau Soleil so his mother could finally heal, so the smile could finally reach her eyes and stay there. He wanted to tell her to stop being selfish. But he didn't. Because he didn't know anything about his long-lost sister…nor about what she felt. He'd always been a Dufrene. Always had an identity. So he bit his tongue. "If your grandmother is stable enough, why not drive up this weekend? You said you have a boyfriend, right? See if he might escort you to the Arch Angels Feast Day at St. Aquinas."

"Will you be there?"

"Yeah, I'm on the committee. Mom is chairing the event so she can't have a meltdown when she meets you. Abram won't be there—ULB's playing Florida—and Darby's still in Spain."

She sighed. "Okay. I can do this. I'm scared as hell, but I can do it."

"Of course you can. You're a Dufrene," he said.

This time she didn't correct him. Instead they confirmed times for a meet-up at Beau Soleil before going to St. Aquinas for the festival, where there would be a shrimp boil and several crafts booths, plus bouncies for the kids. Perfect time for strangers to be in town. No one would think it odd they hosted friends or a cousin or two, especially since Picou chaired the committee.

Nate hung up and turned the shower on. He had a full day ahead—one that didn't need the complication of long-lost sisters or the comparative prices of bounce-house rentals.

No, he couldn't think about those things.

Because today he'd figure out who in the hell had been sending the threats to the Keene family.

Because one thing was certain—whoever it was was in his town.

THE FRENCH RESTAURANT on the main drag was closed at two, as was tradition in the small villages of France. The owner, Madame Jacqueline, bustled in the back cleaning up from lunch while Nate and Annie hunkered at a table for four, notes and files spread out before them.

Annie took a sip of the decaf coffee Madame Jacqueline had placed in front of her and eyed the doberg cake sitting in front of Nate. Seven layers of yellow cake covered in chocolate ganache. She should have asked for her own piece.

"You can have a bite," Nate said, not bothering to look up.

"I shouldn't," she said, trying to refocus on the lab report from the second threat—the one with the dead mockingbird.

"It's worth it. Jacqueline makes the best."

"Oui," Jacqueline called out, clinking glasses together behind the bar.

Annie grabbed the fork and stole a bite. She felt speechless for a moment. It was that mind-blowing.

"Told you," Nate said, jotting something down on her notes. She was surprised he could even read her chicken scratch.

"Yeah. Mind-blowing," she said, licking the fork.

"Don't do that," he warned, his gaze meeting hers above the piece of paper he held in his hand. His brown eyes had melted into chocolate pools of want. It made her pelvis hum. Not good.

She tossed the fork onto the plate. Its clatter broke the moment.

"Thank you," he said.

She glanced out the window at tourists hurrying by. Busy for a Wednesday. Jacqueline had told her in broken English that many came in the fall because the summer was too hot. Today a ladies' church group from Denham Springs antiqued along the crowded storefronts lining the Bayou Tete. Several paused, peering in to see why the bistro was closed.

"Okay, let's go over what we know and what we don't know," she said.

"We don't know who the person threatening Spencer is."

"Uh, yeah. But let's go over the suspects."

"Mick is out. He has an alibi for the night you were attacked."

"I wasn't necessarily attacked, plus I still have my eye on him. Besides, what's his alibi?"

He glanced up, his expression changing, growing fierce. "Anything that leaves you looking the way you do we call assault. And Gemma Dubois is his alibi."

"What was he doing with— Oh." Anne nodded. "I see."

Annie tapped the table. "You read Jimmy's report?"

"He thinks Jane is jealous of Tawny. Big deal."

"But it's not mere jealousy. It's deep-seeded anger."

He shrugged. "I'm not buying it. We'll need something concrete to get a search warrant for her hotel room. I can bring her in for questioning, but we don't have enough to move a judge. She's barren. That's it. Probably one or two others in the production company with fertility issues. Doesn't seem like motive to me."

She frowned. "Well, you weren't there. You didn't see the way she looked, and it's not just the not-having-babies thing. It's Carter. Tawny snaked him from Jane. Tawny got the roles, the diamond and the Beverly Hills dream. Jane got a douche commercial."

Nate made a face. "I'll concede that point, so maybe."

Annie nodded.

"I've read through your files from Sterling, and I see this Rudy guy as a viable suspect. Any chance he's hanging around down here?"

Annie shook her head. "He was in Oregon filming during the initial threat and has since popped up in Indiana visiting for his brother's wedding. He's off the grid as a suspect."

Something flitted into her mind and skipped away again before she could grab it.

"What?"

She shook her head. "I don't know. Just have this thought that keeps flirting with me, but I can't pin it down. Something's been bothering me but…"

Annie hated that feeling—knowing something that was in the back of her mind. An elusive question.

Nate grimaced but said nothing. He had to know what she meant since he'd spent countless hours in investigation. Nothing worse than feeling so close to a break but having it dance away.

"So I see you have background on many of the key employees at Keene Bandit Productions. Any interviews conducted with number crunchers, administrative assistants, or other personnel still in L.A.? Anyone there nursing a grudge against Tawny? Some lonely secretary who had her sights on golden boy?" he asked.

"No. Not that we could tell." She bit her lip. "You did some phone interviews with family, but what about past romances? High school grudges?"

"Takes a lot of manpower and time. Right now we're relying on Tawny and Carter being honest with us about their past. We feel as though they are, but sometimes people hold things back, even inconsequential things."

They stared at the files in front of them.

Nate glanced at her. "Let's allow things to marinate and get out of here for a bit."

Something fluttered in her stomach. His subtle cologne had played with her senses for the past hour, not to mention the accidental touches as they passed files between them. She wanted to ignore the desire unfurling in her belly, but it was damned hard to do with the way his presence dominated the space. She'd spent a good three minutes studying his hands. The well-manicured nails, the crinkly hairs on the back, the veins—all of which made her yearn for them on her body. The craziness was back. "And do what?"

Her question brought a sharp glance. Then heat. Lots and lots of heat.

"Not what we want to do."

She smiled. "So?"

"Let's go to church."

She laughed. "Now, that's definitely on the opposite end of the spectrum. What are we going to do there? Confession?"

He snorted and started gathering up the papers in front of them. She followed suit, tucking her laptop into the side of her small rolling suitcase and fastening the luggage lock so prying eyes couldn't see her true purpose in working for the Keene family. "We could, but I'm not sure I'm altogether sorry for what we've done."

She glanced up. How could he not be sorry about their lapse in judgment? The ramifications of their indiscretion were tucked in the back of her mind, but they came out to float up front during the quiet moments in between everything else she had on her mind.

"Probably the best place to keep my mind off sin, and it's a great place to sort things out. Maybe something will occur to us. Something that will give us a new angle to work." He snapped his leather accordion file and dropped a twenty-dollar bill on the table. "Besides I'm on the committee for the Arch Angels Feast Day this Saturday. It's kind of a big deal around here. We'll have people from all over, including my newly found sibling."

Annie raised her eyebrows. "She's coming?"

He nodded. "I hope. I haven't told Mom yet. Scared to get her too stirred up. She's the committee chairperson, but I've got some things to check on at St. Aquinas. I may need your expert opinion."

"Huh?"

"You know, as a nanny. I got bounce-house problems."

"You're joking, right?"

He smiled and called out to Madame Jacqueline. "Later, Mademoiselle. Thanks for the cake and coffee. The best in the parish. If you ever leave that old coon-dog Frank, I'll make an honest woman of you."

"You are a rascal, Lieutenant. Somezing I admire in a man." The older woman grinned and wagged a finger as he opened the door for Annie. She waved her thanks to the French café owner. The coffee had been divine and she didn't want to think about how much she'd have to run if she'd eaten more of the cake.

"Ride with me?" Nate asked, unlocking the doors of his SUV with the remote.

She nodded, opening the trunk of her rental sitting next to his and setting the rolling suitcase with her files inside. She grabbed her sunglasses and slipped inside the already cool interior of Nate's car.

They didn't talk as Nate wove through the small town streets. They didn't need to. There was a comfortable kinship between them frosting over the throbbing desire they had for one another.

Nate pulled in front of an old chapel, framed by the ever-present twisted live oaks with their lacy shawls of moss. The stained-glass cathedral window was subdued in the bright midafternoon light, but would likely be spectacular from within when the sun set through the multifacted colored glass. The weathered white stone of the façade seemed to hold Gothic secrets, and the double doors were held open as if inviting passersby to lay down burdens and come inside. Annie loved it on sight.

"My church," Nate said, climbing from the car and waving with flourish. In his eyes she saw his love for the quaint building before them. "St. Aquinas."

She stepped from the car. "It's beautiful."

They walked toward the open doors as Annie took in the intricate scrollwork framing the doors, along with the frolicking cherubs. The architecture was very European, almost if transposed from a village in Italy or France.

"His great-great-grandfather built it," the voice said from behind them. They spun to find a priest gazing up at the church, a twinkle in his bright green eyes.

"Father Benoit," Nate said, holding out a hand.

The young priest took it. "Nate."

Then he turned to Annie and offered his hand. "Phillip Benoit."

"Annie Perez," she said, hating herself for lying to a man of the cloth—the best-looking man of the cloth she'd ever met. Father Benoit looked about thirty with dark hair, a strong chin and broad shoulders. He had to have the local ladies clamoring for a shot at the confession booth. "I'm—"

"Annie's staying with my mother. She's the nanny for the Keene family and generously agreed to give us her expert opinion on the children's activities."

Annie thought Nate very restrained for not laughing as he blurted the last statement. Expert opinion was stretching it by a mile. She nodded like a trained seal.

"Glad to meet you, and thanks for coming with Nate. He should have attended the first committee meeting and he wouldn't have ended up in charge of children's activities," Father Benoit said with a laugh before turning to Nate. "By the way, I got emails from two different companies about doing the jumpy blow-up things, and they're both under the impression we want all their bouncers for the day."

Nate's expression reminded her of the time her father had been constipated. "Great."

"Let's go inside." The priest shooed them up the concrete steps and into the church where the dimness blanketed them in welcome air-conditioning. Father Benoit closed the doors behind them, trapping inside a mesmerizing space. A full Raphaelite mural graced the expanse of the high arched ceiling while worn mahogany pews gleamed with what smelled like lemon oil. Candles flickered fervent prayers while soft lights illuminated the beauty of the altar.

"The exterminators just left. Those pesky sugar ants, God's creatures or not, have caused way too many problems for the parishioners. I always air out. Never know about those chemicals." Father Benoit motioned them toward the altar, through the room where the sacristy and vestments sat and into his inner sanctum, which was vastly different from the holy beauty of the sanctuary. The priest's office was very minimalist with cheerful modern art.

"Sit," he said, settling himself behind his desk, unwrapping a lollipop before offering them one from his candy stash sitting on the corner of the desk. Both she and Nate waved them off. Father Benoit shrugged, jabbed the grape lolly in his mouth and propped his brown bucks on the desk. He pulled the treat from his mouth and used it as a pointer. "Now, let's go over the schedule and make sure you have everything set for the children's activities and the shrimp boil. Both companies are sending someone to meet with me, but this is yours to handle. I'll give you the numbers for the bouncer rentals."

Nate slid his eyes to Annie. "Sure you want to help?"

"Do I have a choice?"

Father Benoit looked puzzled, but charged forth, pulling out a list and checking and double-checking all that would go on in the next few days. Annie listened with half an ear, the rest of her focused on Nate and what the devil was going on between them. She'd petitioned him to let whatever they had between them simmer until after they found the person threatening Spencer, but things kept bubbling over. It seemed only a matter of time before they found themselves drunk with passion, consumed by overflowing emotions. She didn't want to end up sprawled under a tiki bar hunting for her panties again.

The major question: Was it more than sex between them? She thought so. But was it enough to pin her hope for a future on?

The thought scared her.

Great irony of her life—Anna Mendes, fearless in the face of threat, able to stare down the barrel of a rifle or tangle with an unfeeling predator, was afraid of having her heart broken.

She could step outside her body and see why—the death of her mother, the absence of her father, the colossal disaster of an engagement—and know why she feared hurt, but that didn't make it any easier to unlock the fortress she'd built around her.

"Annie?"

She jerked her head toward Nate. "Huh?"

"I asked if you think we need both the Beary bouncy-bear bouncer and the All Sports bouncer. They're the same shape."

Annie narrowed her eyes. "Does it matter?"

Nate and Father Benoit looked at each other and shrugged.

"You're a woman," Father Benoit stated as if that explained everything.

"And?"

"You're supposed to know about this stuff." Nate shoved an advertisement showing a range of blow-up bounce houses. She took the brochure, glanced at it and then back up at the men.

"I don't know. Um, why don't you get the Supreme Super Jumper? It's got a slide, an obstacle course and a bouncer."

Both men nodded and she almost laughed at the absurdity of her sitting in a Catholic church as an undercover nanny with a good-looking priest, the man she could love and a brochure of bounce-house rentals. All they needed was a bar and they'd be a joke of the day.

She handed the brochure back to Nate. "I'm going to take a walk."

Both men looked blankly at her.

"Um, to check on room for the bouncers." She needed to get away for a moment. Sitting next to Nate as if she were more than a temporary partner in solving a case made her feel weird. She needed air.

She didn't wait for either man to respond, merely walked out the door in which she'd entered. Stepping into the place where vestments and brass candlesticks awaited polish, she spied a screened door with a heavier door behind it and pushed through. It led to a small garden courtyard with a statue of what looked to be the Virgin Mary but could have been any other martyred saint. Water flowed cheerfully at her feet.

Annie crossed the garden, passing several benches and flowering urns before pushing through a creaking iron gate to the side lawn of the church. The lot was shaded by live oaks and flanked by a pea-gravel parking lot. Thick woods held back in places by aging brick partially enclosed the area to be used for the feast day. Orange port-o-lets hunkered far away near a stand of trees and two funeral home tents sheltered heavy folding tables. Several booths sat near the church while a huge barbecue pit bearing a purple-and-black panther paw squared things off toward the back.

As Annie closed the gate, something flashed beyond the perimeter. Someone was in the woods. She saw movement and then a large man moved in the open, peering at the setup. He almost looked as if he were canvassing the area.

Maybe he was one of the bounce-house guys scouting for the best spot. But why would he come out of the woods? Strange.

She started toward him.

When he saw her, the man jerked his head and took off running.

What the hell?

Her senses tingled and instinct kicked in.

People didn't run unless they had something to hide. She sprinted toward the outskirts, angling in the direction the man headed. Her forethought paid off, and she caught a glimpse of a fairly large guy in athletic shorts and T-shirt. He had dark hair closely shaven and fair skin. He moved pretty well but not as fast as Annie. He shot through the trees, limbs cracking underfoot. When he attempted to vault a felled tree, his shoe hung and it slowed him down. Annie used it to her advantage, spying a huge limb off the fallen tree, hitting it perfectly and flying through the air toward the man scrambling to his feet.

She tackled him low and he went down, rolling in the dusty leaves. She held on, clamoring up his body, reaching for his arms in classic takedown procedure. She wasn't fast enough. He got a hand up and swept her off to the side. She jumped to her feet and tackled him again as he tried to lung away.

"Freeze," she said, grabbing for his hand. She missed again and instead snapped his waistband. Something fell to the ground as she managed to get a hold on his wrist. "Freeze!"

But the man didn't cooperate. Instead he swung his

elbow, hitting her hard in the chest, sending her sprawling backward, skidding on the fallen leaves. She tripped over a root and fell hard on her ass, trapping one leg behind her. Before she could jump to her feet, he'd sprung free, disappearing into the dense foliage. She finally gained her balance and rose, but her foot wobbled. She'd twisted her ankle.

"Shit," she muttered, grabbing onto the trunk of the fallen tree and steadying herself. She wiggled her foot. Not too bad, but she wouldn't catch up to the guy. She sighed, cursing her bad luck.

She heard Nate coming before she saw him. He held his gun at his side and when he caught sight of her, he applied his brakes, sliding on the leaves carpeting the wooded area much as she had. He righted himself and an arched a questioning brow.

"He got away," Annie said, pointing toward where the man had disappeared into the woods.

"Who?"

She shrugged. "Not sure, but he didn't want to be caught."

Nate holstered his gun before vaulting the tree as easily as an Olympic athlete and following the path the man had taken. She slumped against the rough bark of the tree, her hands trembling with a surge of adrenaline, her breathing ragged from exertion.

She'd forgotten she was no longer FBI. Old habits die hard and all that. Sweat dripped in her eyes. As she swiped them with the hem of her t-shirt, her gaze caught on what the man had dropped.

Her gun peeked out from behind a large maple leaf.

The realization slammed her—that was the guy who had taken her gun several nights ago. He was the person sending the threats. She almost reached out to grab her weapon before remembering the guy hadn't worn gloves. There was a good chance they could get prints off the piece.

Nate crunched back into view, drawing her attention from the gun lying in the leaves. He shook his head. "He made it to a dirt road. Had a car and was halfway down the road before I broke out of the woods. Plates were covered in mud, so I didn't make the tags." Nate slumped next to her, breathing hard, wiping sweat.

"He's the guy."

He slid his eyes to meet her gaze. "The guy making threats?"

Annie toed the maple leaf off the gun. Filtered light hit the barrel glinting like a clue in a movie. "My gun fell from his waistband."

"Ah, hell. We could have had him."

She nodded. "Yeah, but we'll get the bastard. He wasn't wearing gloves, and we've seen him. We can ID him."

They both sat in silence, the enormity of the situation soaking in.

"What was he doing? At a church?" Annie asked.

"No clue. Doesn't make sense, but none of this does. I need to get back to the station, call Blaine and get a sketch artist to sit with you. We'll plaster this guy over several parishes and see if we can get a hit." He pulled a kerchief from his back pocket and bent toward the gun.

"You carry a handkerchief? Who does that? It's not hygienic."

He wrapped the white linen around the stock of the gun then checked the safety, before tucking the cloth around the entire firearm. "I always carry one for such cases as this."

She almost smiled, but her ankle had started throbbing. It was a slight sprain, but it would be no picnic trudging back to the church. She took a step, winced, then took another, determined to get back and assess what they now knew.

"You're hurt?" he asked.

"I fell and caught my foot behind me."

"Hold this," he said, carefully handing her the wrapped gun. Then he scooped her into his arms.

"Whoa," she yelped, unable to steady herself because she held the best piece of evidence they'd obtain for nailing the bastard. "I can walk."

He nodded, starting through the woods, heading back in the direction they'd come. "Yeah, but we'd get there on Christmas. I want to run the latents and get a sketch drawn up. Enjoy the ride."

How could she not enjoy the man's arms around her? Even just a little bit. Her heart pounded with excess adrenaline as sweat rolled down her back. Sticks and leaves tangled in the wild corkscrew curls stuck to her sweaty face, and she was pretty certain she smelled like dirt, but she'd never been carried in such a manner, especially not by a man who could claim her soul.

So even if she should be focused on the case, she enjoyed the feel of his heart beating against her breast, the way his five o'clock shadow made him look even sexier and the smell of citrus cologne mixed with hot, perspiring male.

Father Benoit met them in the clearing of the church grounds. "What happened?"

"Annie saw something and then she tripped and twisted her ankle. Women," Nate said with a smile. Annie elbowed him in the ribs, causing him to grunt and set her down.

"Why is she holding a gun?"

Annie lowered her weapon, still carefully protected by the clean white linen. "I found this in the woods."

"Good gracious," Father Benoit said, which sounded very odd coming from such a vital, young dude's mouth—priest or not.

Nate raised a brow, a habit that was both annoying and

oddly seductive. Father Benoit cleared his throat. "Guess Sister Mary Regina is rubbing off on me. I meant to say 'What the hell?'"

"Better," Nate said, steadying Annie with a hand on the elbow. She handed him the gun.

Father Benoit stared at the wrapped firearm. "Who do you suppose had a gun in those woods? Nothing back there for miles, except an old oil pump. Kids sometimes park and make out. Think one of them was screwing around with a gun? Or do you think it might be a weapon used in a crime of some sort?"

Nate shrugged. "Won't know until we run some tests on it and trace the number, so we better get going, Padre. Don't worry about Saturday. Everything will go smoothly. Picou is on it."

They said goodbye and Annie managed to walk gingerly to the car. She slid into the heated car facing the afternoon sun, and felt an urgent need to get back to Spencer.

The guy had a face and now the threat felt even more real. The guy was here in Bayou Bridge, up to something but ready to do whatever it took to remain at large. If she'd been faster and less clumsy, she could have caught him and it could have been over. But she'd failed. As had Nate.

Nate had already bagged the gun, using the kit in his trunk. He climbed into the car and cranked it, punching up the AC. "We need to secure Spencer before we go to the station. Call Tawny and ask if he can come with us to the station. We'll fingerprint him and give him a fake badge while you meet with the sketch artist. I don't want him out of our sight. Time to lock him down."

She nodded. "We missed this guy today. Let's make damn sure we don't miss again. You need to pull strings with the lab to get this guy made. By the looks of him, I'd say he's in the system."

Nate pulled from the curb and headed toward Beau Soleil. Annie put in a call to Tawny, who sounded frazzled enough to agree to whatever Annie suggested as long as it meant taking Spencer off her hands. She knew how Tawny felt. As much as Annie adored Spencer, he could drive a woman to drink.

Kids.

Can't live with them, can't let a lunatic take them.

CHAPTER SEVENTEEN

THE NEXT DAY NATE SAT at his desk studying the report from the parish crime lab.

Sean Shaffer. Six-foot-two, two-thirty and wanted for hot checks and forgery in Cobb County, Georgia. Affiliated with a biker gang, the twenty-seven-year-old had served time for drug possession with intent. He'd been charged with aggravated assault and battery, but charges were dismissed. Sean Shaffer was not the sort of fellow a gal brought home for Sunday dinner.

So why was he in Nate's parish messing with the Keenes?

Nate hadn't a clue. He could find no associations with Carter or his family.

Wynn breezed in to the pit with a coffee cup in one hand and a stack of sketches in the other. "I've gone all over town and no one has seen this guy. One trucker said he might have seen him outside Lafayette, but he wasn't sure. He said the dude rode a fine-ass Harley and had a fine-ass broad in his bitch seat." He tossed the sketch on Nate's desk.

"We don't need the sketch anymore. We got a positive ID from the prints. Just sent the mug shot to everyone's P.D. Maybe we can freeze him, but I bet he's gone."

"No shit," Wynn said, sinking into his desk chair. "So who is he?"

"Not sure. I put in a call to Kennesaw P.D. One of the

guys there said he was a local punk who'd spent year after year getting into trouble. They think he was in on a meth lab, but couldn't make him on it. He did a little time. Nothing hard. Associates are still stinkin' it up in Cobb County and haven't seen Shaffer in months."

Wynn thumbed through the report. "So how's he connected with Keene?"

"No clue. I called the FBI guy Keene's been pushing on this case. Also put in a call to Hollywood division to see if they can hunt something up on this dirtbag." He'd also talked to Ace, Annie's boss, and given him the information. He had a feeling the case meant much more to the man. Meal tickets had value and their firm would pull out all the stops to nail Shaffer.

"So…"

"If he's lying low and being careful, we got to smoke the bastard out. Bayou Bridge P.D. and every guy in our department are on alert. Got guys rousting motels and bars as we speak. If he's still here, we'll find him."

Wynn stuck a toothpick in his mouth and eyed his wife who tapped on a computer. "I hope this don't turn out bad. We need to do this by the book or we'll have spit on our neck for all the breathing people will be doing. Anything you need to tell me?"

Nate glanced up. "No. Think I'm holding back?"

"You're holding something. I've been with you too long to not know."

Nate shrugged. He didn't want to reveal anything about Annie to Wynn. He trusted the man with his life. He just didn't trust him not to tell his wife. Kelli lacked self-control at times. It was one of the things that had hooked Wynn. He clearly loved the way his wife embraced everything with wild abandon. That and her cavernous cleavage.

Nate wanted everything between him and Annie secret.

Maybe later they could creep out from their blanket of anonymity. And then creep back under the blankets for some responsible fun. Maybe. "Everything's cool."

"Right." Wynn spun in his chair and tapped a few keys on his computer. "You never told me what you found out on that Cheramie chick. Didn't you go down to Lafourche?"

Hell. Nate took a deep breath. Too much going on. Sally Cheramie would be there in two days. How could he keep everything under wraps? Annie's true identity. Sally's true identity. The damn bounce-house owners who were now at war over who was hired first. Picou. Spencer. A possible unplanned pregnancy. Like a snowball rolling downhill, everything meshed together to form something he couldn't control. He felt as if he stood in its path with no hope of saving himself.

It was a helluva way to feel.

Everything coming to a head.

Bursting. Exploding. Raining shit on him.

"Wynn, you trust me, don't you?"

Wynn looked back at him. "Always been integral."

"Give me some room on this. I'm asking not in a work-related capacity, but as your friend. Things are coming unraveled and I can't stop them."

Wynn looked hard at him and nodded. "I got your back."

At least someone did.

Nate pushed his chair back, tossing his phone messages to the side. Abram had called once. Darby not at all. The other calls dealt with a few active cases and many cold cases—something he'd had no time for. Guilt flooded him. Radrica Moore waited. Along with Emile Brossette, Timmy Hargon, Sheridan Kinney. So many waiting for him to figure out what had happened to them.

But he had no time for the dead.

The living demanded his present.

He grabbed his gun. "I'm heading out to Beau Soleil."

"Later," Wynn said, not looking from his screen. Nate saw him searching for info on Sean Shaffer. Maybe Wynn would have luck. "I'll catch up with you. Oh, and Abram called—said you weren't answering your phone. He wanted to know if his sister was still coming this weekend."

Nate slammed his hand on the desk. "Damn it."

Wynn turned with a shit-eating grin. "No, I didn't tell Kelli. She'd be planning a damn party. But you should have told me. Trust, and all that."

Nate shook his head. "Abram talks too much. It's going to get him in trouble one day."

"You really found her? No kidding?"

Nate nodded. "Yeah, but it's complicated. We're trying to get our feet under us. She's coming to see Picou this weekend, during the feast. We're going to hope everyone thinks she's a distant relation or something."

His friend nodded. "I'll be your smoke screen. I'm your guy, you know?"

"I know."

Nate turned and walked out of the station, feeling as if the chill of the giant snowball had permeated his defenses—picking up speed, erratically changing course but destined to crash into him.

He shivered despite the heat.

ANNIE WAS LOCKED AND loaded. And sweating her butt off. She wore a thin jacket over her jeans and tank, but nothing was lightweight enough to keep her from sweating like a thoroughbred after the derby. Still, the gun beneath her navy blazer made her feel secure.

Of course, it wasn't her gun. Hers was tagged and sitting in an evidence locker, with no prints other than Shaffer's and a serial number belonging to Anna Mendes. Nate had suggested it had been stolen, which was true, if not mildly fabricated. Only a matter of time before everyone found out Anna Mendes was a former FBI agent and current employee of Sterling Investigations and Security. Her undercover status was in jeopardy.

The Sig-Sauer P226 she now carried was one of Nate's. Twice as expensive as a Glock and heavier in her holster, the gun was fairly accurate with a quick trigger. He'd loaned it to her earlier, right before he went in to talk to Picou about Sally Cheramie's visit. She hadn't seen him since.

It felt good to have a partner again.

"Annie, let's play soccer some more."

"Let's not, bud," she said. The late afternoon shadows fell across the lawn, but it was still Louisiana hot. She wondered when it cooled down in this neck of the woods. Sure would make wearing a blazer easier. "It's too hot and I'm ready for supper."

Spencer frowned. "I don't want supper. I wanna play soccer."

Tawny and Carter would be shooting well into the night for the next four days, then the movie would wrap. In one way, it worked out well Spencer's parents were abnormally busy. Annie now wanted to be with Spencer at all times. Unfortunately, Spencer wanted to do things outside involving her running, kicking and tweaking the ankle she'd already banged up.

"I'll fix you mac and cheese," she said, using his favorite temptation.

Spencer kicked the ball at her. "No!"

Annie placed her hands on her hips. She'd had enough. She didn't know anything about raising children, she'd admit to as much, but she knew how a decent human should behave—and Spencer needed to learn he wasn't the center of the universe. She picked up the ball and walked toward the shady porch.

"Hey, give me the ball."

She didn't stop, didn't speak.

"Annie!" Spencer screeched. She heard him stomp his feet. She stomped hers, too. Up the porch steps. She sank in a rocking chair, placed the ball on her lap and watched as Spencer threw himself down on the grass and pitched a royal fit. It was quite the spectacle. Finally, after several minutes, he looked up at her, his cheeks wildly flushed, his hair plastered to his head.

Not failing to do her job, she watched the perimeter like a hawk while the little boy rose to his knees. Finally, he stood and started walking toward the porch.

She waited.

He clomped up the steps, wiping his nose against his short-sleeved shirt, before stopping in front of her. "Please?"

She shook her head. "No."

His lower lip trembled and she felt something tug at her insides. She almost rose, but didn't. "Why not?"

"Because you're not acting nice. You're acting like a spoiled brat, and no one likes a spoiled brat."

"I'm not a brat," he sniffled, tears filling his eyes. She'd never seen a kid cry so easily. His damp eyes narrowed. "What's a brat?"

"Someone who insists on getting his way all the time, every day, and when he doesn't, he throws himself down on the ground, kicking and screaming until everyone is miserable. No one wants to play with a brat."

The boy cocked his head like an inquisitive puppy. "But I thought you liked soccer?"

She nodded. "I do, but I'm hot, tired and my ankle hurts.

I don't want to play. I want you to consider how others may feel and alter your behavior to show you care about them."

"Oh," he said, walking toward the other rocker and sitting down. "I didn't know you had a hurt ankle."

"Because you don't listen. I told you this morning."

At that Spencer frowned. Such a little man already. Didn't want to hear he was in the wrong. Probably would never stop for directions either. "I listen. I just didn't hear you."

"Oh, well, that explains it."

They sat for a moment. Annie felt the gun against her side, the back of her tank stuck to her like new skin, and mosquitos buzzed in her ears, but she didn't move.

"I'm sorry," he said, propping his elbows on his dirty knees and looking plaintively at her.

She nodded. "I accept you apology. Saying you're sorry is very non-brat-like."

"I don't want to be one of those guys. When I go to kindergarten, I want kids to play with me and stuff."

"If you learn to listen to others and use their ideas sometimes, you shouldn't have a problem." She stood and held out a hand. "Ready for mac and cheese?"

He took her hand and turned, wrapping his arms around her thighs. "You are a good nanny, Annie. I'm glad Mom fired Sophie. She never played with me at all and she called me a brat all the time. I didn't know what that was."

Annie didn't know whether it was all the crap that had been going on, or the thought she'd done something right for a change, but emotion welled in her throat. She stroked Spencer's sweat-soaked head. "I'm glad I'm your nanny, too."

And for once she meant it.

Spencer dropped his arms and tilted his face to her. "I want extra cheese on my mac and cheese."

She crossed her arms and lifted an eyebrow.

"Um, please."

She smiled. "Okay."

They turned to go inside and found Nate watching them. His expression was warm, and something about his catching her having a good moment with Spencer rather than her normal incompetency pleased her. "Hey, Mom made spaghetti with Italian gravy for dinner."

Annie looked at Spencer. "Spaghetti and meat sauce."

He thrust both fists into the air. "Score!"

Spencer disappeared like free beer samples at a bar.

"Guess he was hungry," Nate commented, moving onto the porch and closing the door behind him. "I don't know why you think you're not good with kids. I overheard the conversation. Pretty good if you ask me."

"I didn't ask." She didn't want his praise. Or maybe she did and that's what made her feel so confused. Everything felt tense, as if she walked a minefield, expecting to be blown to smithereens. "Sorry. I'm tense."

"Preaching to the choir," he said, sinking into the chair she'd occupied minutes before. "Picou has been dragging out all the family recipes since I told her about Sally coming for a visit. She's determined to make copies of her great-grandmother's praline recipe along with Uncle Reuben's shrimp creole. She made Aunt Cecile's Italian gravy and meatballs in celebration. Why would food matter?"

Annie leaned against the door frame. "Soothes her and she needs something to keep her hands busy. Food is comfort. My mother did the same thing. Made chocolate chip cookies every time she was upset or nervous."

He smiled. "I don't know much about your family."

She shrugged. "I don't talk much about them. My mother passed away and everything fell apart."

He didn't respond, maybe because he knew about things

falling apart, about holes unable to be filled. But all that had changed when he walked into that school nearly a week ago. He would no longer carry the burden of an empty place. Sally would fill that one when she finally realized she had a family who'd loved her once…one that would love her again. And Nate would carry guilt no longer.

She cleared her throat. "So, you hear from the lab?"

"Got a hit on the prints early this morning."

She stiffened. "You didn't tell me earlier."

"I am now. We've got uniforms canvassing the neighborhood surrounding the church. More hitting hotels surrounding I-49."

She felt aggravation creep up her spine. "You should have briefed me this morning. Instead I spent the day drawing stick figures and playing Candy Land. We're partners."

"In a way," he said, flicking leaves off the porch with the toe of his loafer. "You couldn't do anything. Your job is to stay with Spencer. It's the only thing that gives me comfort. I looked at your record. You were a good officer in the Air Force and a good agent. I know he's safe with you."

"You should have told me. My firm has files and this guy might be in them. You didn't even give me a name to check." She couldn't believe he was cutting her out of the investigation. What the hell? They'd worked together the whole day before, and her instincts to give chase to the suspect gave them the lead. So now he was taking over and giving her the babysitting job?

He shook his head. "I didn't see anything on a meth head named Sean Shaffer from Georgia. Besides I already sent the info to Ace this morning."

"You what?"

"Saved you the trouble of sending it to him. It was no problem. I've been intending to speak with him anyway. He said he'd run the dude through his—"

"We were working together," she said, unable to stop the flood of anger. He went over her head to her boss? How would that look to Ace? Like she was an incompetent fool who couldn't do her job well enough. Another woman who had to depend on a man to do it for her.

"You're angry?"

She glared at him. "No, why would I be? You reported information on my case to my boss. I'm sure he feels confident I'm handling things down here. Bet I get a gold star by my name for having my job done for me by the capable Nate Dufrene."

"I thought I was doing you a solid. This isn't about ego. It's about Spencer and solving the case."

"You think this is about my ego?"

He arched a brow.

"No, dumbass, this is about my job. I'm in the middle of a probationary period and I need to look like I can handle this without some other guy doing it for me. I make my own reports."

He stood. "You're acting irrationally."

"Irrationally? You're overstepping your bounds. I never told you it was okay to talk to my boss. This is my case." She jabbed her pointer finger into her chest. "Step off."

"This is my case. I wasn't stepping on your toes. Just doing my job. Expediency is critical at this stage and I took time to come here and give you an update. Because you feel sidelined doesn't give you the right to snap my head off."

Annie bared her teeth. "I knew there was a reason I didn't like you. You're an asshole."

Anger shone in his eyes. They were no longer warm and chocolaty. "Nice. I'm covering your ass and you're acting like Spencer. Do I need to give you a lesson on being a brat?"

"I know you didn't just say that," Annie said. Rage ate

at her and she wanted to hit him—partly because he was right. She felt sidelined and useless. Relegated to bodyguard status, no more important than Brick. But the other part of her was furious he'd failed to see what this case meant to her. It was her trial period, her key to a future with a firm of good standing, a ticket to getting her life back on track.

"Look, there's no need to get your panties in a wad over this, Annie. I'm sorry I didn't let you report to Ace. I didn't think it was a big deal."

She didn't want to talk to him anymore. Calling Ace and repairing the damage Nate had done was more important. This was her fault. Again. She'd let her emotions get in the way, and like a misty-eyed romantic, had forgotten she had one reason to be in Louisiana—and that was her job. She pulled the gun he'd loaned her earlier from the shoulder holster beneath her jacket, holding the stock out to him. He took it and looked up, confused. "I don't need this anymore. I can do my job without you."

Turning on her heel, she pushed through the screen door, refusing to acknowledge knot in the pit of her stomach, trying to forget she'd put her faith in a man who obviously didn't get who she was. Didn't matter his action had been unintentional. It was a wake-up slap to the face.

And she had a case to solve.

On her own.

Only then could she go back to California and start her life again.

Nate didn't follow her, and she didn't blame him. Maybe she had overreacted, but what he'd done had been worse. He'd taken what he knew and ran with it, leaving her behind kicking a damned soccer ball.

Whatever she and Nate had between them was over before it started. No need to discuss anything after they closed the case. If she didn't focus on her job and moving ahead, she'd get left behind. She'd already sacrificed her career once. She wouldn't make the same mistake twice.

So why did it feel like a piece of her had died?

Maybe because it had.

Her hope for something genuine and good with Nate had just withered. It left a bitter taste in her mouth.

But it was for the best.

She needed to go home. Forget Louisiana. Forget the hunky detective and his high-handed tactics. Absolutely. Soon Beau Soleil, the Dufrenes and the case would be a fading memory.

But then she remembered she could be pregnant with Nate's child.

She walked into the kitchen where Picou sat eating spaghetti with a child who probably wore more sauce than he'd eaten and wanted to cry.

But Anna Mendes didn't cry.

She sucked it up and moved ahead.

CHAPTER EIGHTEEN

THE FEAST DAY ARRIVED with no other developments in the case. Nate had gleaned some information but nothing leading to apprehending Shaffer. The man was in the wind.

Nate had done his own legwork, talking to a few people who had seen Shaffer around town, sometimes accompanied by a dark-haired woman. No one could describe her other than she dressed scantily, looked like an addict and had brown hair often covered by a baseball cap. One storeowner said she looked familiar but in a generic way. Whatever that meant.

Normally with such a description, he'd assume her to be a prostitute, but there were no working ladies in Bayou Bridge. Shaffer could've picked her up in Baton Rouge or Lafayette, so he'd sent a request for help to those cities, hoping for a bite.

So far, they'd made no progress.

But, this morning he'd take a small break. He had shrimp to boil, ladies to hoodwink into running the face painting booth, and a sister coming home for the first time in twenty-four years—even if Wynn had told everyone it was a cousin of the Dufrenes down from Monroe.

The weak morning sunlight hadn't broken through the clouds yet and reminded Nate of the rainy days they hadn't had in weeks. The sun would break soon, heating up earth that was already dry and crunchy. He needed to call the fire department before they started the fire for the boil. Thankfully, they'd scratched the plans for the *cochon de lait*.

Father Benoit met him at the church door. "Morning, Nate. Looks like the rain will hold off. I know we need it terribly, but I'm thankful the Good Lord didn't see fit to send it on the Arch Angels Feast Day."

"True. Maybe we'll get some later this week."

With the obligatory talk of the weather aside, they got down to business. Several parishioners were busy setting up more tents. A few vendors had come from around the area, selling candles, hot sauce and handmade lace. The Feast Day had originally involved only a picnic, but in typical Bayou Bridge fashion, it had evolved into something much grander. Bayou Bridge folks liked a reason to get together, cook and make merry.

Picou met him under one of the tents. His mother's excitement was palpable. "Have you heard from her?"

He couldn't resist. "Who?"

His mother punched him. Hard. "Don't mess with me, Nathan Briggs Dufrene."

He rubbed his arm. "No. I haven't spoken with her since Wednesday. I told her we'd meet at Beau Soleil around lunchtime. Once we get everything going here, we'll slip back home. She's bringing her boyfriend and hopefully they'll come to the festival and see the community. Might make her more comfortable to be around others. You have to remember how she feels, Mom. Be patient with her."

Picou's violet eyes flashed with irritation. "I will."

"I mean it. She's skittish. Treat her the way you did the injured fawn you found several years back. And try not to look all googly-eyed at her the whole time. I promised her we wouldn't let the cat out of the bag until she's ready."

His mother nodded. "I'll try, but I feel so full, like I'm bursting at the seams."

"I know, but this will be harder than you think for her."

His mother narrowed her eyes before turning away, pointing several men with tables toward what was to be the eating area. His mother was hardheaded and never liked to be told what to do.

Told what to do.

He did a lot of telling people what to do. It was his father in him, he supposed. So he was high-handed? Did that give Annie the right to treat him like an insufferable ass? Maybe. But he'd treated her like any other partner he'd ever had. Wynn had never accused him of cutting him out of an investigation, nor had anyone else. Partners consulted with one another, but they didn't seek permission to move forward when there was a lead. He'd never considered Annie would think he was undermining her when he'd called Ace. He'd only thought of the case.

Lord, he didn't understand women at all.

He tried to tuck the thought of Annie out of his mind, but her memory was as stubborn as his mother. He needed to talk to her. Apologize for going over her head, but she wouldn't return his phone calls. She meant what she said. She was through with him.

And that hurt more than he wanted to admit.

Luckily, his shrimp-boil experts showed up and took his mind off women and placed it squarely on the crustaceans awaiting their hot bath.

Three hours later, he sat with Picou on the porch of Beau Soleil, telling his mother for the fifteenth time that, no, she didn't look old, and "yes, the blue caftan was a good choice."

"I'm not sure. It's unconventional. Did she seem conservative to you? Should I have put on my linen pants with the khaki tunic?"

He had no idea what she was talking about. "You look fine, Mom."

Picou stared down the empty road. "She's not coming. She changed her mind."

He folded his hands over his stomach and tried to look calm. Picou had him in knots. "She'll come. She's a Dufrene. She's been curious, you can bet."

Silence fell, only to be broken by Spencer, whooping onto the lawn, followed by Annie.

Nate's heart pinged when he saw her. She wore jeans, a sleeveless orange shirt and a frown. Her hair curled in ringlets around her face and all he could think about at that moment was putting his lips on the delicate collarbone peeking out from beneath her blouse.

She parked her hands on her hip. "Spencer, I told you to stay in the back. Picou and Lieutenant Dufrene are busy."

Oh, it was Lieutenant Dufrene now.

Spencer ignored her and ran up the steps. "Annie says we can't go to the Feast Day. That it's dangerous. I want to go. Will you take me?"

Picou didn't take her eyes off the road. "You have to mind Annie, Spencer. She knows what's best for you."

"But I wanted to get my face painted like a tiger, and Lucille said they have cotton candy there. Please!"

Annie climbed the steps, not bothering to glance Nate's way, and grabbed Spencer's arm. "I said you have to stay in the back."

Spencer jerked away. "Not fair. You said we'd go to the festibal."

At that moment a Toyota Prius rounded the curve in the drive.

Picou sat at attention. "Oh, God, she's here. She came."

Nate rose, stepping around a wriggling Spencer, and walked toward the steps. He caught Annie's light floral scent on the breeze stirring through the oaks. Even though she was mad enough to spit at him, it somehow calmed him. He tapped Spencer on the noggin. "Do what Annie tells you to do."

The child's eyes grew big and he allowed Annie to take his hand and tug him toward the front door.

"Who's that?" Spencer said, digging his heels in once he saw the car stop in the graveled parking area.

Picou stood up, her hands clasped. "That's my daughter."

ANNIE HADN'T PLANNED ON witnessing the reunion between Della and Picou, but for some reason, she couldn't look away from the woman she'd grown so fond of in a few short weeks. Picou's face held a sort of ethereal light that spilled around her. The woman had talked of auras ever since Annie had been at Beau Soleil, and at that moment, Annie saw the older woman's aura—it was pure light.

She stopped tugging Spencer and watched as the doors of the small blue car opened. Nate walked down the stairs, toward it. A man stepped from the driver's side, offering his hand to Nate, who took it immediately. The man was whip thin and wore wire-rimmed glasses. He was handsome in a yuppy-accountant sort of way.

Then Della emerged from the passenger's side.

Annie heard Picou's intake of breath and couldn't stop herself from closing the screen door and watching the older woman see her grown daughter for the first time.

It was an intensely personal moment, but Annie couldn't go inside. If she left she'd miss seeing God's hand at work. Even Spencer fell silent.

Nate approached his sister and gave her a brief hug. She could see that the woman's smile was tremulous and her hands shook. Della wore her long dark hair in a low ponytail, silver hoops flashed in her ears. The sleeveless dress she wore, showing off elegant, tanned arms, was the exact color of the lavender still blooming along the walk. The three turned and moved toward the porch and Picou.

The Dufrene matriarch stood still as the crane Annie had once imagined her to be, watching, waiting with amazement on her face. Her lips tilted at the corners and pride shone in her eyes. Annie recalled the same look in her own mother's eyes. Maternal bliss.

Della climbed the steps, ahead of the two men. She saw Annie and gave her a small smile. "Hi, Annie. Nice to see you again."

Annie nodded. Her voice seemed stuck. Spencer grabbed her leg, uncharacteristically shy. Della looked down at him. "You, too, Mr. Spencer."

Then Della's gaze slid to her mother's.

Annie watched as Picou swallowed hard and tried to smile, failing. The older woman nervously licked her lips.

Della glanced back at the man who'd come with her and he gave her an encouraging nod.

She walked to her mother. "Hi, I'm—"

"You're beautiful," Picou said, tears choking her voice. She pressed a hand to her mouth, trying to quiet the suppressed emotion. She shook her head, swallowing convulsively, trying to hold herself together, but not quite achieving.

Della stood, unblinking, unsure. She extended her hand. "This is, well, it's—"

Picou nodded, but didn't speak. She reached out and took her daughter's hand. The older woman looked beyond words.

"I look like you," Della said. Tears sat like dew on her thick lashes.

Picou nodded. "You do."

Finally she dropped Della's hand and lifted both hands

to her daughter's face, framing it, smiling, not caring tears streaked down her face. "You always did get brown as a berry in summertime."

Della smiled and covered her mother's hands with her own. For a moment, the two women, so similar in stature, stood savoring the sacred moment of being together once again. Annie felt tears on her cheeks. She didn't even realize they'd spilled past her lashes.

No one else moved. They all were too entranced by the display in front of them.

Picou nodded at her daughter, dropping her hands. "This will not be easy for you, but you must know this is the happiest day of my life. I always professed it to be the day I gave birth to each of my children, but to lose one and then miraculously get her back is the most overwhelming, pure emotion I've ever experienced. You have come back to me, and I am satisfied with that for now."

Della pressed her lips together before swallowing. "I can't promise anything. It's like everything I am has changed and I'm on a Tilt-A-Whirl. Inside I feel out of control, like I can't stop things. Yet, I was the one who bought the ticket. I started all this."

"And thank goodness you did," Nate said.

"Is there a Tilt-A-Whirl at the festibal?" Spencer asked. "Wanna ride it with me, Annie?"

Della laughed and the tenseness, the sacredness of the moment was broken.

"Can we go? Please, Annie," Spencer asked again, letting go of her leg and looking up at her.

She grabbed his hand and opened the screen door again. "Come with me and stop the pestering."

Nate had looked good wearing worn blue jeans and a light blue polo shirt that made his skin look vibrant. He'd not shaved, instead leaving a scruffy sexy beard that reminded Annie of lazy mornings in bed, wrapped naked in sheets, languidly stretching—

She cut off her thoughts. Nate Dufrene might look good enough to gobble up, but he was also an arrogant, controlling man who could sidetrack her too easily. She needed to remember it was business between them. Well, not even that anymore.

She entered the house, shutting the door on the Dufrenes and their guests, ignoring Spencer's pleas as she dragged him to the kitchen. Maybe she could plug him up with food. Or *SpongeBob* on the little TV in the kitchen Lucille used to watch soap operas.

She sat him at the table and pressed the on button, finding the channel that played the show. Spencer stared in rapt attention, his festibal-going temporarily on the back burner.

Annie grabbed a honey bun from the snack basket and sat it in front of him. So much for being a good nanny. She went to the sink, grabbed a glass and filled it with water. Her throat hurt from the unshed tears as much as her mind throbbed with tangled images of Nate, Spencer, Jane and failure.

She'd tried to repair the damage done by Nate's presumptuousness. She'd called Ace, who didn't seem to think it a big deal the detective had contacted him with the break in the case. He also didn't sound impressed by Annie's effort, only relieved she'd managed to get the gun back. He'd run info on Shaffer but had come up empty-handed. The only info he'd obtained was Shaffer's rap sheet, which, though extensive, showed no leaning toward violence.

So what was the connection? Again, a fleeting thought nudged her brain, but she couldn't grab hold of the wisp that curled around her mind before evaporating like smoke.

"Annie?" Nate stood in the kitchen doorway.

She turned from the sink.

"They just picked Shaffer up in Little Rock."

She pressed a hand against her chest. "You're kidding."

He shook his head. "They found him passed out in some dive on the outskirts of the city. A Harley registered to Sean Shaffer was in the lot. He must have dumped whatever car we saw him in. Wynn's going up to talk to him. We'll charge him on assault and theft. Then we'll explore the threats. Maybe he'll get smart and confess."

"Did he say why he was doing this? Beyond money, of course. About why he—" she lowered her voice "—targeted Tawny and Spencer?"

"He was tanked and is sleeping it off. Wynn just left, so maybe we'll know more by this afternoon."

Annie felt a burn in her gut. Something didn't feel right, but there was little doubt Shaffer's prints were on her gun. They'd gotten the guy, so why did she feel as though they'd missed something. She nodded. "Thanks for sharing the info."

He nodded, but his eyes looked sad. "No problem."

For a moment, they stood silent, so much unsaid between them. So much that would remain so.

"So," she said, "I guess I'll see you around. Maybe this afternoon. Since they picked up Shaffer, I can probably take Spencer to the festival."

He nodded. "But until we talk to this guy and get the story, let's keep a close watch on him. See if Brick can accompany you."

"I don't need you to tell me how to do my job," she said, bristling despite the sense in his words. "I wouldn't go without being careful. But I would appreciate your sharing what you find out about Shaffer. If you don't mind."

"Why would I mind?" he said, pushing through the kitchen door without even saying goodbye.

Annie felt her heart break. This was what she wanted.

Distance between her and Nate. Yet, it felt so wrong. They'd been good together as partners. She'd sensed how well they balanced. In another time, another place they could have been really good together.

But it wasn't another time or another place. Reality always won over dreams. Her life was in California, hopefully still employed by Ace, working, building value, finding a small comfortable life for herself. She could live that way. Would have to live that way, remembering she wasn't a woman with girlish dreams of the perfect man who'd give her a perfect life. Anna Mendes was a realist.

"Okay, Spencer. Let's go to the festival."

The boy didn't answer because a squirrel with a glass bowl on her head was dancing the hula.

Yeah, reality trumped.

CHAPTER NINETEEN

THE FESTIVAL WAS CROWDED, not totally unexpected, but still presenting certain problems. Like the trash cans. They didn't have enough.

Nate lifted the clear plastic bag and took it to the Dumpster he'd had the foresight to rent. Too bad he'd miscalculated the trash-can situation.

All around him people laughed, yelled, and one particular toddler screamed. Apparently for cotton candy, if Nate's bleeding ears could be trusted.

He chanced a glance at his mother, where she sat beneath the canopy of a tree with Della and her boyfriend, Jason. She titled her head and listened as his sister talked. He'd never seen his mother at such peace, not even after the tranquility retreat she'd spent with an order of monks outside of Ponchatoula. Oddly enough, people steered clear of his mother, no one interrupting or barging in. He wondered how many people suspected the young woman with his mother was her long-lost daughter.

A glance around the festival site told him not many. Everyone seemed intent on having a good time with their own families, just as intended.

"Everything's going well," Father Benoit said, appearing at his elbow. Nate glanced at his friend. The priest wore shorts and a T-shirt reading Does This Shirt Make Me Look Too Catholic? on it. His running shoes were bright orange-and-green. He didn't look like a priest.

"Except we needed more trash cans and they ran out of bubbles in the tiny-tots' tent."

"But still, everyone looks happy, especially your mother. Who's the girl with her? Wynn said a cousin?"

"Something like that," Nate said, grabbing another bag from the box at the first aid and information table. He caught Annie and Spencer out of the corner of his eye. They were shooting water guns in a race to fill up a paper cup. Brick hovered nearby looking like a large dump truck. Spencer bit his lip concentrating on the task, while Annie encouraged him.

Regret pinged inside him, along with many other emotions. Everything pointed toward Annie being the woman made for him, but her stubbornness drove him nuts.

Still, he wanted her, with a longing he didn't understand.

"Excuse me, Father," he said, shaking out the plastic bag and heading toward the nearest can, which happened to be very near Annie and Spencer. He quickly relined the can, but before he could move over to his target, someone tapped him on the arm.

"Hey, there Lieutenant Dufrene," Jane drawled, batting her eyelashes. Tawny stood next to her, looking like an ad for a down-home fashion doll. She had high heels, cutoff jean shorts, a tight tank top and a cowboy hat perched on her blond locks. Jane was dressed in a similar fashion.

The parishioners and visitors all stared at the two actresses and he could hear the whispers.

"Carter told me they got the guy," Tawny said, with a genuine smile. "You don't know how much I appreciate all your hard work. It's like clouds have parted and let the sunshine back in my life."

He nodded, wishing Jane would take the hand she'd curled in the crook of his elbow away. Jane didn't budge. Instead she tugged him. "Come sit with me and Tawny.

Have you eaten yet? We just bought a boatload of tickets
for Spencer and have enough to spring for a beer."

"Yeah," Tawny chimed in, waving to Spencer, who ran
over, squealing about winning a piece of bubble gum. He
wrapped his arms about his mother's nicely-toned thighs
and beamed. "I owe you, after all. You've kept my birdie
safe."

She stroked Spencer's head. Annie stood several feet
away frowning at them. Something satisfying ignited inside
him when he noted it was mostly Jane she frowned at.

"It wasn't just me. A lot of people helped in this investigation." He looked purposefully at Annie.

"But I've been telling Tawny there was something mas-
terful in you. I knew you would find the guy," Jane said,
stroking his arm. He felt more than uncomfortable, but
liked the side effect of Jane blatantly coming on to him.
Jealousy was written all over Annie's face. He arched an
eyebrow at her, and her expression shuttered. She walked
their way, chin high, shoulders straight. Defensive.

"I didn't know you were coming to the festival, Tawny."

Tawny glanced at Annie. "I hadn't planned on it, but
Carter finished shooting ahead of schedule and wanted to
do some retakes of shots we weren't in, so what's a girl to
do with an afternoon off when there's a festival in town?"

Jane tittered. "Come to where we can find a drink and
a good-looking man. Say, who's that guy over there in the
orange running shoes? Is he single, by chance?"

Nate smiled. "Yeah, he's single."

Annie's lips twitched but the smile didn't make it to
her eyes.

"I wanna stay with Mommy," Spencer said, trying to
blow a bubble with the huge gum ball he'd crammed in
his mouth.

Annie looked at Tawny. The blonde shrugged. "Sure. I'll take you to get your face painted. Would that be fun?"

Spencer nodded his body.

Annie looked over her shoulder at Brick with a nod. "That's fine. I promised Picou I'd try some of the gumbo her friend made. I'll be with her if you need me. Have fun with your mom, Spencer."

She left without even bothering to say hello to him or Jane. Guess that was their punishment. And although he knew it wasn't funny, he smiled. Because whether Annie knew it or not, she'd told him exactly what he needed to know. She was jealous. She was still into him. And that renewed hope in him.

"Well, I've got more trash cans to empty. You girls have fun," he said, pulling away from Jane and heading for the overflowing trash can next to the beer stand. He noted Jane heading toward Father Benoit as Tawny took her son's hand and crossed over to the face painters.

He glanced back at Annie, who'd sat down at a table with Picou, Della and Jason.

Maybe he should try the gumbo, too. After he emptied the trash can, of course.

ANNIE WATCHED NATE. She didn't want to. Her eyes kept going his way of their own accord. It was as if she had no power over her body. She wanted his scent. His touch. And, oh, yes, his taste.

"Hungry?" Picou asked, shoving a bowl of steaming seafood gumbo in front of her. "Try this. My friend Gracie made it, using fresh oysters her son sent up."

Della nodded. "I've had good gumbo, but that's a great gumbo."

Annie obligingly slurped up a spoonful. Tasted like ashes, but she nodded. "Very good."

She watched as Nate passed a family, stopping to shake hands. Nate belonged in this happy town. He may have given up a career in a large hospital or morgue for running his family interests and chasing speeders, but he'd gained so much more. She could feel the goodwill of the community, and it made her sad. Sad for herself. That she could never have this. That connection to friends and—she glanced at Picou who smiled radiantly at her newfound daughter—family.

She shoveled down the gumbo and drank half of a lukewarm Abita beer, watching the families around her while around her flowed talk of teaching—tales of playground disasters and classroom successes. She felt so alone.

"I need to go to the bathroom."

Picou pointed toward the orange portable bathroom sitting near the woods Annie had chased Shaffer through. "You'll have to use that one. They should be clean, though."

Annie tossed her bowl into the almost-overflowing can. Obviously, Nate had wanted to stay well away from her. She hadn't seen him in a while...and she hadn't seen Jane.

She tamped down on the jealousy and crossed to the temporary bathroom facilities. No one waited in line. Perhaps they, too, found it repulsive to potty in a plastic box. As she approached the area, she heard a muffled noise. Then she saw one of the port-o-lets shaking as if someone were kicking from inside. The sign on the outside read Occupied. Perhaps a child had locked himself inside and couldn't figure out how to unlatch the door?

She knocked. "Hello?"

The kicking became more furious, shaking the entire plastic frame. She heard furious, garbled screeching.

What in the hell?

Using her palm, she pushed the round spinner that

locked the door from inside. She felt the plastic mechanism move and heard the plastic wedge pop. The door flew open.

Annie stepped back to keep from getting hit and then saw a very enraged Jane sitting on the commode, gagged and bound. Annie reacted, leaping inside and ripping the duct tape from Jane's mouth.

"Ow!" Jane yelled, standing up, nose to nose with Annie.

"Jane, what—"

"She took Spencer!"

"What?" Annie stepped out of the port-o-let pulling Jane with her. Jane stumbled, but maintained her balance. Annie saw a plastic restraint cinched around Jane's wrists. "Who? What are you talking about?"

"A woman took Spencer. He had go to the bathroom. Tawny went to meet Carter so I took him—"

"Where's Brick?"

"Spencer pitched a fit for cotton candy. He went to get it. Here he comes now."

Brick moved incredibly fast for a big man. And he carried a bag of cotton candy in one hand.

"Who took him, Jane?" Annie shook her arm, bringing her back to the immediacy of the situation.

"I don't know. I couldn't see. She shoved me in and held a knife to my throat. She said she'd cut my face, so I let her bind me. My face is my livelihood and—"

"Get Tawny and Carter," Annie interrupted, turning to Brick. "I'll call Nate."

Annie slid the phone from her pocket and dialed Nate's cell. When he picked up, she said, "Come to the port-o-lets. Someone took Spencer."

Then she hung up and tried to cut the plastic strap off Jane's wrists with her keys. She also tried asking her about the woman who taken Spencer, but Jane wouldn't stop cursing about being humiliated, locked in with "all that piss."

Annie had been around Air Force guys and spent years in law enforcement and she'd never heard such an inventive and crude lambasting as she had from the actress with the "trusting, wholesome" face.

"Jane?" Annie said.

"Huh?"

"Shut the hell up."

NATE HAD BEEN PICKING UP overflowing garbage in the front of the church when he got the call from Annie. A dog or two had already snuffled through the paper plates and bowls, scattering them all over the front lawn.

As soon as he heard Annie's words, he tossed the bag down and sprinted for his car, where he'd left his gun and radio. He put the call out to the station as he rounded the corner of the church, streaking through the festivalgoers who look bewildered by the scene playing out.

He reached Annie at the same time Carter and Tawny did. Annie ran her keys over the plastic restraint on Jane's wrists.

"Here," he said, taking a knife from his pocket and slicing through the cuffs easily. "What's going on?"

Jane turned, flexing her wrists. "I took Spencer to the bathroom. He was in that one." She pointed to the stall next to her. "I had to go, too, so I called out for him to wait on me."

Tawny whirled on Brick. "Where were you? You were supposed to stay with him."

Brick flushed. "I went to get the damn cotton candy he wanted."

Carter stammered. "I thought you caught the guy. How did this happen?"

Jane shook her head. "I don't know. I stepped inside and she shoved me from behind. I tried to turn around, but she kneed me in the back of my thighs and slapped a piece of tape over my mouth and I hit my head on the seat." Jane stopped to shiver. "Then she held the knife to my cheek."

"Give us a description," Nate said.

"I don't know. She had on shorts and a T-shirt with maybe a logo on it? I think her hair was brown. Just plain brown."

"Plain brown," Annie said, getting that faraway look he'd seen before.

"I couldn't see anything else," Jane said. "But she sounded Southern."

"Plain brown hair," Annie repeated looking at Tawny. She tilted her head. "Plain brown. Like mine. Like your sister."

"Who?"

Tawny's eyes widened. "Teri? No. She wouldn't."

Carter had remained silent, looking ashen and non-Carter-like. "Teri? You think she's the one who's been doing this? She's not smart enough."

Tawny stiffened. "Yeah, she is, and she's capable of anything when she's using. Not to mention she's pissed at me."

Jane cocked her head. "You know, she did look a little like you."

Tawny shook her head. "Oh, my God. I can't believe it, but it makes sense. The last time I spoke to her, I told her I wasn't going to send any more money because she used it for meth. She told me it didn't matter. She had a new man and he had a plan."

"That bitch," Carter growled, thrusting a hand into his sunny hair. "When I get ahold of her, she'll wish she'd stayed her hillbilly ass in Crowder, Arkansas."

"So how did no one see her?"

Annie looked at the port-o-let. "The woods. That's why Shaffer was there. He was scouting out the vicinity because they knew about the festival. Knew it would be a good time to take a kid."

"But Teri didn't know Spencer would be here," Tawny interrupted.

"But there was a good chance a kid would show up where there's cotton candy and bounce houses. They'd probably been scouting out a couple of opportunities." Nate pulled his radio out, stepped away and called in the description. He put an APB out for the car, basing it on the one he'd seen Shafer driving days before. He was certain the car was a rental or one Teri had borrowed.

He stepped back and looked at Annie. "We've got uniforms coming. Bayou Bridge P.D. is patrolling the city limits. She can't have too much of a jump on us."

Annie nodded, but then stopped. "Shouldn't there be a ransom note?"

He turned toward the port-o-let Spencer had used. Sure enough, a piece of paper was stuck to the door, held by duct tape. He left it hanging but read the missive.

Birdie, birdie in the sky
Tawny's too dumb and let him fly
Leave five hundred grand in the old sugar mill
Or sweet, sweet birdie I'll have to _____.
No police. No trace. No funny business.
Leave money where they found Della's shoes.
You've got till 5:00.

"Oh, my God, she's crazy," Tawny cried, her shoulders shaking with sobs. "How could I let this happen? How did I not know?"

Carter put his arms around his wife. "You didn't. It's not your fault, baby. We're going to get him back."

Carter Keene's eyes met Nate's over the bowed head of

his wife. The message was unmistakable. Whatever means necessary. Nate felt a chill run through him. Tawny's sister knew about Della, about the Dufrenes' history with kidnapping. Of course, most everyone in the area knew the story. Billy and Sal had left Della's shoes beside the evaporators as proof they had his sister. Why would Teri set it up there? Was she needling him? Reminding him what he'd lost long ago? Proclaiming a dark harbinger?

The old Dufrene sugar mill was ten miles away. If they could get to Teri before she got to the mill...

"So she took him through the woods. Maybe we can get to her before she gets to the mill. Annie?"

Tawny looked up and blinked. "Why do you keep flippin' asking Annie what she thinks? She's a nanny."

Everyone turned to look at Annie, but she looked caught up in her thoughts. Again.

She cocked her head. "Tawny, this is important. The night Spencer made Play-Doh spaghetti, did you sneak out to meet up with someone? Mick, perhaps?"

Tawny frowned. "Of course not. I don't even like Mick. He's been a shit to Jane."

Jane nodded. "Yeah, he's pretty much a shit."

"I took Jane gumbo that night so I could poke around a bit."

He heard Jane huff, but couldn't tear his eyes from Annie.

"I had to get gas and saw a woman going into a motel room. The light caught her face, and I thought it was Tawny. She wore a ball cap and looked extremely cautious. But it wasn't Tawny. It was Teri."

Tawny looked confused. "Why were you spying on Jane?"

Carter sighed. "Annie's not a nanny, babe. She's an undercover private security officer. Former FBI."

Tawny shoved Carter. "And you didn't tell me this? Why?"

By this time quite a crowd had gathered. All were whispering low, including Picou, Della and Jason.

Nate turned as Carter tried to soothe his distraught wife and addressed the crowd. "Look, everyone, we need your help. Spencer Keene is missing." A collective intake of breath came from the crowd. Nate caught his mother's eyes. They were unfathomable. She'd been here before and she didn't want to be here now. "He's five years old and we think he's with a woman wearing shorts, T-shirt and a ball cap. She has dark hair."

"I saw them," Father Benoit said, pointing past the bounce houses still wiggling with jumping children. Already some parents ran toward the inflatables. "She didn't seem threatening because they were laughing. I thought nothing of it. They walked toward the woods. I stopped watching because Mrs. Honeycutt came to speak to me."

"Okay, we need some of you to spread out and search the woods. We're going to treat this as if it's a missing child until we get more information. Keep a phone with you and if you find anything, call 911."

Several in the crowd nodded.

He felt Annie before she touched him. "I'm going to the Super Six to see if she's there. Can you call ahead and get me a key?"

"As soon as Blaine gets here, I'll follow behind you, but don't do anything until I get there with backup. She's likely not there, but if she is, we don't know what to expect. Get information from the desk clerk, get the key and then wait on me."

Annie's eyes flashed irritation. She didn't like taking orders from him, but she nodded before hurrying off. He felt itchy about letting her go alone, but if she could do the preliminaries with the motel clerk, they'd be clear to search the room when he got there. They wouldn't need a warrant.

He turned back to his community. "The sheriff's office and Bayou Bridge P.D. are canvassing the streets. Let's see what we can do here to help."

Carter had Tawny back in his arms. "What do we need to do?"

"Get a suitcase. I'll call my cousin at Community National Bank and get the money...just in case."

Carter nodded, his eyes determined. "No problem. I'll cover with a check."

Nate walked toward his mother. "This isn't going to happen again."

His mother grabbed his arm. "I have faith in you, Nate."

"And I do, too." Della touched his arm. Somehow her fingers on his arms, so like the ones that had gripped him twenty-four years before in much the same way, gave him strength. He'd gotten his sister back. He'd get Spencer back, too.

CHAPTER TWENTY

ANNIE FELT LIKE AN idiot for not having seen the threads to pull in this case. For God's sake, she'd heard Tawny tell Carter she'd cut her sister off. Annie hadn't made the connection and she should have. First rule of law enforcement—suspect the family.

And they had. They just hadn't found anything on Teri that would make them suspect her of threatening her nephew. Annie should have dug harder, spent more time with Carter and Tawny. Then she would have picked up on Tawny's relationship with her sister.

Maybe Nate had distracted her.

Nate definitely had distracted her.

She shook her head and concentrated on what she needed to do in the next few minutes, no time to get sidetracked on what she should or should not have done.

The Super Six motel was shoddy and run-down. The lobby had plastic palm trees, badly in need of dusting, and a tired-looking kid slumped behind the check-in desk.

"Need a room?" he asked, not bothering to look up from the phone he held in his hand.

"No, I need a key."

"What key?" He glanced up and eyed her with spaced-out muddy eyes. "You the chick the police dude called about?"

"Yeah. I'm the chick."

He nodded. "Cool. Here's a key. You know how to use it? Just stick it in the card slot."

Annie took the card. "What room number?"

"Um, let's see. 162. She also got another room a few days ago. Wanted the adjoining room." He shrugged, pocketing the phone. "The maid said no one's used it yet."

Annie held out her hand. "Give me a card for that one, too."

He tapped on the computer, slid a card through and handed her the second room key. "It's 160. Is there gonna be any shooting or anything?"

She stared blankly at the kid.

"Right." He sat, pulled out his phone and started tapping on the screen.

Annie stepped outside the lobby and climbed back into her car, cranking it and pulling it around, parking near the large blue Dumpster, kitty-corner from the room Teri had presumably been staying in. She didn't see the silver Chevrolet the woman had been driving. Strong possibility Teri would never come back, but her room might hold a clue to her plans.

Had she hurt Spencer?

Just thinking about it made Annie hurt. Surely Teri wasn't so callous, so evil as to hurt a small boy, a boy whose own blood ran in her veins. But Annie knew differently. She'd seen too many cases end badly. Too many times someone stepped over the broken body of the innocent to get to what he or she wanted. The thought of what humanity could do froze her blood.

She glanced down at her watch. Two hours, thirty-five minutes left.

Where was Tawny's sister?

Where was the boy she, despite all her vows, had grown to love?

The minutes ate at her—tick, ticking away until she felt shrink-wrapped by her own skin.

Then she saw the car. It did not roll cautiously into the parking lot—it roared, the gears grinding as the driver shifted into Park.

Teri, sporting dark sunglasses and the ball cap, threw the car door open and climbed out. It might as well have been a normal day, maybe a beer run or a quick trip out for a burger—not a kidnapping with a ransom. The woman looked positively unconcerned. Then she cast a glance about before opening the back door of the car and pulling Spencer out.

Annie covered her mouth.

Not unexpectedly, he'd been crying. Annie couldn't see the tears from the hundred or so yards between them, but she saw his scraped, bleeding knees. The woman had likely pulled him when he'd stumbled. Maybe in the woods. But it didn't matter.

Annie was pissed.

Spencer wasn't her child, yet he was, and Teri the Meth-head had messed with the wrong kid's nanny.

Annie pulled her phone from her pocket.

Nate hadn't called yet.

He said he'd be behind her, so where was he?

She glanced up as Teri dragged Spencer into the room adjoining the one on the end. Annie saw the door slam.

Looking back at the blank screen, she wondered what to do. She had no gun, no badge, no true authority. And that pissed her off even more.

She dialed Nate, drumming her fingers on the steering wheel, eyeballing the motel door the whole time. The call went to voice mail. What the hell?

The man knew where she was and what she was doing. Voice mail? Really?

She looked around her rental for anything she might use as a makeshift weapon. There was nothing, save an umbrella. She knew Teri had a knife, and she doubted springing an umbrella her way would serve as much defense.

Annie was screwed. Spencer sat yards away, and she was helpless.

The door of Teri's room opened and the woman stepped out again, casting a look in each direction before walking back to her car. Annie ducked down, praying having her car in place before Teri arrived had given the woman false security.

Annie peeked over the steering wheel.

Teri was back inside her car and backing out without even so much a glance toward the Dumpster or Annie's vehicle.

Huh.

She'd left him?

Or...

Annie didn't want to think about anything other than getting to the child. She looked down at the console where the plastic key cards sat. She snatched the one that would open the room where Teri had stashed Spencer then she looked back at the nearly empty parking lot.

Strike hard. Strike fast. No hesitation.

Annie unlocked the door just as her phone started jittering in the cup holder.

Nate.

She pressed the button. "He's here at the motel. Just saw Teri take him from the car, put him in a room and leave."

"Hang tight. I'm almost there."

"She drove away. I'm going in. You get her. She turned toward the interstate, heading for the drop-off. She's really a dumbass. How did she think she'd pull this off?"

"Wait for me. You're not carrying, no backup, and you can never predict the behavior of someone as desperate as this woman."

Annie knew it was the sensible thing to do. All her years of training had taught her to rely on the rules of engagement, taking precaution. Nate had a point, but Spencer was scared and bleeding. And this could be a matter of life and death.

She looked back at the key card.

"I've got to get him out. He's hurt. No telling what she's done, Nate."

"Don't. Wait for me. I'm close. Two minutes out."

But it was too late. She pressed end. She respected Nate. He was smart and knew his job, but if he were minutes away, it was close enough.

She opened the door and ran for the room Teri had roughly shoved Spencer inside, clutching the key card, making sure it was in the right direction. She jammed it in, heard the lock mechanism move, click and give a green light. She pushed the door open into a darkened room.

Spencer was crying.

Fumbling for a switch at the bottom of a ceramic lamp, she flicked the knob, illuminating the water-stained ceiling with dim light before hurrying to where the sound was coming from.

His crying broke her heart. She pulled the mirrored door of the closet open to find a little boy balled into a knot in the corner. His body shook with terror.

"I'm here, Spence," she said, not touching him.

He stilled, cupping his hands over his ears, eyes screwed tight.

"Annie?"

"It's me, baby."

He unwound, reaching blindly for her. Annie figured

there had never been such a good feeling as those two hands twining around her neck. She lifted him, pulling him for a quick hug.

"We've got to get out, Spencer. Come on, sweetie."

But he clung to her, wrapping both legs around her waist in a death grip.

She sensed the movement before she felt something slam into her temple.

Pain blinded her as she staggered toward the ratty flower-strewn spread on the bed. Spencer fell away.

Shit, it hurt. Teri knew where to hit. But what had she used to hit her? A gun? A bat? Darkness spotted her vision, but she fought it off.

No time to think.

Move.

Annie bounced on the mattress and came up swinging. Her fist landed right in the middle of Teri's windpipe. Yeah, Annie fought dirtier.

"Argh." Teri gasped for breath, clutching her throat. Annie saw her mouth open and close, desperately trying to drink in a breath. She fixed on Annie with pain-crazed eyes before reaching behind her, withdrawing a gun from her waistband.

Instinctively, Annie crouched, launching herself at the woman's knees. *Get low. Center of gravity.* She used her left hand to sweep above her, hopefully colliding with Teri's right arm, the hand most people used to shoot with. Annie heard the gun clink against the bureau at the same time Teri crashed into the ancient TV stand. They both went down.

"Get off me!" Teri shrieked, thrashing beneath her. Annie rose, going for the gun, which had landed at the foot of the bed. Spencer stood pressed against the wall, eyes big, knees bleeding. A keening emerged from his throat.

Teri's hand opened and closed, searching for the gun, but

she wasn't faster than Annie. Annie's hand closed around the grip before the woman could scramble close enough. Annie kneed her hard in the stomach and rolled to her knees, fixing the gun on the woman, aiming for a body shot.

Teri stilled.

"Get up. Show me your hands." Annie's voice was cold. She felt the surge, felt the confidence in the training, the experience. She had control of the situation.

"He's my nephew. I wasn't gonna hurt him. I just wanted the money. I swear."

"Hands up where I can see them. Now."

Teri raised her hands. "See? See?"

Annie nodded, but kept the gun steady on the thin woman. It was her first close look at the woman who resembled Tawny, just rougher, desperate and jacked up on something. Teri's thin hands shook.

Annie heard the squeal of tires outside the motel room. Help had arrived. "Sit on your bottom, cross your legs, keep your hands where I can see them."

Teri did as she was told. Maybe she wasn't too dumb. "I wasn't going to hurt anyone. I—"

"Shut up."

Annie heard a crash, then Nate appeared at the connecting door to the room, gun drawn, expression fierce. His eyes surveyed the room, processed the situation. She returned her gaze to the woman in front of her.

"I screwed up, Nate." She kept her eyes on Teri. "She made me while I sat in the car, doubled back and ambushed me."

Spencer continued to whimper. Each sound pricking between her shoulder blades a confusing need.

"Go to him. I've got her," Nate said, reading her like he'd done so many times before. Annie lowered the gun, her thumb sliding against the safety, securing the weapon. She dropped back, her butt connecting with the thin mattress. She reached over and set the gun on the nightstand and went to Spencer.

He'd plugged his fingers into his ears, but his eyes were wide. She'd seen enough victims to know he was in shock. There were things one did for victims, but he was not any victim. He was her Spencer. She gently tugged his fingers from his ears.

"Shh, shh," she whispered. "It's okay, baby. It's okay."

She could hear Nate behind her, cuffing Teri, reading her the Miranda, along with a few other choice words that normally would have made her smile. But she had no smile left in her. Only an unfathomable need to hold the child in front of her. She didn't understand it, but it had to be done.

"Baby," she murmured, folding him into her arms, easing him onto the bed. His fingers clutched at her.

"Annie, Annie," he said over and over.

"Shh," she whispered against his hair. He smelled like sweaty little boy, a very welcome scent.

Annie had done many things in the aftermath of a takedown. She'd laughed. She'd felt the power, the rush, embraced it. She'd even delivered a gut jab to a man who'd grabbed her boobs, but she'd never sat on a bed with a terrified child, rocking him and loving him.

And for the first time in her life she did something on the job she'd have been horrified to have witnessed.

She cried.

She couldn't stop herself. Her heart had overridden her brain. So the tears came, mingling with the sweat and, perhaps, even a bit of Spencer's snot. She didn't care—because it was something she'd had no control over, that sweeping feeling of absolute love. She'd forgotten how much it hurt, bittersweet in its ripping at the soul, absolutely raw and splendid.

So she didn't stop it. Just held on to Spencer and the ironic beauty for a moment.

Finally, she glanced up at Nate.

He had Teri face down on the ground, cuffed and still. He knelt, pressing the woman down, but his eyes were on Annie.

Annie shook her head, but didn't move to wipe the dampness from her cheeks. She felt slightly embarrassed by her lack of control, absence of professionalism.

But the expression in Nate's eyes washed over her and all unease faded. Suddenly, it wasn't about love for Spencer. It was about those same emotions stirring for the man with his knee in the back of the woman who'd started this whole crazy journey.

"I'm so sorry," she mouthed, tucking Spencer's head beneath her chin.

Nate gave her a quasi smile. "Ah, Annie, you're killing me."

NATE SIGNED OFF ON Teri's arrest and sought the sanctuary of his cleared desk. A Windows icon bopped around on the screen, the stack of files stared at him and the phone was silent.

Same desk. Different man.

When had he changed?

Was it the discovery of his sister? Or falling for the nanny who wasn't really a nanny?

Both?

"Good day, eh?" Wynn sank into his chair and rubbed his face. "I've got statements from the folks out at the Feast Day festival. No problems there. Padre said tents are packed up, bills settled and trash cleared. He also said you'd have to chair the activities for the children next year since you bailed."

"To catch a kidnapper."

Wynn shrugged, chewing on his customary toothpick. "Just what he said."

Nate shook his head and shoved a file toward his friend. "Here are the reports. Hand them back when you need signatures."

"Shit," Wynn moaned, staring at the thick file. "You're joking, right?"

"You're the one who offered."

His friend frowned. "Me and my big mouth."

"I wouldn't talk about Kelli that way when she's standing right behind you." Nate waggled his fingers at Wynn's pregnant wife. Kelli shot him a particular finger.

"Why didn't you tell us the nanny was on our team?" she said, lightly tracing the shaggy hair on the nape of her husband's neck. "Didn't have a clue myself. Guess I suck at being a detective."

Wynn visibly relaxed into his wife's caress. "Yeah. Why didn't you tell us?"

"Need to know basis."

"Humph," Kelli snorted. "Like we can't keep stuff under wraps."

Nate merely stared at Kelli. She blinked first and turned her gaze from his.

"Talk about conflict of interest," Wynn said, focusing his attention on the pages within the file he'd opened. He thumbed through them, his frown growing more pronounced the further he progressed.

"How so?" Nate asked.

Ever inquisitive, Kelli cocked her head. "Yeah, how so?"

Wynn shrugged. "He's been sleeping with her."

"Get out," Kelli said, tweaking her husband's hair. "Why didn't I know about this?"

Nate didn't say anything. What could he say? It was the truth. Kind of. They weren't sleeping together, only had sex. Once. Still, to admit any sort of relationship other than secretly professional seemed wrong. Like a breach in confidentiality. Easier to say nothing.

Kelli studied him with bright blue eyes. He didn't shrink under the duress of her probing gaze. Nor did he blink. Finally, she wagged a finger. "I knew something was different, but I couldn't put my finger on it. You've been distracted, but I thought it was the case. Now I can see things clearly. She's awfully pretty, but I just don't see it. Too much alike."

"And that's a problem why?" he asked.

Kelli shook her head. "Don't you know anything? Opposites attract because they balance each other out. Look at me and Wynn."

"You're both annoying. Doesn't that count as a similarity?" He crossed his arms and glared at them. "In all seriousness, you don't know her, so how can you make a judgment about how well we'd suit?"

Her brow crinkled. "Oh, wow, you really like her, huh?"

Wynn's steady gaze joined that of his wife's. "Uh-huh, he's probably practicing writing their names together. Mr. and Mrs. Nathan Briggs Dufrene. Aww."

"You know my middle name?" Nate spun around in his chair, grabbed his gun and pulled a protein bar from his desk drawer. He ripped the package with his teeth and pocketed his keys.

Kelli's mouth hung open. Wynn grinned. "Oh, man. You got it bad."

Nate didn't bother looking back as he strolled out of the

detective's bull pen. "Don't forget I need that paperwork on my desk by Monday. Have a good weekend."

Then he left the office to the sound of his friend's colorful phrasing. Somehow, though his life was tangled like the line on both his fishing rods, he felt okay. A bit as if he'd popped free of the spot where'd he'd stuck all those years ago. For so long, he'd been weighted down, unable to move, by the guilt and responsibility in his life. But now, he felt different. Maybe life could be something other than Bayou Bridge, Beau Soleil and the Sheriff's Department. Maybe he could be a different Nate.

And maybe he could get Annie to stay.

Or maybe he could go with her.

The thoughts piled up in his mind.

What if… What if…

He had some thinking to do. Then he had some action to take. No more sitting still, waiting for life to pass him by while he twiddled his fingers on the front porch.

Della had been found. Spencer was safe. And Anna Mendes was meant for him.

He just had to convince her.

CHAPTER TWENTY-ONE

ANNIE WALKED SLOWLY along the unpaved drive of Beau Soleil, reveling in the coolness of the breeze enveloping her. The moon sat low in the sky, orange and mysterious, lighting the way for her evening walk. The day had been overwhelming, and she needed some very alone time to process everything that had occurred.

She shook her head to start the process. Beginning with the emotional homecoming of Della Dufrene and ending with the apprehension of Tawny's sister, the entire day had been dipped in crazy and laced with danger.

And then there was Nate.

Her emotions skydived into the pit of her stomach. She didn't know what to do about him. She'd fallen for him, but...

The thought floored her.

Yeah. Anna Mendes had fallen in love for the absolute first time in her existence, and it was impossible.

The heavy oak branches swayed in the gentle evening breeze almost in harmony with what stirred inside her.

Hell. She had no recourse. No direction. No real hope or promise of anything from Nate. Not to mention she could be having his child. Possible. But not probable. She knew her body and was nearly certain she'd start her period in a week. Her boobs didn't lie.

But that didn't solve anything with her heart.

The old cemetery appeared when she rounded the corner. It stood in stark contrast to the soft blue of the darkening sky, jabbing with rusted pronged posts and weathered stones, reminding the living of lives once well spent… or perhaps misspent. An owl hooted, bringing mysticism edged with creepiness to the hallowed ground. Annie stopped before the gate.

She unlatched the handle, expecting the stereotypical creak, but the gate swung open effortlessly. Of course. The expected didn't happen at Beau Soleil, did it?

Picou's words from the first day still haunted her. *What seems benign can sometimes bite.*

"Annie?"

His voice carried over her shoulder like a caress. She turned and there he stood, the planes of his face harsh in the light of the harvest moon.

She didn't reply, only watched as he walked toward her, his footfalls crunching in the gravel and dry leaves.

"What are you doing here?" he asked.

She lifted a shoulder. "Nothing in particular. You?"

He lifted a finger and stroked her cheek. His eyes held words unspoken. Worry, befuddlement and, dare she hope, love. "I worried about you."

"Did you?"

He held her gaze but didn't answer.

She turned from him, too afraid to allow him to see into her soul, and pointed to the crypt. "What do you suppose Henry Laborde wanted out of life?"

She stared at the engraved marble. Another similar in style sat directly beside it, two hearts overlapping etched into the faded stone. Henry David Laborde's loving wife, Emily Ann.

"He wanted what every man wants. A roof overhead, food in his belly, a baby at his knee, a woman in his arms."

"That's it?"

"What more is there?"

She jerked her gaze to his. "Love?"

"That, too, I suppose."

Both fell silent, the night cloaking them in intimacy, accompanied by the woodlands at night. Annie walked among the tombs, reading the names, feeling her heart wrench at the tiny cherubs perched above the names of infants and children. Here was a family who gasped first and last breath at Beau Soleil—living, laughing, sobbing their way through life.

She paused before the tomb of Martin Briggs Dufrene. Nate appeared at her shoulder. "My father," he said.

"How did he pass?"

"Heart. I was in my last year of med school at Tulane when Mom called me from Baton Rouge. He died before I could get there."

She nodded. "I'm sorry."

He shrugged. "My father was a hard man and expected a lot from people, including his own family. He could be an absolute son of a bitch, but I knew he loved us. I tried to take care of things for him. Felt he wanted me to see to Mom and take care of the estate. That's why I declined my residency."

She didn't say anything. She'd sensed Nate felt he stepped in the footprints of his father, but she didn't see him that way at all. He was flawed like every man, but he was his own man. "You think you're like him?"

Several seconds ticked by. "Maybe."

"But you're not." She turned to him. "You still angry with me?"

His eyes remained unreadable. "You didn't trust my judgment. When I saw you in confrontation with Teri, even though you had the upper hand, I couldn't help feel as though you disregarded my request as some kind of punishment."

"But I didn't."

He sighed. "I don't understand you."

"I don't understand myself."

She turned and looked at the moon barely visible through the trees before rubbing her upper arms. She wore a thin T-shirt and the cold front sweeping through the parish earlier that evening had brought cooler air. Nate draped his jacket over her shoulders. She felt the warmth of his body in the light fleece, savored his smell enfolding her much as his arms had done once.

"I acted out of character," she said, sliding her arms into the comfort of the sleeves. "I led with my heart and not my head. My fear for Spencer crippled me."

She glanced back at him. "My love made me weak."

"Or made you stronger."

She shook her head. "Every word you said was correct. I had no weapon, no backup, no concrete knowledge of Teri's whereabouts. I should have waited for you, but I didn't. I could have gotten us both killed. I almost did."

He nodded. "Maybe. But you also showed conviction, and your analysis of the situation was spot-on. Teri had means and opportunity to harm Spencer. You took that away from her."

She shivered. "But—"

"What? You took her down, using experience and decisiveness. You did what you were hired to do. All along, you busted leads for us." His dark eyes were fierce in her defense. Something moved inside her so hard and fast, she clasped her chest.

"But I made mistakes." She clenched the front of the jacket.

His lips twitched. "Oh, you mean you're human?"

She pressed her lips together but said nothing. She allowed the gathered material to fall.

"So I've been thinking," he said, shoving his hands into the front pocket of his khaki pants. He wore a striped piqué polo shirt that made his shoulders broader than normal. She looked away, afraid she might touch him and give her emotions away. "I'm good at my job. I do fine under Blaine and I've got a nice little pension tucked away."

"Security's good."

"Yeah, it is, but I also have these boxes stacked in my house, full of missing persons and cases long gone cold. I work them in my spare time."

"Weird hobby."

"It's not a hobby. It's a quest. Mostly, it's on my own dime, but there are grants I could likely pursue if I had the time. I feel convicted about helping others get absolution from the burdens they carry."

"Like you never had."

"Things have changed, haven't they? And with them, I feel the need for a new chapter for myself...and maybe you."

She jerked her head toward him. "Me?"

"You."

"What are you talking about?" Panic inched into her thoughts. Marriage? Was he talking something like that... just because she could possibly be pregnant? Or was there more?

"An arrangement similar to what you have at Sterling, but more of a partnership."

"You're offering me a job?"

He laughed. The sound didn't suit the mood or the night around them. Something flapped in a nearby tree, rising higher in the thick canopy overhead. "Sort of."

She took a step back. "But I have a job. In fact, I'm leaving in a few days to head back. What would keep me here?"

His expression split and she saw his vulnerability. It slammed her, kick-starting her heart with the rawness of his love. But he didn't say anything, merely watched, trying to shutter his expression, but failing to do so.

"You," she said.

"What's that?"

"You want me to stay for you."

Nate tore his eyes from hers and looked around. As if he'd rather look at scraggly weeds and faded artificial flowers than acknowledge the truth in her words.

"But we have no…that is to say…we barely know each other really. I've never seen your house. Don't know your favorite color or your birthday. I can't leave everything I've ever known or the new career I've managed to salvage from the ashes of my old one for a person I…" She trailed off because she wasn't ready to say those words. A person she'd fallen in love with.

It was all very impractical, ridiculous and stupid.

They'd gotten caught up in the moment, ambushed by passion, shoved together by shared purpose, linked by like personalities. Those did not translate into a relationship. It could not emote into a happily ever after.

He grabbed her shoulders. "Listen up, Annie, because I'm only going to ask this once."

She blinked.

"What I feel for you is illogical, absurd and possibly silly." He paused, swallowing the words. "But what I know without doubt is the feeling is true. From the moment you walked into my life, I've been pulled toward you like a magnet to iron. It's not merely the urge to bend you over this crypt and mate with you like a…a primeval wolf."

"Really?"

He blinked. "Okay, maybe not here, and not like a wolf, which was a strange thing for me to say, but I want you with a need so strong it scares me. But it's not just that, Annie, it's the way you smile. The way you crook your head when you're thinking. The way you stare longingly at Spencer when you think no one is looking. It's your stubbornness, your scent, your taste. It's everything. And all that combined tells me you were made for me."

"I—" She closed her mouth because his descended.

His hands slid up to cup her face, not gently, but possessively. She felt every word in his kiss and she welcomed it, felt passion stir and rise within her body.

He broke the kiss, but kept her face cupped in his warm hands. "So I'm going to say this once, Annie."

She nodded.

"I love you, or at least I think this is love. I've never felt it before."

She nodded again.

"Stay with me and be my partner, in all ways."

She felt her heart thud, hard and heavy, and it felt as if it might burst from her chest. Or was it already clogging her throat? She wasn't sure. Then the panic came again.

"Can I have a little time to think this through?"

He dropped his hands, took a step back and then started laughing. "That's your answer?"

She slumped. "It's who I am. I have to think. You said you've thought, but I haven't. I've been briefing Ace, watching *Barney* with a too-quiet Spencer, consoling your mother on Della leaving. All those things have crowded my mind and I'm all cloudy. I—"

"If you have to think about it, what does that say?" he asked, finally ceasing his somewhat profane laughter among the departed.

"It says I want to be sure. I mean, I think I feel the same way, but I have to give my mind the same credence I've given my heart. It's only fair."

Nate folded his arms, shook his head and watched her with a tinge of amusement in his gaze. "See? Another reason why we suit."

"You're okay with it?"

He smiled. "I think I'd prefer it."

"Right now at this very second, my heart says yes. So this is a risk."

"But one worth taking. I want you beside me, mind, heart and soul. Anything less would be unacceptable. So, think. Think hard." He turned back toward the house where he'd grown into a man.

Annie felt the vise in her throat loosen. This was a man not accustomed to handing a decision to someone else. This man usually got what he wanted, so she knew it was a rare gift. He'd given her power over his fate. "Hey, Nate?"

He turned.

"You're nothing like your father."

She couldn't see his expression in the shadows. "Oh, but I am. I go after what I want, and what I want most in this world is you."

NATE DIDN'T SLEEP WELL for the next two nights as the mirror attested early Monday morning. He looked like an extra in Michael Jackson's "Thriller" video. Pale, tense, with luggage under each eye. He may or may not have lost a body part.

Specifically, his heart.

"Hell," he said to himself before scrubbing the fuzz from his teeth. Afterward, he rubbed his scruffy jaw thoughtfully, turning right then left. He wouldn't look too bad with a beard. Hunting season was around the bend. Maybe he'd visit the old salt lick and see if any deer had sniffed around, providing him a store of venison he'd not had in many years. Of course, he didn't really hunt much and, outside of Lucille's summer sausage, wasn't a big fan of the sometimes too gamey meat. Never mind.

It had been two days since he'd seen Annie and already he was going Grizzly Adams. Or crazy.

The peal of the doorbell interrupted his contemplation of beards, hunting and wallowing in sorrow. He slid on the wrinkled pajama pants lying over the hamper and padded out to the living room.

Probably his mother. He'd called in sick, something he so rarely did he had stockpiled months of vacation. She'd likely made gumbo—her one good soup recipe she pulled out for all people under the weather.

But it was Annie.

She wrinkled her nose. "You look terrible."

"And you don't," he replied, meaning it. She looked great. Her hair curled around clear gray eyes and a pretty pink mouth. His heart played a game of hopscotch in his chest. He swung the door wider. "Come inside?"

She lifted one shoulder. "Should I? You look like that wolf you mentioned a few nights ago."

"Well, then, by all means come in."

She slid past him and he inhaled her sweet scent. Definitely baby powder. Then he stopped because it was quite wolfish behavior.

"You weren't lying," she said, turning a circle in his living space. "There are a lot of cases here."

He closed the door and turned to her. "Too many."

"Should we get started right away? Is this going to be our office?"

He spoke before he registered her words. "It will... Wait, are you staying?"

She leaned against the arm of an overstuffed chair. Her gaze dropped to his bare chest, and he felt the pilot light go on deep in his pelvis. He wanted her, but this was greater than lust. She redirected her gaze. "Yeah, against all better judgment, I am."

He stood for a moment, allowing the information to filter through his fuzzy brain. Did this mean only as a business partner? He'd wanted more. "So..."

She folded her arms. "You know what convinced me to stay? Henry and Emily Ann."

"Who?"

"Your great-great-aunt and -uncle."

He tried to connect the dots but failed. His face must have shown as much because she sighed and shook her head. "The cemetery. Two hearts interlocked. Good food and a good woman. Remember?"

"Yeah, and you said, 'What about love?'"

She stared at him for a moment. "You know what single women everywhere want?"

He shook his head. He really, really didn't know that one.

"We don't want to be found one day dead in our apartments with a cat eating our faces off."

"What?"

"Stay with me," she said. He eased himself on the couch because, though he knew Annie to be quite logical, he had no clue where she was going with this.

"I tried over a year ago to circumvent the whole spinster dead on her couch surrounded by hungry cats thing. I forced myself into a relationship thinking I didn't have to have love. I could have a husband, a kid, a dog and a life not spent alone watching reruns of *Titanic* while eating Lean Cuisines. I tried to squeeze my foot into that slipper thinking love didn't matter because I wouldn't be alone on Christmas. Thing is, when you try and do that, you get blisters and bunions and you don't want to even walk around."

Now he followed her. She'd tried to force something and it didn't work.

"So I didn't want to put on the slipper anymore. It was easier that way."

"We're talking about relationships, right?"

She blinked. "Yeah."

He clasped his hands between his spread knees and nodded. "Go on."

"So I spent the last day and a half doing some thinking, which seems contrary to what you should do when you are in love, but this is important, you know?"

"Absolutely."

"I thought about what I thought I wanted, that whole pretty-packaged life, and then I thought about what you said. Or what I said. About love. See, that's what I lacked all along, and when I started feeling like I was falling for you, it scared me and I threw up all kinds of barriers. The case was an important barrier. We're talking about saving a life here, so that wasn't necessarily a barrier. But still, I convinced myself that it couldn't be real. It was lust. Or the damn heat. Or whatever straw I could grasp, but the deal was—"

"We fell in love despite common sense."

"Yeah," she said, finally smiling. "We did, and it's crazy, but it's true."

His heart expanded in his chest, but he didn't move toward her. Not yet.

"So what it boils down to is I want to lie beside you every night, and when we've passed into the great beyond, I want our hearts still overlapping. I want to be next to you in that cemetery at Beau Soleil as your loving wife, Anna Maria Dufrene. I want that more than a career or California sunshine."

He almost cried. Almost. "I want that, too."

"I'll have to go back to California for a week or so. I have to make arrangements for my dad, have to meet with Ace and deal with my grandmother's house and the stupid condo I bought. I know you haven't said anything about marriage, and that's okay for now because we've not even gone on a date. Unless you count Madame Jacqueline's."

"I don't count that."

Annie's eyes were damp. Sweet, damp gray eyes, shining with a new beginning for him. "Oh, good, because I was hoping to get another opportunity at that doberg cake."

He rose. "Whatever you want."

She stood, toe to toe with him. "I like the sound of that."

And then she smiled up at him. Not Annie the competent undercover nanny, but Anna, slightly unsure, possibly scared but wonderful in so many ways he couldn't possibly begin to list.

"It may be rough. I'm not an easy man to deal with."

"Then you'll understand when I'm as difficult."

He twined a curl around his finger. "We are much alike."

She rubbed a finger over his bottom lip. "We are. So it might get…passionate at times. I'm stubborn."

He tugged her T-shirt from the waistband of her jeans. Sliding his hands over her tight stomach, up her ribs to just under her breast. She gasped, her eyes widening, as he murmured, "I'm planning on passion. Lots and lots of passion."

She watched his mouth. Hungrily. "Oh, good. That's a nice side benefit of being in a partnership."

He couldn't stop the smile at his lips. "You've made me a very happy man, you know that?"

"I hope you still feel that way next week."

He lowered his mouth and kissed her. She tasted like toothpaste and sweet, sweet Annie. She rose on her toes and wrapped her arms around him. Fireworks went off and he knew this was what had been intended for him.

"Anna, I will forever be a happy man because you chose me with both your heart and mind."

"Call me Annie. My mother always called me that, and I like who I am as Annie." She looked up at him. "Besides, my body chose you long ago."

He chuckled. "Yeah, our bodies knew exactly what was right for us, so let's go to my room and give them an opportunity to have their way again."

She smiled. "You don't want to work on cases? Get our new business, Mendes and her Wolf Investigations, off on the right foot?"

He gave her a smoldering look, the only wolfish one he had in his arsenal, and then snatched her hard against his body. "I'd rather play the big, bad wolf and you can be Little Red Riding Hood."

She slid her hands around to his ass and wiggled against him. He couldn't stop the groan or the surge of hot liquid pouring into him, heating him. She peeked up. "Okay, but I refuse to tell you how big your…um…teeth are."

"You're definitely suited for me. Too much alike."

She turned and pulled him toward the back of the house. She didn't know where she was going, but it didn't seem to matter. "I know one way we are way different. I'm a woman. And you're a man."

"You are a good detective."

She laughed and pure joy flooded his soul. "Yeah, but I'm going to need to rediscover those difference for my-self."

"Lead on, partner."

* * * * *

*There's more to be told about the Dufrene family
and Beau Soleil! Look for Abram's story,
UNDER THE AUTUMN SKY,
book two of THE BOYS OF BAYOU BRIDGE series.
Available in July 2012 wherever
Harlequin Superromance books are sold.*

HEART & HOME

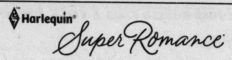

COMING NEXT MONTH
AVAILABLE JUNE 12, 2012

HSRCNM0512

REQUEST YOUR FREE BOOKS!
2 FREE NOVELS PLUS 2 FREE GIFTS!

Harlequin

Super Romance®

Exciting, emotional, unexpected!

YES! Please send me 2 FREE Harlequin® Superromance® novels and my 2 FREE gifts (gifts are worth about $10). After receiving them, if I don't wish to receive any more books, I can return the shipping statement marked "cancel." If I don't cancel, I will receive 6 brand-new novels every month and be billed just $4.69 per book in the U.S. or $5.24 per book in Canada. That's a saving of at least 15% off the cover price! It's quite a bargain! Shipping and handling is just 50¢ per book in the U.S. and 75¢ per book in Canada.* I understand that accepting the 2 free books and gifts places me under no obligation to buy anything. I can always return a shipment and cancel at any time. Even if I never buy another book, the two free books and gifts are mine to keep forever.

135/336 HDN FC6T

Name	(PLEASE PRINT)	
Address		Apt. #
City	State/Prov.	Zip/Postal Code

Signature (if under 18, a parent or guardian must sign)

Mail to the Reader Service:
IN U.S.A.: P.O. Box 1867, Buffalo, NY 14240-1867
IN CANADA: P.O. Box 609, Fort Erie, Ontario L2A 5X3

Not valid for current subscribers to Harlequin Superromance books.

**Are you a current subscriber to Harlequin Superromance books and want to receive the larger-print edition?
Call 1-800-873-8635 or visit www.ReaderService.com.**

* Terms and prices subject to change without notice. Prices do not include applicable taxes. Sales tax applicable in N.Y. Canadian residents will be charged applicable taxes. Offer not valid in Quebec. This offer is limited to one order per household. All orders subject to credit approval. Credit or debit balances in a customer's account(s) may be offset by any other outstanding balance owed by or to the customer. Please allow 4 to 6 weeks for delivery. Offer available while quantities last.

Your Privacy—The Reader Service is committed to protecting your privacy. Our Privacy Policy is available online at www.ReaderService.com or upon request from the Reader Service.

We make a portion of our mailing list available to reputable third parties that offer products we believe may interest you. If you prefer that we not exchange your name with third parties, or if you wish to clarify or modify your communication preferences, please visit us at www.ReaderService.com/consumerchoice or write to us at Reader Service Preference Service, P.O. Box 9062, Buffalo, NY 14269. Include your complete name and address.

HSR11

SPECIAL EDITION

Life, Love and Family

USA TODAY bestselling author

Marie Ferrarella

enchants readers in

ONCE UPON A MATCHMAKER

Micah Muldare's aunt is worried that her nephew is going to wind up alone in his old age...but this matchmaking mama has just the thing! When Micah finds himself accused of theft, defense lawyer Tracy Ryan agrees to help him as a favor to his aunt, but soon finds herself drawn to more than just his case. Will Micah open up his heart and realize Tracy is his match?

Available June 2012

Saddle up with Harlequin® series books this summer and find a cowboy for every mood!

Available wherever books are sold.

*A grim discovery is about to change everything for
Detective Layne Sullivan—including how she
interacts with her boss!*

*Read on for an exciting excerpt of the upcoming book
UNRAVELING THE PAST by Beth Andrews....*

SOMETHING WAS UP—otherwise why would Chief Ross
Taylor summon her back out? As Detective Layne Sullivan
walked over, she grudgingly admitted he was doing well.
But that didn't change the fact that the Chief position
should have been hers.

Taylor turned as she approached. "Detective Sullivan,
we have a situation."

"What's the problem?"

He aimed his flashlight at the ground. The beam illuminated a dirt-encrusted skull.

"Definitely a problem." And not something she'd expected. Not here. "How'd you see it?"

"Jess stumbled upon it looking for her phone."

Layne looked to where his niece huddled on a log. "I'll
contact the forensics lab."

"Already have a team on the way. I've also called in units
to search for the rest of the remains."

So he'd started the ball rolling. Then, she'd assume command while he took Jess home. "I have this under control."

Though it was late, he was clean shaven and neat, his flat
stomach a testament to his refusal to indulge in doughnuts.
His dark blond hair was clipped at the sides, the top long
enough to curl.

The female part of Layne admitted he was attractive.

The cop in her resented the hell out of him for it.

"You get a lot of missing-persons cases here?" he asked.

"People don't go missing from Mystic Point." Although plenty of them left. "But we have our share of crime."

"I'll take the lead on this one."

Bad enough he'd come to *her* town and taken the position she was meant to have, now he wanted to mess with *how* she did her job? "Why? I'm the only detective on third shift and your second in command."

"Careful, Detective, or you might overstep."

But she'd never played it safe.

"I don't think it's overstepping to clear the air. You have something against me?"

"I assign cases based on experience and expertise. You don't have to like how I do that, but if you need to question every decision, perhaps you'd be happier somewhere else."

"Are you threatening my job?"

He moved so close she could feel the warmth from his body. "I'm not threatening anything." His breath caressed her cheek. "I'm giving you the choice of what happens next."

What will Layne choose? Find out in
UNRAVELING THE PAST by Beth Andrews,
available June 2012 from Harlequin® Superromance®.

And be sure to look for the other two books
in Beth's THE TRUTH ABOUT THE SULLIVANS series
available in August and October 2012.